broken pieces

ALSO BY KATHLEEN LONG

broken pieces

kathleen long

LAKE UNION
PUBLISHING

Published by Lake Union Publishing, Seattle

www.apub.com

Amazon, the Amazon logo, and Lake Union Publishing are trademarks of Amazon.com, Inc., or its affiliates.

ISBN-13: 9781503937178
ISBN-10: 1503937178

Cover design by Danielle Fiorella

Printed in the United States of America

For Ingrid

One day someone is going to hug you so tight that all of your broken pieces will stick back together.

—Author Unknown

CHAPTER ONE

My father stood at my front door as if he'd simply run out for bread and forgotten his keys.

A slight gray stubble dappled his chin and the line of his jaw, his appearance a far cry from the practiced, clean-shaven face he sported the one time I saw him each year.

Frustration and disbelief tangled inside me.

I didn't need a surprise visit. Not tonight. Tomorrow would be one of the biggest presentations of my career, and the last thing I wanted was to find the mighty Albert Jones on my doorstep.

Yet there he stood.

I'd rarely seen my father during the twenty years since he'd handed me to my grandmother and walked out of my life. Last year the man had lingered for several awkward hours during his annual Christmas visit. The year before he'd stayed for fifteen minutes, leaving me to dine alone at the local café, which was, quite honestly, a relief.

I couldn't help but wonder what he wanted, considering that he'd never before stopped by in the middle of August, much less looking like something the cat dragged in.

A taxi idled at the curb, but Albert stood his ground, feet firmly planted on the top step.

I studied him through the sidelights and thought about throwing the deadbolt and walking away. Instead, I opened the door but blocked his entrance.

"Destiny, my girl," he said, the faux affection in his voice serving as a reminder of why the man had earned a collection of Tony Awards.

I couldn't remember the last time he'd called me his girl.

The realization and reminder sliced me to the core, and I drew in a deep breath and worked to steady myself.

I had neither the time nor the interest to discover why he'd traveled the hour and a half from New York City to my hometown, but the sooner I dealt with him and sent him on his way, the better.

"You're four and a half months early for Christmas, and you haven't remembered my birthday in at least fifteen years, which begs the question: Why are you here?"

His green eyes measured me, their light dim, as though the months since I'd last seen him had stolen their brightness. They focused momentarily, flickered with hope. "*Is* it your birthday?" he asked.

The pain of his not knowing stung, but I'd long ago learned to shove away my disappointment. "No," I said, shaking my head. "Not even close."

His focus faded once more, and I wondered briefly just how much his brain had been affected by the accident that had made front-page news in Paris, New Jersey.

Tony Award–winning native struck down during rehearsal three weeks before opening night.

According to the reports I'd seen, he'd been hit on the head by a faulty piece of scenery, and although he'd given all of Broadway a scare, he'd been treated and released and was expected to make a full recovery.

When he spoke, however, he did so carefully and succinctly, the very act of choosing his words seeming to require effort.

Worry flickered through me, but I tamped it down. This man hadn't cared about me since I was ten years old. He'd never done a thing to earn my concern.

"Can't a father visit his daughter?" he asked.

"A father can, yes. But you lack the basic qualifications, don't you think?"

I cringed inwardly as the words left my mouth. Even for me, they were harsh.

He graced me with the facial expression theater aficionados called *The Albert*.

Stoic. Superior. Put-upon.

Albert Jones might not be a household name, but among people who knew Broadway, he was royalty.

Here, where he was nothing more than an absentee father, he was anything but. He and I were linked by nothing more than DNA—a sad truth I'd accepted long ago.

Fatigue bracketed his famously expressive eyes and might have weakened me momentarily if he hadn't spoken his next words. "I paid for this house."

A knot fisted in my belly. Was this seriously how the man felt? That he had a claim on this house? He'd deserted me when I'd needed him most.

I laughed—a nervous reaction I did my best to control—but his statement was . . . "Unbelievable. Either you're still suffering from your injuries or you're even more selfish than I thought."

He flinched as if I'd slapped him.

Good.

"You may have paid off the mortgage, but this hasn't been your house since you walked away before Mom was cold in the ground. Or had you forgotten that part?"

He looked at me then, really looked at me, the mention of her apparently breaking through his façade.

Before my mother died, I'd been able to tell the difference between my real father and my actor father. Some of my proudest moments had been spent watching him onstage, acting out the emotions of characters he brought to life. My happiest moments, however, had been the times during which I hadn't had to share him with an audience.

He'd been my dad, and the love that had once shone in his eyes had been genuine.

Now, however, I couldn't remember the last time I'd been able to tell whether my father was acting.

"You have her eyes," he said, hitting me below the belt.

I dropped my grip on the door, and he slipped past me, stepping into the house as if on autopilot.

"Don't leave," I shouted to the taxi driver, hoping he could hear me.

"My bags," Albert Jones said, as one might say to a butler or personal assistant.

Alarm bells chimed deep inside my brain.

"Bags?"

I thought of the presentation I planned to make the next morning before the opera board, picturing the designs and budget materials spread across every available inch of my office.

"What do you mean, *bags*?"

"I'm staying for a visit," he said matter-of-factly, dismissing my question with a wave of his hand.

"A visit?"

My father hadn't slept under this roof in twenty years.

While I'd never moved into the bedroom he and my mother once shared, the sheets, curtains, and carpet had long ago been replaced, erasing all memory of the happy family we'd once been, leaving behind nothing more than a sterile guest room that had never been used.

"Life is short. I want to know my daughter." He raised his arms majestically, like a Disney hero who'd arrived to save the day.

Sadness pushed at my frustration, and my voice faltered on my next words. "Don't you think you're a little late?"

A horn blared from outside, and Albert blinked. "My bags," he repeated.

We stared at each other, our eyes locked. His were a cool, pale green, so unlike my mother's warm, dark-brown gaze.

"A visit, Destiny. Surely you're not going to deny a tired old man a visit."

And so, Albert the actor returned.

"One night," I said as I turned for the door.

I fantasized momentarily about hoisting my father into the air and shoving him back into the waiting taxi, but I wasn't about to give him the satisfaction of knowing how deeply his appearance had rocked my state of mind.

"Has he paid you, at least?" I asked the driver as he exited the car upon my approach.

The man, a silver-haired gentleman with a generous smile, tipped his hat. "Quite handsomely, miss."

"Lovely," I said beneath my breath as I waited for the trunk to open.

I expected an overnight bag, perhaps a weekender, not a large wheeled suitcase and an oversize leather duffel.

Holy cow.

Albert Jones apparently planned on far more than a quick visit.

What the hell was going on?

The driver hoisted each to the curb, then slammed the trunk shut. I hesitated, half in the street, half out, as the taxi pulled away and faded into the distance.

"Selling luggage, darling?" a sweet voice called out from beside me.

Something soft and fluffy brushed against my ankles, and I instinctively bent down to scratch the head of Marguerite Devine's poodle mix, Picasso.

I met Marguerite's quizzical gaze and laughed, at a loss to do much else. "The great and mighty Albert Jones has returned for an unexpected visit. Apparently he wants to spend time with his daughter."

Marguerite's eyes widened, and she pressed one hand to her chest, as though I'd told her the sky was falling. Then she narrowed her eyes suspiciously. "Have you questioned his motives?"

I nodded. "Most definitely."

"And?"

I shook my head. "I'm not sure he's capable of telling me the truth."

Marguerite nodded. "He rarely was."

My next-door neighbor and my mother had been best friends since their days at Paris Elementary. While Marguerite had never married, she'd been part of our family for as long as I could remember. She'd always insisted I call her Marguerite. Not Aunt Marguerite. Not Mrs. Devine. Just Marguerite. As if we'd always been equals, when in fact, we had not.

Marguerite had been the bright beacon that guided me through my darkest years, and for that, she would forever sit upon a pedestal in my mind's eye.

She pointed to her head. "How about the injury? Maybe he's suffering from lasting damage."

I shrugged. "He's speaking a bit more slowly than usual, but that's about it."

She screwed up her features.

As close as Marguerite had been to my mother, her friendship with Albert had been tenuous at best. Once my mother became ill and my father began spending more and more time in New York, Marguerite had stopped trying to hide her dislike of the man.

After he'd handed me off to my grandmother, Marguerite had never forgiven him.

"Want me to march in there with you?" she asked.

Affection warmed my insides, but I shook my head. "I've got this. Thanks."

Picasso trotted to her side and sat up on his haunches, urging his mistress to continue his walk.

Marguerite grasped my elbow, giving it a squeeze. "I'd tell you to give the mighty one my regards, but why start pretending now?" She leaned close, our heads touching. "You, however, I love like my own, so if you need me, holler.

"You have a big day tomorrow. Don't let him throw you off your plans, and do not let him stay a second longer than you want him to."

She released my elbow, but pressed her palm to the small of my back.

I stared at my house, the weight of Marguerite's touch bringing with it a flood of memories.

While I was a fairly accomplished craftsman entering her thirties, I suddenly felt more like the frightened ten-year-old who'd hidden in the corner of Marguerite's garden as mourners filled my parents' house with platitudes and respects paid.

It had been Marguerite who'd found me that day, not my father. It had been Marguerite who'd held me tight and dried my tears, Marguerite who'd held my hand and led me back to where my father commanded the sitting room like a man on center stage.

While everyone else had seen a strong, grief-stricken husband and father, I'd seen an actor pretending to be brave when he was not.

You are enough, Marguerite had whispered in my ear.

When my grandmother moved in the next week and my father moved out, Marguerite had held my hand and said it again.

You are enough.

And I had been. Without my so-called father.

Marguerite held her ground as I walked toward my front door, Albert's luggage in tow. I glanced back over my shoulder once. Her ruffled, lemon-yellow skirt flounced in the breeze, and one hand gripped the wide-brimmed sun hat that covered her auburn curls. With Picasso by her side, she looked as though she belonged not in Paris, New Jersey, but in the real Paris, thousands of miles away.

You are enough, I thought.

Then I braced myself for the man who waited for me on the other side of the door.

I found Albert in the sitting room, standing beside what had once been his favorite chair.

He studied a pair of framed photographs, his fingers touching a treasured shot of my mother cradling a newborn me in her arms.

We'd been happy once. The three of us.

My father had been my hero—taking me for adventure walks, carrying me on his shoulders, helping me tie old towels around my neck in my superhero days. He used to take my hands and spin me until my feet and laughter flew.

Then Mom got sick, and he faded. First from our games, then from our home, eventually from our lives. He spent more and more time in New York and less here in Paris.

Once Mom died, he left for good.

"Why are you really here?" I asked.

He answered without turning to face me. "Sometimes life is so hard you simply want to go home."

The delivery of his line was flat, defeated, and I couldn't help but wonder if they weren't the first honest words he'd spoken since he appeared at the front door.

Another person might offer a soothing word or ask what was wrong.

I was not that person.

When he turned toward me, a shadow crossed his features, and I remembered the look from the days when my mother had been failing.

Albert Jones was done talking.

My insides quaked with the unwanted emotions I'd long ago done my best to shut down. The truth was, if the man wasn't going to honestly answer my question, I had better ways to spend my time.

I was due before the Paris Opera House Board of Trustees at ten the next morning. They'd put out requests for bids for the complete renovation of the opera house's once majestic paneling, box seats, and trim. I intended to make the best presentation of my life, and I intended to win the bid.

The sudden appearance of Albert Jones was not going to derail those plans.

"One night," I said, turning for the hall and my office.

"May I have a cup of tea?" he asked.

As much as the ghost of the ten-year-old inside me might want to please her father, recapture his affection, and race to fix him a cup of tea, I did nothing more than quicken my pace away from him.

"You remember where the kitchen is, don't you?" I asked.

Then I steadied myself, silenced the unwanted memories, and shut myself behind my office door.

CHAPTER TWO

I'd worked most of the night, my mind a jumble of presentation plans and conversation snippets from my father's sudden appearance. Sometime after four o'clock in the morning, I'd curled into the over-stuffed chair in my office, where I'd attempted sleep.

I'd hoped Albert would be gone, but based on the noise that woke me now, he hadn't gone anywhere except outside.

The morning sun slanted brightly between the blinds. Too brightly. I scrambled for my phone and pressed the screen to illuminate the time.

Nine o'clock.

I was due at the opera house in one hour.

Adrenaline spiked through my veins. I'd need every minute to get showered, dressed, and figure out who in the hell Albert was yelling at.

Based on the shrill yapping that answered every one of his baritone commands, I imagined that the object of his displeasure must be Picasso.

Albert's luggage remained where I'd left it in the hall.

The front door, however, sat open wide.

Albert and Picasso faced off beside a bush that had marked the line between properties for as long as I could remember, their shouting-barking cacophony rattling my exhausted brain.

Where my father had looked only slightly unkempt the night before, he now looked completely disheveled.

His silver hair stuck out in choppy clumps, suggesting he'd recently dragged his fingers through the hanks. His shirt hung untucked from his trousers, which were wrinkled and creased as though his restless night had matched my own.

Good.

"What are you doing?" I shouted.

"This little pisser is going to kill your mother's favorite azalea," he called out over his shoulder, projecting his voice so loudly I was quite sure every one of my neighbors heard.

Mom's azalea.

I pictured the once-vibrant fuchsia flowers and wondered exactly how many years it had been since the plant stopped blooming.

On cue, Picasso lifted his leg, then disappeared around the end of Marguerite's hedge toward home.

Albert's cheeks puffed out and reddened momentarily, and I couldn't help but think he resembled a child—a spoiled child. Then his features smoothed, his composure returned, and he shifted his attention to me. His eyes narrowed as he studied me from head to toe.

My bare toes peeped from beneath the tattered hem of my jeans. I'd worked and slept in my favorite Derek Jeter T-shirt, and while I was grateful to my mother for the head of sable hair I claimed as my own, I shoved the violet-streaked strands behind my ears, not wanting to imagine what I must look like at this particular moment.

Then I reminded myself that I didn't care. Albert Jones had no right to say a word about my appearance. Hell, the fact that I no doubt appeared more than a little bit haggard was due to his sudden visit just as much as it was to my impending presentation.

I held my ground as he walked toward me. He stopped so close nerves fluttered in my stomach.

Ridiculous.

Yet, even though we saw each other once a year, we hadn't stood this close since we'd clasped hands beside my mother's coffin decades earlier.

Albert took a hank of my purple-streaked hair between his fingers. "Did you know this was her favorite color?"

Something deep inside me cracked—something I'd thought long healed. "No," I answered, working to keep my voice solid. "I don't think I did."

Silence beat between us. Awkward, uncomfortable silence.

The memory of how much I'd once loved him echoed through my mind. Haunting. Unbidden.

"I have a meeting," I said, stepping away from his touch and the unwanted memory. "Have a safe trip back to New York."

Then, before he could say another word, I tucked the loose strand of purple behind one ear and headed back inside.

A short while later I walked the four blocks to the Paris Opera House. I hustled past open shop doors and brightly decorated windows in the center of town, keeping my conversations brief and my feet moving.

I was determined to be on time. My presentation was polished, organized, and practiced.

A few years earlier I'd worked with a partner, but after his move to New England I'd reorganized my business into a sole proprietorship and never looked back.

I'd made a name for myself by designing and installing custom cabinetry and doing other carpentry work, but found myself wanting something more than residential contracts. Something bigger.

Landing the renovation and restoration at the opera house would provide just that. More. Much more. The stage renovation presented an opportunity for me to leave my mark on Paris, the chance to give back just a small measure of all the town had given me.

I'd prepped for today's meeting by pulling my hair into a somewhat stylish topknot and trading my usual blue jeans and work boots for a long skirt, tailored blouse, and dress boots.

The morning had already turned hot, even for August, and a breeze had picked up, bringing with it the promise of a summer thunderstorm. The leaves on the trees along the Delaware River had flipped, showing their silver-toned underbellies.

"Rain coming," Manny the barber called out from the door of his shop as I hustled past. "Knock 'em dead, Destiny," he added.

I shot him a smile, my facial expression belying the nerves building inside me.

Most everyone in the small town knew how much landing this job meant to me. I'd researched historical photographs and documents, I'd made countless measurements of the space, and I'd interviewed town elders. The project was definitely a step outside my comfort zone, but I wanted my shot, and I intended to get it.

The Paris Opera House sat on the main thoroughfare at the corner of Bridge and Front, a location as beautiful as it was practical. The majestic spire rose into the heavy summer sky, and I held still momentarily, fantasizing about what it might be like to add my name to the list of architects, designers, and carpenters who had helped create and shape the structure over the more than 150 years the opera had inhabited this space.

The building had been fully restored back when I'd been in first grade. I could still remember watching the construction from the opposite sidewalk as I clutched my father's hand. We'd visited weekly during the months of work—as the renovation came to life and we stood side by side, observing.

I often wondered if my six-year-old brain hadn't decided then and there that carpentry would be my life.

That renovation had modernized the interior, and the historical society and opera house board had recently voted to restore the theater to its once ornate glory. That's where I came in.

The fact my father had suddenly reappeared the night before my presentation was disconcerting, but I was more than capable of shutting off my emotions long enough to do the job I needed to do today.

My father had once performed here, and my mother and I had sat in the front row, applauding, just days before our lives turned upside down with her cancer diagnosis.

Perhaps part of me wanted to erase that memory. Perhaps part of me wanted to honor it by creating a work of beauty she would have loved.

A shiver whispered through me as I stood at the bottom of the steps and stared, as if the ghosts of my past were about to throw open the massive glass doors and invite me inside.

Instead, Nan Michaels appeared at the center door and yelled: "Hurry it up, Ring Ding. You're three minutes late."

The grandmother of one of my oldest friends and a proud Paris Opera Guild member, Nan had a tendency to call those she knew by the names of the sugary treats Doc Malone had made her give up years earlier.

She studied me with kindly eyes, and I wondered if she knew how forcefully butterfly wings beat inside my belly.

Nerves. I mentally berated myself.

I didn't do nerves.

I'd once been afraid of thunderstorms, dark corners, and shadows in the night, but after my mother's death I'd sworn off fearing anything ever again.

I wasn't about to start again now.

I anchored my portfolio beneath my arm, sucked in a steadying breath, and headed inside.

I'd been told to report to the executive offices, where I found the rest of the Paris Opera Guild gathered around a long conference table, collating newsletters. The group met weekly to label envelopes, organize mailings, and gossip.

"Good morning," I said, using my perkiest voice.

Because most guild members had known me since birth, and perk was not part of my usual repertoire, my tone was met by several pairs of raised eyebrows.

"Leave the acting to your father." Mona Capshaw, another beloved, albeit grumpy, Paris grandmother, pointed to the large clock on the wall. "Chop, chop."

I hesitated, wondering if they knew about Albert's unannounced visit. Then I realized there was no need to wonder. There were no secrets in Paris. Never had been. Never would be.

"Feeling all right, dear?" Nan asked.

"You'd better hurry," Mona added. "Byron doesn't like to be kept waiting."

Byron Kennedy . . . a fixture in Paris for as long as I could remember. Descended from one of the town's founders, he'd been the president of the opera house board for several years, complementing his luminous career as the foremost expert on regional history.

"Don't let him rattle you," Millie Carmichael chimed in from the far end of the table. "You've got talent."

I'd done a whole-house renovation on Millie's original floors, baseboards, and wainscoting, and she'd been bragging about my work ethic ever since. Bless her heart.

"Thank you, Mrs. Carmichael."

There'd been a time in my life when I'd called the man *Uncle Byron*. I'd seen him at family brunches and backyard picnics. I'd seen him at my father's shows and sitting at our kitchen table playing chess late at night. I'd seen him sober. I'd seen him drunk.

He and my father had belted out drunken songs and laughed uproariously late into the night on many occasions.

Yet after my mother died and my father left, Byron Kennedy had never so much as checked in on the daughter of his supposedly closest friend.

And while I wasn't one to hold grudges, I also wasn't one to hide my true feelings.

The man was a blowhard, more worried about appearances and social connections than people. I might not like him, but I'd never let Byron Kennedy rattle me.

At that moment the conference room doors opened, and Byron Kennedy emerged.

A hush settled over the gathering of guild members, and all collating and envelope-stuffing activity fell silent. Spines were straightened and hair smoothed.

Byron Kennedy fancied himself town patriarch, and most everyone in Paris treated him with a respect to match that title.

While I wasn't one for bullshit titles, I was smart enough to know I had to play the game if I wanted to work with the board of trustees.

"Destiny," he said warmly.

"Mr. Kennedy."

He twisted his features. "Whatever happened to Uncle Byron?" he asked.

Good question, I thought.

Outwardly I merely chuckled, pretending I found his words amusing. Then I shook his hand, centered my thoughts, and stepped inside the conference room.

The selection committee sat along the far side of the conference table. Jack Maxwell, owner of Maxwell's Mortuary; Polly Klein, of Polly's Klip and Kurl; and Erma Leroy, of the Leroy Inn.

Byron sat at the head of the table and gestured for me to begin.

Even though I knew everyone at the table, a frisson of anxiety zipped to life inside me. I did my best to tamp it down as I set my portfolio on the empty end of the table and opened the long edge.

"Good morning, ladies and gentlemen of the selection committee," I began. I carefully set out my designs, talking as I positioned each in precise order.

"Thank you for the opportunity to address you today. I am confident the renovation concept I am about to present captures not only the history of this fine building, but also the character and personality of Paris itself."

I worked flawlessly through my presentation, not needing to refer to the index cards I'd prepared. I spoke from memory, and I spoke from the heart.

I loved carpentry and the art of shaping a whole from what had once been pieces of wood. The Paris Opera House would be my largest project to date. It would also be my most creative.

"If you'll notice," I said, holding up my artist's rendering of the massive panels that framed the stage, "I'm proposing something I believe the committee and the town will find spectacular and fitting for the opera house. Reclaimed maple from the Paris Mill."

Abandoned for twenty years, the mill had become more than an eyesore along the river just outside Paris city limits: it had become a danger.

Originally constructed in the 1920s, the building boasted spectacular rough maple planks throughout, wood that, for the most part, had withstood the invasion of the elements, time, and the occasional family of squirrels.

Having already made plans to salvage as much of the mill's maple flooring as I could, I reached into my portfolio to pull out a small piece of sample wood I'd refinished to a spectacular sheen.

Even Byron's expression brightened.

"I propose we purchase the wood from the salvage company stripping the building. By upcycling, we'll not only have the caliber of wood this fine building deserves, but we'll preserve a piece of Paris history at the same time. And we'll save money."

I pulled out the sheet on which I'd made my financial notes, detailing the difference in expenses between ordering and installing new wood and reclaiming the old.

Excitement danced inside me. By using material from the old mill, I'd developed what I suspected was a completely unique approach—one that would keep not one, but two pieces of Paris history alive. I felt sure the next few moments would push my proposal into the win column.

Byron held out one hand. "The rendering and the financials, please."

Jack, who had reached for both, slid them to the end of the conference table.

Byron tapped his expensive pen against the tabletop as he studied every angle on my design and digit on my financial projections.

Yet I continued my presentation unfazed. Adrenaline pushed aside my exhaustion as I moved from point to point, design element to design element.

I'd married my love of reclaiming old materials with techniques I'd honed through years of practice—making multiple cuts on the same piece of wood to yield intricate trim and scrollwork, and fabricating large finished projects from carefully designed sections.

Excitement surged through me, and I felt more alive than I'd felt in years, my confidence shining, my words flowing. I'd finally captured Byron's full attention by the time I made my closing remarks.

"We'll be in touch," he said a few moments later, after I'd gathered my materials and shaken hands with each member of the committee.

I ended my presentation more forcefully than I typically concluded potential client meetings. After all, the renovation was most likely a once-in-a-lifetime chance.

"I want this job," I said, meeting each of their gazes in turn. "I will deliver a product that exceeds your expectations. I look forward to your call."

Then I gathered up my portfolio, held my head high, and walked out.

CHAPTER THREE

Moments later I sat at the counter inside the Paris River Café and soaked in the murmur of the early lunch crowd. Coffee brewing. Dishes clattering. Voices raised and dropped in earnest conversation.

I'd been sitting at this counter at some point each day since Jessica Capshaw, the owner and one of my oldest friends, had opened the restaurant.

I worked alone. I lived alone. I liked it that way. Yet here, cozied up to the counter in the company of my dearest friend, I enjoyed the buzz of activity that filled the restaurant.

After she'd lost her heart—and her life savings—to her ex-husband, Jessica had returned to Paris with two small children. With the help of her family, she'd rebuilt the café, turning the once empty storefront into a gathering place for good food and great people.

I studied her as she worked her space, taking orders, making small talk, and pouring coffee. Her smile never wavered, and the life in her eyes shone brightly.

There were times when I envied Jessica, but mainly I admired her. I knew myself well enough to know I could never be her—juggling work and motherhood. In our circle of friends, she was the one who inspired calm and hope and positive thinking.

Personally, I had no patience for that crap.

"How are the kids?" I asked as she pulled out a twenty-ounce mug and poured me a cup of coffee.

Eight-year-old Max and six-year-old Belle were the lights of her life, and while I knew her routine to be exhausting, she rarely showed the strain. Even now, she appeared effortlessly fresh and happy.

"Amazing," she said on a sigh. She waved her hand dismissively. "Don't get me wrong, they're driving me crazy and growing up way too fast, but they're just . . ." Her voice trailed off as her blond brows pulled together. "Amazing."

"I don't know how you do it." And I meant that.

But Jessica grinned and shrugged. "I just do."

I nodded, letting the questions of my past flash through my mind for a split second.

How different might my life have been had my mother lived? Would I have married? Had children? Would we have settled in a house not far from my parents? Would we have shared Sunday dinners and backyard dances?

Jessica's smile faltered and she placed her hand on top of mine for the briefest of moments, evidently reading my mind. "I want to hear all about your presentation." She hesitated momentarily. "And Albert."

Paris, New Jersey, population 1,326, give or take a few, was notorious for the speed at which news traveled.

Her brows lifted as she waited for me to bare my soul, like a bartender who could read her customers' woes simply by the set of their shoulders or the tone of their voice.

"So you've heard?"

She leaned forward. "Honey, everybody's heard." She gestured toward a wall of photos where another of our childhood friends had hung a collection of photographs documenting special moments in the town's everyday life.

"I'm surprised someone didn't capture his arrival and post it front and center on the wall. One of Paris's most famous sons," she said in a mock announcer voice.

"And lousiest fathers," I added.

"There is that." Her expression turned serious. "He was in here this morning."

"Here?" I frowned. "I was hoping he'd be on his way back to New York."

Jessica shook her head. "Stopped by for a stack of pancakes and a cup of coffee. Said he'd see me tomorrow."

Disbelief pushed at the high I still felt after my presentation. "You have got to be kidding me."

"Nope." She slid a chocolate-glazed doughnut with sprinkles in front of me. "Why the surprise visit?"

I took a bite of doughnut, gave Jessica the thumbs-up, chewed, and swallowed. "To quote the mighty Albert Jones, 'Can't a father visit his daughter?'"

Jessica glanced from one end of the counter to the other, checking on her customers; then she wiped the counter in front of me, by all appearances working a stubborn spot.

"It's a valid question," she said, her voice soft.

All my life, she'd had a knack for saying exactly what I needed to hear. This statement, however, was ridiculous.

"You're kidding, right?" I set down my doughnut.

Two new customers settled at the counter. Jessica gave each a warm greeting, handed them menus, then moved back to where I sat.

"You used to complain about not seeing him," she said.

I laughed. "I haven't complained in a very long time."

"Fair enough," she said. "Look, I'll never forgive him for the way he faded from your life, but what if he wants a second chance?"

I held up a hand to stop her train of thought.

Had I ever considered what I'd do if my father did ask me for a second chance? Sure. Twenty years ago. Hell, even ten years ago.

But now?

"Too little, too late," I said flatly. "Ask me about the opera house instead."

Jessica's brows wrinkled momentarily, suggesting she didn't quite believe me; then she smiled. "Tell me. I've been dying to hear."

I shoved away all thoughts of Albert Jones and relived every moment, doing my best to ignore the fact that a measure of my excitement had faded after talking about my father.

"I've got a good feeling," Jessica said.

She gave my hand a pat just as a gathering of Clipper Club members hooted and hollered from the back corner of the restaurant, their favorite meeting place.

"Bucket-list day," Jessica explained. "Mona had this crazy idea that if she added 'theme' days, the club would take on a new life."

Jessica's grandmother had started the coupon-clipping club at the height of the extreme-saving craze, but the group's focus had become more social than anything else.

"What's on yours?" I asked.

"Healthy kids. Happy family. You?"

I ignored her question. "What about your plans to take over the restaurant world?"

She grinned, pulling a snapshot from her apron pocket. In it she stood behind her son and daughter, her arms wrapped tightly around their shoulders, pride and love shining in her posture and expression.

"I've got everything I need right there." She tapped the photo. "Your turn," she said, as she tucked the picture safely away.

I frowned, as if I didn't understand what she meant.

She simply said, "Answer."

I took a swallow of hot coffee.

A long time ago there had been only one thing on my bucket list—one thing I could never have again.

My mother. My father. My family.

Just as we'd once been. Happy. Whole. Untouched by illness, and death, and life.

"Nothing," I said with a shake of my head.

Jessica pursed her lips and studied me, apparently seeing right through me, a skill she'd perfected back in first grade.

She leaned across the counter and spoke softly. "Be careful what you don't wish for."

Not quite ready to see Albert again after I left the café, I set out for the place I'd loved my entire life.

Situated beside the asphalt walking trail that ran along the Delaware, parallel to Front Street, the massive boulder perched above the river like a sentinel charged with keeping an eye on the Pennsylvania side of the river.

Lookout Rock, the river, and the trail sat just across the street from the opera house.

My heels sank into the soft ground leading from the path to the rock, and thunder rumbled in the distance as I set my portfolio against the boulder's base.

Ironically, the person who'd first brought me to the rock was the very person I'd come here to avoid.

Albert Jones.

As soon as I'd been old enough to climb the massive object, he'd introduced me to the spot, and all my life I'd come here to reflect, to plan, to celebrate.

Even now, as the river rushed past and the breeze picked up, rustling the dense summer foliage, part of me wondered what it might be like to hear Albert ask how my presentation had gone.

How might it feel to tell him how visibly impressed Byron had seemed by my proposal to upcycle reclaimed wood from the Paris Mill, even though he kept his verbal responses stiff and noncommittal?

I squeezed my eyes shut. My father had never asked about my work. Not once. Instead, our annual dinner conversations had consisted of little more than a rundown of his latest awards or upcoming show schedule.

Perhaps we were safer sticking to the superficial.

Before each Christmas visit, I reinforced my emotional walls. Last night's pop-in, however, had put a serious crack in my defense.

My cell phone chirped an incoming call, and I glanced at the screen. Surprise whispered through me; Marguerite hated talking on the phone.

"Hey," I said. "Everything all right?"

"I was going to ask you the same thing. Are you out celebrating? My sources tell me you dazzled the committee."

It wasn't just her words that soothed my nerves. It was her voice— the voice that had been my sounding board, rock, and counsel for as long as I could remember.

My grandmother had been so shattered by my mother's death she'd seemed unable to shoulder my grief in addition to her own.

Marguerite, however, had kept the promise she'd made to her best friend—to be there for me.

Even now.

I sighed. "Too soon to celebrate."

"You're not sitting on that big, damp rock contemplating life, are you?" she asked.

I looked around me, momentarily considering a twist on the truth, but opting for a straight answer instead. "It's not damp, and I'll be home soon."

"Storm's coming," she said. "Don't sit by that river too long."

Even at age thirty, I found the maternal tone of her voice insanely comforting.

"Plus," she added, "you have company."

I sat up straight. "He's still there?"

"Yes, he is, along with a young man in a zippy white sports car."

I did my best to slide off the rock gracefully, then gathered up my portfolio.

"I'm on my way."

It was bad enough that Albert was still at the house. I sure as hell wasn't going to encourage him to have company.

CHAPTER FOUR

A sleek white Tesla with New York plates sat in front of my house when I arrived back home.

Even though the car stuck out like a sore thumb along tree-lined Third Street, part of me wondered if the anger I felt was irrational. An even bigger part of me knew I was fully validated in being pissed. After all, I'd given Albert one night. I hadn't said, "Stay awhile. Have some friends over."

Marguerite, who hadn't missed a thing in her almost sixty years, sat on her front porch, sipping a glass of iced tea.

Today's outfit included a pair of vivid lime-green Capri pants, a loudly flowered top, and enough chunky jewelry to open her own boutique over on Artisan's Alley.

"No movement in or out," she said, in her best secret operative voice.

I knew her well enough to know she was trying to cool my anger before I walked through the door. After all, she'd spent the last two decades cooling my anger.

"Did you get a look at the driver?"

She nodded. "Young guy. Little bit older than you." Her eyes widened. "Handsome."

I waved as I hurried past. As long as he was here to take my father back to New York, I didn't care if the guy looked like the Creature from the Black Lagoon.

As I pushed through the front door, a tall, apparently frustrated man paced back and forth across the width of the sitting room.

Albert sat in his chair, appearing more annoyed than anything. His coloring had gone red and splotchy, and for one quick moment fear flickered through me. Was he all right?

I shook off the question and focused.

"What's going on?" I asked loudly as I stepped inside.

The man was as polished as his car was sleek.

He appeared to be several years older than I was, yet his dark, close-cropped hair showed not a trace of gray. He wore crisp blue jeans, a T-shirt, and a tweed jacket, even though it had to be close to ninety degrees outside.

"Jackson Harding," the new arrival said, giving my hand one quick pump. He emitted an air of familiarity despite the fact he was a stranger standing uninvited in the middle of my home. "You must be Albert's daughter. Your father speaks of you often."

The man's statement took me by such surprise my anger slipped, and the warmth in his eyes left me momentarily speechless, but I held my ground. Found my voice. "And you are?"

"Your father's manager." He gestured grandly to Albert, who remained sitting, arms crossed, eyebrows locked in a fierce scowl. "Surely he's spoken of me," Jackson continued.

"Mr. Harding"—I shrugged and fisted my hands on my hips—"my father hasn't *spoken* to me about anything substantial in years."

Surprise flashed across Jackson Harding's classic movie-star features, yet he quickly regained his composure.

The flush in my father's cheeks, however, had morphed from a rosy pink to bloodred.

Jackson raked a hand across his face. "Has your father shared with you that he moves closer to breach of contract each day he misses rehearsal?"

"Do tell." Here was a topic directly in line with my desire to end Albert's visit.

"Your father is scheduled to open on Broadway next week in a Howard Carroll classic, yet he's chosen this moment to return to his roots."

I nodded. "I'm sure he'd be happy to drive back with you right now."

My father stood, shooting me a sharp glare. "I owe those people nothing."

His hostile tone stunned me.

"You owe those people the return of your signing bonus if you don't go through with this performance," Jackson said, his voice steady, soothing.

My father waved one hand dismissively, then turned his back. "Fine. Send back the money."

I may not have known much about my father, but I knew he took his reputation in the business seriously. Based on the rising color in Jackson's cheeks, my father's words had left him similarly surprised.

"If you are truly unable to fulfill your contract, Albert, I will, but you haven't even tried."

My father pulled himself taller, sucked in his gut, and spoke slowly and deliberately. "There are some things in life more important than money or reputation."

"Like what?" I asked before Jackson had a chance to reply.

He turned to me, then pointed to the small, framed photos that sat on the table beside the chair. "Like family." He gave an exaggerated shrug. "Perhaps there comes a time in every man's life when he feels compelled to return home."

Home?

Paris hadn't been his home in two decades.

Anger burst to life inside me. How dare he stand here and pontificate about home as though his life here had mattered?

"This isn't your home," I said. "You made that abundantly clear twenty years ago."

Albert looked as though I'd slapped him, a reaction I was sure he'd perfected in one role or another.

Jackson, however, jumped through the window I'd opened.

"Your daughter is correct," Harding said. "New York is your home. Broadway is your home. I understand if you're nervous about the time you've missed because of the accident, but they aren't going to wait for you much longer."

Annoyance simmered in my father's eyes, an annoyance I'd seen in my own reflection many times. "I do not get nervous."

His words echoed the internal dialog I'd had earlier at the opera house, and I realized his was the voice I carried in my head. Back when he'd been my hero, he'd taught me to be brave, to be strong.

Well, I was strong now. Without him.

As quickly as he'd bristled, Albert shrank before my eyes. "I just need more time."

The momentary light at the end of the tunnel dimmed.

"To do what?" Jackson's voice went gentle, the exact opposite of the reaction I'd expected. "You can't hide forever. Either you learn your lines and go back, or you don't."

Learn his lines? Some of my clearest memories of time spent with Albert had been watching him learn his lines. The man had been a natural, making each role his own within moments of opening a script.

Since when had he had trouble learning his lines?

My father slapped his chest, pulling himself taller. "I am an artist. I will not perform until I feel ready to give my audience my best."

"I'll run your lines with you," I blurted before I could stop myself.

My father's actor façade slipped, and for the briefest moment I saw him, the dad I'd once known. Surprised. Proud. Genuine.

I flashed back on the images of my childhood, back when my mother had helped my father run his lines. When she'd grown too weak to continue I'd taken over her role, sitting out on the patio or in this very room with my father, helping him rehearse.

I'd never felt more important.

That was the only explanation I could think of for my ridiculous offer.

Jackson clapped my father's shoulder. "I'll see you tomorrow at ten. I'll send a car."

"Miss Jones," he said, reaching to shake my hand, "I apologize for the intrusion. It was a pleasure to meet you."

He was partway down the front walk when he turned and jogged back up to the top step, stopping several inches from where I stood. "Perhaps you'd like to come with your father tomorrow—see where he works his magic?"

Works his magic.

The words tapped into a loss and longing I'd worked to deny, but in spite of that I found myself nodding.

I did want to see where Albert worked his magic, where he'd chosen to make his life instead of here. "No need to send a car, then," I said. "We'll see you at ten."

I stood in the doorway until Jackson Harding's car drove out of sight, then I turned to face my father.

"OK," I said. "Let's run your lines, but first I need you to tell me the truth. Did you come here to see me? Or was this just a convenient place to hide?"

Albert sank back into the chair, going pale.

I shut the front door and stepped into the sitting room. "For God's sake, don't act."

His gaze snapped to mine. "What is that supposed to mean?"

"That means I'm fairly confident everything you've said since last night has been said in character. Everything," I added, "except for that one quick moment back there when I saw you. The real you."

My father stood and turned his back to me, plucking the photograph of my mother and me from the end table. I fought the urge to tell him to set it down.

"I'm having trouble with my lines." He returned the frame to its place on the table and pivoted toward me. "Since the accident."

The frustration I'd felt a split-second earlier softened, but I caught myself, bolstering my resolve. He didn't deserve my sympathy.

Yes, I felt bad for the man if, in fact, what he said was true, but where had he been all my life? Did he honestly expect he could come back now and gain my sympathy?

"So this is a habit of yours?" I asked. "Hiding from things that are difficult?"

He sank back into the chair, folding his hands in his lap. Something purple speckled his slender fingers and covered a few nails.

"What's on your hands?"

He lifted his pale eyes to mine, even as the shadow fell. He was done with the conversation. Done with the truth.

"I painted the chairs on your patio."

I blinked. "You show up unannounced, after years of merely stopping by for Christmas dinner, and you paint my patio chairs?"

Albert tucked his hands into the pockets of his chinos and looked down at the floor.

"I wanted to do something to thank you for letting me stay."

In that moment he looked like a young boy, unsure of himself, frightened. He looked nothing like the imposing image I'd held inside my memory for most of my life.

He appeared broken, and the ten-year-old inside me wanted nothing more than to run for a towel to tie around his neck to remind him of his superhero status, even though he hadn't been my superhero in a very long time.

For all I knew, he was still acting.

I pushed away the past and focused on the now.

"You painted my chairs?" I repeated.

He looked up and our stares locked. "Want to see them?"

I threw up my hands. "Sure," I said, wondering if the chairs were nothing more than a diversion to shift our conversation away from his career troubles.

"Her favorite color," Albert said proudly after leading me to the patio, pointing to the chairs he'd painted—chairs that had been a faded green that morning and were now the same brilliant violet they'd been in my youth.

He grinned as if my mother might step outside at any moment to happily discover what he'd done. He'd once taken so much pride in our house. They both had, my parents. Ours had been a home filled with love and laughter, a warm, nurturing place where I'd always felt safe.

"She's been gone a long time," I said, wondering if he'd returned the chairs to their original color to somehow bring a piece of her back.

"Seems like yesterday." Sadness flickered across his tired features.

"I guess that happens when you run away."

Silence stretched between us. Silence and twenty years of nothing but stiff holiday meals.

"It's my favorite color, too," I said, wishing I could take back the words as soon as they left my lips.

Albert pressed his hand to my shoulder, the rush of memories his touch brought almost more than I could bear. "I had no idea," he said.

I winced against the sting of his words.

Of course he had no idea. He knew nothing about me, making my earlier moment of sentimentality feel ludicrous.

I walked back inside, away from the fresh paint and the emotional danger it represented. I stopped in the kitchen, leaning hard against the counter, working to regain my composure.

I could do this.

I could run lines with Albert and drive him to New York in the morning. Chances were good I wouldn't hear from the selection committee for a day or two, and the projects waiting for me at the shop weren't anything that couldn't sit untouched for another day.

I thought about the violet chairs and my mother, knowing exactly what she'd ask me to do if she were here.

She'd been kind, gentle. Slow to anger and quick to forgive. Pretty much the polar opposite of the woman I'd become.

When my father stepped back inside, I channeled her spirit and did the exact opposite of what I wanted to do.

Straightening, I gave him my full attention and said, "Let's do this."

CHAPTER FIVE

That evening, over an awkward dinner of pizza and mozzarella sticks, Albert and I set about the task of practicing lines.

We sat at the kitchen table, and images from my childhood played through my mind as I ran my hand across the script's cover.

Like still shots from a movie, I remembered my father's head bent low over a new script, my mother's soothing voice coaching him, bolstering his confidence with her unwavering belief in his abilities.

There would be laughter out back, when they'd break from rehearsal to join me in a game of hide-and-seek.

There would be dancing and music and dress rehearsals after the lines had been learned.

Then, after everything changed and everyone was gone, there had been silence.

Most nights after dinner my grandmother cleaned, mopping the kitchen floor until it shone, a seemingly futile attempt to erase the pain of our past by wiping away the dirt.

My grandfather had died a year earlier, and I often wondered if the weight of losing her husband and her daughter so close together had been the reason she'd lived for only another ten years. She'd survived just long enough to raise me, then checked out.

"Destiny." Albert's voice broke through my thoughts. "You all right?"

His simple question tightened the knot in my throat, but I nodded. "Lost for a moment," I said, doing my best to hide how affected I felt, sitting here with him at the kitchen table as though our estrangement had never happened.

"*The Squeaky Door*," I read aloud from the script's cover. "By Howard Carroll."

"A genius," my father said, shifting smoothly from his concerned tone to his actor's voice. He pushed to stand, closing his eyes as he warmed up with a flourish of hands and posturing.

I shook my head and said, "Never heard of him," pretending somehow I might have, when in fact I'd purposefully avoided the theater all my life.

My father launched into a soliloquy on the artistic significance of the oft-neglected Howard Carroll.

"Which is why this production is so important," he said, pacing from one end of the small sitting room to the other.

I refocused my attention and narrowed my concentration on the prize at the end of this particular exercise.

Early tomorrow I would load Albert Jones and his luggage into my car, and I'd drive them to New York. After a quick visit to the latest theater to hire him for its stage, I'd return home to Paris alone.

Eventually the voices of these two days would fade, disappearing along with the voices of the past. With any luck at all I'd move forward with the opera house work, and my father's anomalous surprise visit would go down in the history books as just that.

An anomaly.

An undeniable melancholy pulled at my heart, but I shut it down, focusing instead on the words printed on the pages before me.

"Well, then," I said. "We'd better get to it, so you can do his genius justice."

"Which is precisely why I thank you," he said with a dramatic bow. Then he added, "A bit like old times, isn't it? You helping your old man with his lines?"

I nodded, not trusting my voice.

Albert closed his eyes and breathed in slowly through his nose, then out through his mouth. He drew his arms into his chest and out. Into his chest and out, diaphragm expanding with each inhalation.

Drama. The man had always loved his drama.

After the sixth inhale/exhale production, I decided it was time to forgo the theatrics and get down to business.

"In this scene, your character—"

"Bob Drummond."

"Bob Drummond," I repeated. "In this scene, Bob Drummond and Helen Carter are about to meet. It seems that Helen has fallen and injured her ankle."

"And Bob will carry her to safety," Albert interrupted.

"Very well. Shall we?" I raised the script and waved it in the air.

He nodded.

"Helen Carter is on the ground, writhing in pain, dragging herself toward a set of stairs, when you say . . ."

Albert gathered himself, pulled himself taller, and I'd be damned if he didn't make himself appear younger. "Hello, there . . . Miss," he proclaimed loudly, his theater voice exploding inside the small space.

I shook my head. "Not even close."

"Give me the line, and I will deliver it with perfect recall."

Perhaps he wasn't exaggerating about his difficulty with lines. Genuine concern whispered at the back of my brain. I squinted at the script and then up at my father. "How long have you had this script?"

He tapped his head in a manner suggesting I'd forgotten about the incident.

"How long?" I repeated.

"Weeks."

"Have you looked at it since your accident?"

"I have been . . . distracted."

Hadn't we all.

"OK. Here we go." I walked to the window, cradling the script in my hand. "If I remember correctly, I used to feed you the first few words and you'd take it from there."

Albert nodded.

I began. "Perhaps I can . . ."

I waited, studying my father's expression. If the man weren't so darned stubborn, he'd simply admit he couldn't remember a word. Instead, he improvised.

"Perhaps I can call you a cab," he said, baritone voice booming.

"No," I said, moving to where he stood, stopping in my tracks when he gave me the palms-in-the-air-don't-come-any-closer warning.

Frustration crossed his features, frustration and fear.

He hadn't been exaggerating.

Albert Jones had no idea what his first line was, and it was a simple line.

Sympathy edged through me, softening the hardness I'd worked to maintain since he showed up at my front door.

"The goal of the scene is to come to her aid, if that helps you remember."

He looked at me blankly.

"OK. I'll give you the line, and you repeat it back to me." I forced a reassuring smile. "Simple, right?"

He nodded, and I read the line. "'Perhaps I can be of some assistance.'"

Albert shook his head. "I don't think that's quite right . . ."

"I'm reading the script."

He frowned.

"That's your line. 'Perhaps I can be of some assistance.' Try again?"

He nodded.

"Helen Carter is on the ground," I repeated, "dragging herself toward a set of stairs, when you say . . ."

I held my breath and waited. My father's face fell blank.

He had to be kidding me.

"Albert?"

Color rose in his cheeks, and he blinked. He moved to the refrigerator and opened the door, pulling out a bottle of beer.

Fear quickly replaced my concern—the sort of fear a child learns after her world shifts.

I flashed on the image of a favorite figurine, shattered in a drunken rage, and remembered how he'd changed after my mother's diagnosis, and even more so after it became evident she wasn't going to survive.

"What are you doing?" I asked.

He held up the bottle. "Is this all you have?"

"I thought you didn't drink anymore."

He'd quit the day of the funeral, promising me he'd never drink again.

A tangle of frustration and shame played out across his features, and I realized he might drink every day for all I knew. Just because he'd quit drinking once didn't mean he hadn't started again.

"Do you still drink?"

"No," he answered.

Much to my relief, he set the bottle back down on the counter. He shoved his hand through his hair, leaving the strands in utter disarray. "No," he repeated, as his features fell. "I'm going to bed."

I took a backward step. "What about your lines? What about rehearsal tomorrow?"

"I'll reread the script on the drive." Then the light faded from his eyes. "I've put my bags in your grandmother's old room. I hope you don't mind."

"Not at all," I said, understanding why he'd chosen that room instead of the one he'd shared with my mother.

Ghosts.

I reached for his arm as he brushed past me, and he hesitated momentarily.

"You'll go back to your life tomorrow. Right?"

Sadness washed across his gaze, and he shook his head. "I've sublet my apartment. I have no place to go back to."

I dropped my hand from his arm, my mind fumbling to understand his intention when I understood it all too well.

"I should have told you sooner, but I'd like to stay here with you, Destiny. If you don't want me, I'll go to the inn."

Jessica's question ran through my head. *What if he wants a second chance?*

I could only manage one word. "Why?"

"I want to spend time with my daughter."

Too little, too late. I thought, exactly the same thing I'd said to Jessica. But by the time I'd recovered from the shock of his words and the knowledge that he had no place in New York to go back to, he'd disappeared down the hall and up the stairs.

I thought about following him. Thought about ranting and raving and demanding an explanation for why on earth he thought he could sublet his apartment and barge back into my life. But the truth was, the day and Albert's presence had wrung me dry, and a very large part of my being simply needed to shut off the noise in order to survive.

I grabbed the beer he'd left on the counter and headed for the one place I'd find quiet.

I found Marguerite sitting on her back patio, a glass of iced tea puddling condensation on the table beside her. The line of storms that had threatened all day had not yet broken, but the night sky flashed in the distance, the accompanying rumbles of thunder drawing nearer and nearer.

I curled up on the bench beside her, remembering countless days spent in this exact spot or inside, wrapped in a blanket on her sofa.

Until I'd been old enough to stay alone, I'd walked straight to Marguerite's every day after school while my grandmother worked to supplement the money my father had sent from New York.

Marguerite had stepped wholeheartedly into the void my mother's death had left behind. She'd never once complained about her space or her time or her life being crowded by a grieving young girl's presence.

Instead, she'd opened her heart and her home, and she'd pulled me inside.

"So," she said, as she'd said to me more times than I could count, "How was *your* day?"

I looked at her loving eyes and wild auburn curls, and I let loose a sound that was half-laugh, half-sob.

Marguerite wrapped her arm around my shoulders and pulled me close. I leaned hard, as if I were once again ten years old, hiding inside the safe borders of her backyard as my motherless world raced by.

Then I told her everything.

The storm finally broke a little after ten. Fat splats of raindrops hit the panes of my bedroom window, and I wished they could wash away the past twenty-four hours, somehow returning my life to exactly what it had been the day before.

Solitary. Uncomplicated. Comfortable.

The rain quickened, and a sudden image of my mother's violet chairs popped into my mind.

I pulled a pair of jeans on under my nightshirt and raced for the stairs, reaching the back kitchen door just as lightning flashed and crashed close by.

I carefully tucked them close to the back wall of the house, one by one, where they'd be safe beneath the overhang as the long-anticipated summer storm raged outside.

CHAPTER SIX

Albert and I made most of the hour-and-ten-minute drive from Paris to the city in silence the next morning.

He studied his script while I focused on the road, thinking about how special our trips into New York had once been.

Sure, I'd had occasion as an adult to travel into the city with Jessica and her kids or for conferences, but the streets and crowds had never again held the allure I'd once experienced standing in Times Square, holding my mother's and father's hands.

When Albert shut the cover on the script, I shook off the past and dove into the present.

"Well?"

"I think I've got it," he said, although he didn't sound terribly convincing.

"Good to hear."

I navigated onto the ramp for the Lincoln Tunnel, then charged headfirst into the questions that had been bombarding my brain.

"Do you plan to commute daily from Paris to the theater?"

Silence.

"Albert?"

"Why don't you ever call me Dad?" he asked.

I answered with a sharp look.

"The commute?" I asked.

"I'll arrange for a car."

And even though he'd told me he hadn't started drinking again, I needed to ask one more time for my peace of mind.

"What was that beer all about?"

My father's voice fell soft. "That was a weak moment."

"I hope so," I said, although I couldn't shake the feeling that it had been something more.

We were in a lot and parked before I had a chance to ask the rest of my hard-hitting questions, like did he plan to stay in Paris forever, and if so, how soon would he be taking a room at the inn?

Jackson Harding stood waiting at an unmarked burgundy door, the opening almost imperceptible along the expanse of wall edging the sidewalk on West Forty-Fourth as we made our way from the lot to the theater.

He wore an outfit much like the one he'd worn the day before. He appeared pleased to see us, his smile genuine as he held open the door and ushered us inside.

"Welcome to the Manchester," he said, his deep voice rumbling in my ear.

A shiver danced across the back of my neck as I walked into the air-conditioned space.

Jackson led us through a cluttered room and past a desk covered with clipboards, empty candy wrappers, and partially full soda bottles.

"So this is where the magic happens," I said, taking in the backstage area.

Narrow passageways stood tightly lined with props. Small changing areas were framed only by well-worn curtains. Dresses and jackets and suits hung on the wall in collections by character.

Theater employees hustled past, chattering about staging and props and moving equipment.

Although the brick walls showed their age, the space felt alive. For a fleeting moment, I understood my father's love of this place and other theaters like it.

Here, he could inhabit a different world for weeks or months, taking on the persona and clothing and life of a character in a play. Here, he could shed that same world after the show had finished its run and left audiences entertained.

Here, he never had to be himself.

Jackson had been saying something, explaining who did what as they rushed past. I snapped my attention back to his words as I followed behind him.

"Is it chaos on show night?" I asked, unable to imagine what the space would be like during a performance.

Jackson pointed to carefully marked pieces of tape beside each chair, vase, and prop. Labels. "Precision," he said. Then he stopped to press his hand to my shoulder. "How were the lines?"

Something fluttered deep inside me, but I ignored the unwelcome sensation.

"A bit rough." I shrugged. "But he spent the entire ride over reviewing the script."

We'd lost sight of Albert momentarily, and Jackson led me beyond the backstage area, up a flight of ancient, sloping metal stairs that led to another narrow hallway.

I caught a glimpse of my father as he entered the second door on the right. Jackson blocked the door with the toe of his polished loafer, then we followed uninvited into the small, stale space.

A dressing table sat against the far wall, complete with a large mirror framed by makeup lights. Jackson flipped a wall switch and the room came to life, dust motes whirling through the air, jostled free by our entry.

He gestured for me to take the room's one seat, a navy-blue velour sofa that looked as though it had seen better days—many, many better days. As touched as I was by his apparent chivalry, I shook my head and remained standing.

"Would you like to run some lines?" he asked Albert. "Warm up a bit before you head downstairs?"

Albert appeared momentarily startled, but quickly recovered. He pulled himself taller, lengthening his spine. He inhaled deeply through his nose, and I watched as his diaphragm expanded. He transformed before my eyes from the broken man who had gone to bed defeated the night before to the Tony Award–winning actor I'd seen mentioned in the Paris news from time to time.

"How about the first parlor scene?" Jackson said.

I flipped through the pages of the script and fed my father the setup.

"You are looking through the curtains, and your mother says, 'Watching the stars, Bob?'"

When I lifted my gaze from the script to the man, he'd transformed fully into the character of Bob Drummond. He stood tall, his stance younger, stronger, and he gazed toward the wall as if peering through an invisible window.

"There's nothing like the night sky," he said, his baritone stage voice rumbling through the small room. "Nature has a way of reminding us how things should be. Like this." He gestured dramatically, taking a few steps to his left and turning. "This is peace."

Life and vitality shone in his eyes, and I stood speechless, staring at the man I hadn't seen in years.

"Nicely done." Jackson gave a single clap.

My father ran through several more pages of the scene, his confidence visibly improving with each passing moment.

"Fantastic," Jackson said when he'd finished. "Perhaps a quick trip back to your hometown was exactly what you needed."

Then he shifted his attention to me. "Why don't I show you the rest of the building while your father heads off to rehearsal?"

I suddenly couldn't wait to get out of the theater.

As impressive as my father's command of his lines had been, his performance served as a stark reminder that this world was what he'd left me for.

Jackson reached for my elbow, his dark gaze showing a hint of concern. "You all right?"

My stomach fluttered again, and I silently berated myself. I didn't do fluttering stomachs. Didn't do the weak female role.

"I just need to something to eat," I said, waving off his touch. "I've gotten a great sense of the place, though. Thank you."

Jackson studied me a moment too long, apparently not fully convinced by my answer. "Tell you what," he said. "I'm a little hungry myself. Want to grab an early lunch?"

He turned to Albert. "I can have you driven home later, since you'll be tied up in rehearsals all day."

Albert nodded.

I hesitated before I answered, but then I thought, *What the hell, a girl has to eat.* "OK."

We walked Albert downstairs, waiting as he disappeared into a small group gathered backstage; then Jackson and I headed for the exit door.

Our arms brushed together in the close quarters, and I pulled my phone from my pocket to hide the fact I felt flustered. I also hoped to see a text or email regarding the opera house renovation, but found none.

"I'm actually glad we have this opportunity to talk a bit more," he said. "How do you feel about hot dogs?"

"Hot dogs?" I laughed nervously.

"Not a fan?" He raised his brows, then smiled. The move lit his face and softened his features.

"OK," I said. "Hot dogs it is."

We headed down Thirty-Fourth toward a group of food carts.

"Somehow, I pictured you as more of a power-lunch-and-cigar sort of guy."

"That's breakfast," Jackson said, deadpan.

I laughed, startled by his show of humor.

He sidled up to a white hot-dog truck, gesturing for me to order first.

"Mustard and relish," I said.

"Ah," he said. "A traditionalist."

Then he ordered. "Heavy on the sauerkraut, please."

He traded the vendor a ten-dollar bill for our hot dogs, and we made our way toward an oasis of green nestled between Broadway and Avenue of the Americas.

I recognized Herald Square instantly.

Macy's giant storefront loomed across the street, and the statue of Minerva and two bell ringers served as an imposing focal point. Two women stepped away from a bench, pushing strollers as they sipped on oversize coffee cups.

"Good?" Jackson asked, tipping his head toward the now empty seat.

"Perfect."

A slight grin pulled at one corner of his mouth, and I caught myself watching him. I shifted my attention to the gardens, hoping he hadn't noticed.

The summer flowers were in full bloom, and if I'd possessed any sort of talent for small talk, I might have made a smart comment about the juxtaposition of color and tranquility with the surrounding craziness of the city.

Instead, I sat down without saying a word, wondering why in the hell I cared about my lack of conversational skills.

"Your father is a Broadway treasure," Jackson said. He pulled a carefully wrapped hot dog out of the bag, spotted the yellow mustard, shook his head with a teasing smile, and handed me my lunch.

He unwrapped his own hot dog and devoured half in one bite.

"Broadway treasure," I repeated, wondering where this line of conversation was headed.

"Albert Jones has been a fixture on these streets for a very long time." Jackson gestured toward the crowded sidewalk and the bedlam of taxicabs and buses maneuvering for position in the traffic rushing past.

"When I was just starting out, your father gave me a chance. Said he liked what he saw. We've never looked back."

"Until now," I said, sensing a definite *but* in his tone.

Jackson polished off the end of his hot dog and set the crumpled paper between us on the bench.

"I know he looked impressive today," he said, "but he hasn't been himself lately."

"Since his accident?"

He shook his head. "Even before the accident."

Words from decades earlier ran through my mind.

She hasn't been herself.

"Is he sick?" I asked, concerned.

"I don't think so." He blew out a sigh, as if he'd run the possibilities countless times. "Distracted, I think. But usually he's never distracted."

"How about since his injury?" I asked. "Worse? Better?"

"He actually seems detached," Jackson answered. "Maybe he's had enough."

"Of acting?" I couldn't imagine. As far back as I could remember, acting had been my father's life.

Jackson's features softened. "He's had a full workup. MRIs. Cognitive tests. Echo-cardiogram. Vascular tests. You name it."

"All for a bump on the head."

"A bump on the head of Albert Jones. Once Broadway's brightest star."

"Once?"

He nodded. "Even the brightest stars dim eventually."

"What are you trying to say?"

"I'm trying to say that maybe he needs a break. Some time off."

"He told me he sublet his apartment," I said.

Jackson studied me seriously. "I think he's sincere about wanting to spend time with you in Paris."

But why? I thought. *Why now?*

"Let me ask you something," I said. "Has Albert ever spoken about me by name? Shown you a picture?"

Jackson met my stare, our gazes holding a moment too long.

He drew in a long, slow breath. "As I mentioned, he's talked about you a few times. Never with a picture, no. And never by name." He chuckled suddenly. "Oddly enough, I was actually under the impression he had a granddaughter."

"Granddaughter?" My laughter matched his. "Maybe he's been keeping a second family all these years."

Our laughter faded then. Perhaps we both realized that what sounded like a crazy possibility wasn't that crazy. After all, the man had led a completely separate life from mine, and I was the last piece of his first family.

I picked up Jackson's crumpled paper, crossed to a trash can, and tossed it along with the remainder of my hot dog.

"What will you do if he stays in Paris?" Jackson asked when we met on the sidewalk to head back toward the theater and my car.

"The same thing I did when he left Paris," I answered. "I'll live my life."

"That's the thing about life, though, isn't it?" Jackson brushed the front of his jacket as we walked, chasing invisible crumbs. "Sooner or later, she throws every single one of us a curveball."

CHAPTER SEVEN

I walked toward the Paris Inn Pub a little after seven o'clock that evening. The long afternoon sun had faded, and the night sky had begun to darken ahead of the coming sunset.

I'd spent the afternoon working in my shop, hoping for word from the selection committee, but I'd received none. No matter, I had two contracted jobs that, while not huge by any stretch of the imagination, were creative enough to keep me occupied.

I was used to spending much of my time alone, both at home and at work. Being alone didn't bother me. As a matter of fact, I'd become fond of the silence.

Tonight, however, I was looking forward to meeting Jessica at the pub for our weekly night out. I was ready for the noise and the laughter, the singing and the inevitable storytelling.

Karaoke night at the pub was one of the many Paris traditions in which I found comfort. Even though I'd become what many people would call a loner, here in my hometown I was never truly alone.

As I walked down the steps toward the pub entrance, I hesitated for just a moment to appreciate the history of the place.

Perhaps it was the thought of how many others had passed through the massive oak doors before me—Pony Express riders, politicians, neighbors, friends. Perhaps it was the knowledge that once I passed through the doors I'd be surrounded by those who knew me best and welcomed me.

Perhaps it was just that I needed the relief of being here, tonight, away from thoughts of Albert, thoughts of the opera house job, thoughts of my thoughts.

Once inside, I made my way through the crowd, headed for my usual seat at the bar. Jessica stood waiting, and Jerry, the world's best bartender, opened a bottle of my favorite beer as I approached. I gave him a nod of thanks and sat down.

"Kids with your mom?" I asked Jessica.

She nodded. "The plan was popcorn and movies for dinner."

I grinned. "Doesn't sound half-bad."

Jerry, doing double duty, as he did every week, stepped to the microphone and called Jack Maxwell to the stage.

As the local mortician launched into a halfway-decent rendition of the Beach Boys' "California Girls," Jessica leaned close. "You owe me over twenty-four hours of updates." She tucked her long hair behind her ears. "Start talking."

I started with Jackson Harding's visit, touched on the violet chairs and practicing lines with my dad, skipped all mention of the beer, and ended with my hot-dog lunch in Herald Square.

A grin tugged at the corners of her mouth.

"What?" I asked.

"Sounds like a cozy lunch." Jessica wiggled her brows. "Anything else you want to tell me about this guy?"

"No," I said, giving a quick lift and drop of my shoulders. "He's just Albert's manager."

But based on the amusement in her face, Jessica wasn't buying a word. "Moving on," she said. "Anything from the selection committee? My sources at the lunch counter tell me one presentation was a perfect fit."

I shook my head and took a long swallow of beer.

"And Albert?"

I met her gaze, warmed by the concern I saw there—genuine concern that had never wavered in all the time we'd been friends. "You may have been right about him wanting a second chance."

"What makes you say that?"

"He gave up his apartment in the city. Said he wants to spend time here in Paris."

"Whoa." She sat back against the bar as if I'd dropped a bomb on her lap. "How do you feel about that?"

I squeezed my eyes shut, but before I could answer, the noise level in the pub fell to almost nothing. Jessica tapped my knee. "Look."

In the doorway, looking more than a little bit lost, stood my father.

I held my breath, expecting a rush to greet him. A solid measure of surprise slid through me when only a handful of people stepped forward.

The music level rose with the next performance, and the conversation level returned to normal.

Albert shook hands with the three men that had stepped forward— the town pharmacist, Manny the barber, and Byron Kennedy.

"Oh, look," I said with more than a little bit of sarcasm. "A reunion with Uncle Byron."

But Jessica said nothing, leaning forward to rest her hand on my arm. "Albert looks lost."

She was right. My father did look lost.

"He doesn't belong here anymore," I said. "And now he knows it."

While she didn't verbally agree with me, we shared a look that said she knew I was right.

Paris folks weren't just loyal; they also had very long memories. If my father had thought he'd receive a hero's welcome upon his return to the pub, he'd been wrong. Most everyone here still remembered how he'd walked away and left his ten-year-old daughter behind.

I hoisted my beer. "To old friends."

"To old friends," she said as she clinked her wineglass against the neck of my bottle.

Marguerite made her way toward me, then wrapped me in a tight hug. "You OK?"

I nodded.

She patted my cheek before quickly turning and walking away.

I understood why a moment later, as my father made his way toward me.

"How was the rest of your day?" I asked when he got close enough to hear me over the music.

"Interesting."

"What do you mean?" I asked, shouting above the noise.

But before he could give me an answer, Byron Kennedy grabbed him by the elbow.

"Good evening, ladies," he said as he steered Albert toward the end of the bar.

They settled at the far corner, and when Jerry picked up a bottle of scotch, the small hairs at the base of my neck bristled.

I relaxed when he set just one glass down. In front of Byron.

"I thought you came here to have fun," Jessica said.

"You're right." I shifted in my seat to focus on the stage instead of my father. "For the next few hours, I don't care about the opera house job or Albert."

But I did care. More than I wanted to admit.

Jackson's words about my father's distraction had stuck with me, and I couldn't help but wonder what Albert wasn't telling me. Although we only saw each other once a year and knew little about each other's lives, he was still my father.

As the night progressed, I continued to sneak glances at him, studying his body language, measuring his expressions.

"Stop it," Jessica said, elbowing my side. "You're staring."

I shot her a frown just as Marguerite approached, heading toward the stage.

She slowed long enough to give my shoulder a squeeze. "Did Byron say anything about a decision?"

I shook my head, and she crossed her fingers.

Then she took the stage with a poise all her own. Her flamboyant skirt swirled, flashing violet as she swayed to the opening measures of the song she'd selected.

Her music choice was a slow melody, meandering and compelling, and I felt myself relaxing. The buzz of voices inside the inn grew quiet, and all eyes focused on her performance.

She and my mother used to sing in our kitchen as they baked cookies, pretending their wooden spoons were microphones. I would clap along, mesmerized by the two women who'd seemed invincible to me. Invincible, as though nothing bad could ever touch either of them.

Applause roared through the crowd as Marguerite hit her final note. But while every other patron inside the bar celebrated Marguerite's performance, my father walked briskly past, headed for the exit.

"Albert," I called out, but he didn't hear me.

Wondering what might have set my father off, I glanced at where Byron Kennedy sat. Kennedy, however, showed no sign that anything was amiss. If anything, he looked more relaxed than usual, applauding with the rest of the crowd as Marguerite returned to her seat.

Had Marguerite's performance brought back the same memories for my father as it had for me?

Seems like yesterday, he'd said the night before.

I'd never stopped to think how fresh all the reminders of Paris would be for him, even after twenty years.

"I need to go," I said, setting down my partially empty beer bottle.

"So soon?" Jessica frowned.

"Who are you kidding?" I said and then kissed her cheek. "You'll be home with your babies before I can figure out where Albert went."

She squeezed my hand. "Think about what I said. About second chances."

As I headed for the exit, I did just that. But someone tapped my shoulder just as I reached for the door.

Byron Kennedy.

"Congratulations," he said brightly as I turned around. "You were the selection committee's unanimous choice."

His pronouncement seemed so out of place for the moment that I remained momentarily silent, too surprised to respond.

He grabbed my hand, giving it a vigorous shake.

I snapped myself to attention, forgetting all about Albert.

"Thank you," I said, returning his shake. "I'm thrilled. Thank you."

I'd done it. I'd won the bid.

At that moment, I was sure my smile must reach from ear to ear.

"The committee would like to talk to you about a production schedule. Can you come in first thing Monday?" he asked.

"Absolutely."

I stepped back into the crowd long enough to tell Jessica and Marguerite the good news; then I headed out into the Paris night in search of my father.

When Albert wasn't at home, I backtracked the four blocks to the river, passing the Paris Inn on my way to the asphalt trail that ran along the Delaware.

I was concerned for his well-being, much as that realization left me a bit unnerved.

I spotted his silhouette as I stepped off onto the grass.

For a fleeting moment I thought about turning back, thought about minding my own business, but I wanted to know if he was OK.

I cared.

That revelation shook me to the core.

I didn't have to like the man or what he'd done, but he was still my father. I'd spent the past twenty years hating the man, but the truth was, I still loved him. Flaws and all.

"Albert," I called out. "Is that you?"

"Over here," he answered, and I made my way across the dark expanse between us, scrambling up onto Lookout Rock when I reached him. "Checking on me?"

"You didn't stay very long." I shrugged. "I wondered why."

He took his time answering. "Too much to take in."

I thought about the beer the night before. "You and Byron did some catching up?"

He sat quietly for a moment. "It's been a long time." Then, anticipating exactly where my question was headed, he added, "I said no when he offered to buy me a scotch."

"I'm glad." I pulled my feet up, wrapping my arms around my knees.

Silence dropped between us.

"Do you remember how they used to sing?" he asked.

"Mom and Marguerite?"

He nodded, and I flashed on myriad memories of moments spent just like this, side by side atop Lookout Rock.

"I remember."

"I actually thought Marguerite's song might have upset you."

He sighed. "It was easier not to miss your mother when I wasn't here. I suppose that's part of why I never really came back."

I dropped my chin, staring at my lap. "It's a lousy excuse."

Another long silence stretched between us.

"I quit the show today," he said flatly.

Quit the show?

Surprise and sadness wound their way through me. *Even the brightest stars dim eventually,* Jackson had said.

"Are you all right? Physically?"

He nodded.

"Were the lines too difficult after all?" I asked.

My father laughed, the sound more tired than amused. "That's the crazy thing. As soon as I decided I was through, I could remember every line."

"Jackson said he thought you might need a break."

"Maybe. Or maybe I'm just done."

I inhaled deeply, then sat back, staring up into the dense trees, searching for stars in the summer sky. "What will you do now?"

"No idea."

"Do you need to work?" I asked, letting myself settle into our conversation, not questioning the ease with which we'd set aside the past for a while.

"Are you talking about money?"

"Yes," I answered. "Money."

"I'm pretty well set in that department."

"Great," I said. I knew nothing about this man. Not how much he made or how many shows he'd performed. I knew nothing about where he'd lived or who his friends were.

He was a shadow of my past who had suddenly taken on solid form.

"How long are you going to stay in Paris?" I asked.

"I'm not sure."

The familiar anger simmered inside me.

I'd expected him to say "for good" or something a bit more definite. Instead, his answer left me wondering not whether he'd be leaving again, but when.

If I let him back into my life and my heart, I was setting myself up for loss. Again.

Even so, I took a deep breath and said the thing Jessica would want me to say, the thing my mother would expect me to say.

"If you want to stay at the house until you figure out your plans, you can."

Silence beat between us for several long seconds, during which I thought about changing my mind, thought about having my head examined, but I said nothing.

Maybe he did deserve a second chance.

"I'm sorry I left." Albert's words bridged the space between us, his voice cracking.

His blunt statement shocked me, and I swallowed against the tightness in my throat.

He'd never apologized before, never acknowledged what he'd done.

"I don't think I knew how to stay without her," he continued.

His words cut me to the core. "What about me?"

"You had your grandmother . . . and Marguerite."

He took my hand, interlacing our fingers. I surprised myself by not pulling away.

"Didn't you ever think I needed you more?"

He said nothing, did nothing. He held my hand, tightening his grip, and stared at the darkness over the river.

After a few moments, I extricated my fingers. "Ready to go?" I asked, when it became apparent he wasn't going to answer my question.

I climbed down from the rock, thought about holding out my hand to steady his descent, but took a backward step instead.

I distanced myself and said nothing on the walk toward Third Street, working to quiet the small voice inside me that wondered if I hadn't just made a mistake.

CHAPTER EIGHT

I heard the rattle of dishes and pans from the kitchen as I headed downstairs a little after seven thirty the next morning.

I'd slept later than normal, but supposed my exhausted brain was trying to make up for the restless nights since my father's arrival.

He stood at the kitchen counter, frowning, a measuring cup in one hand, a large mixing bowl on the counter in front of him.

"Pancakes?" he asked, a smudge of flour on his cheek.

I took a moment to ground myself. In a little more than forty-eight hours, I'd gone from wanting the man in the next car back to New York to inviting him to move in, albeit temporarily.

"Pancakes," I repeated, a sudden image of my mother's coffee-stained recipe card flashing through my mind. "You know how to make pancakes?"

He nodded. Then he grimaced. "In theory I do. I mean, it's been done, but not in a long while. Plus, I found a box of Bisquick in the pantry."

I headed for the coffeepot, where a full glass carafe sat waiting. "You made coffee? I should have invited you to move back years ago."

I winced, then chalked up my overly familiar remark to the fact that I hadn't yet had any caffeine. I filled my favorite coffee mug and leaned back to watch Albert cook, hoping he hadn't given too much weight to my words.

"I looked for some fruit," he said, "but I couldn't find any."

"I work a lot." I shrugged. "And then I eat at Jessica's."

"What about breakfast?" he asked.

"What about it?"

"Most important meal of the day."

I pulled open the refrigerator, pulled out a gallon of milk, and poured two glasses. "You're not seriously going to lecture me on my dietary habits, are you?"

He fell silent then, concentrating on the puddles of batter he'd poured onto a large frying pan.

"I don't suppose you have a proper skillet somewhere?" he asked.

I shook my head, surprised to be enjoying the moment, watching him fumble his way through my poorly appointed kitchen.

"These will be up in a minute. I set the table out back."

Considering that my typical morning consisted of a shower, a quick cup of coffee, and a brisk walk to Jessica's café, I gave my arm a pinch as I headed outside to see the table for myself, just to make sure the past few days hadn't been a dream.

Albert followed on my heels, balancing our plates and a dish of butter with the finesse of someone who'd been serving breakfast for the two of us for years.

I settled on one of my mother's now-violet bistro chairs, doing my best to ignore the echo of earlier times in this same spot.

Instead I focused on the moment, on the man I'd once known so well but now knew not at all.

"Do you want to talk any more about your decision?" I asked, as he set down our plates and sat across from me. "Now that you've had a chance to sleep on it?"

He shook his head. "I wanted to ask *you* a question."

For a moment I imagined he might ask about my work, my friends, my life, but instead he said, "Would you mind if I replanted the garden?"

"The garden?" I blinked, having expected a slightly deeper breakfast conversation after our heart-to-heart the night before.

"I thought it might be nice."

"Nice," I repeated, my thoughts whirling.

"Your mother loved that garden." He spoke around a mouthful of pancakes, answering my question before I'd given it voice. "I thought you might enjoy having it restored."

Even as he spoke the words, I saw through them.

"None of these things will bring her back," I said, setting down my fork, losing my appetite.

He looked at me then, studying my face, seemingly searching for something.

"I'm doing this for you," he said. "I thought you'd like it."

I wanted to believe him, but fought the urge to do so. I'd invested too much time in my self-preservation.

"Thanks," I said, doubt blatant in my voice. I pushed away from the table and moved to clear my still-full plate.

Albert frowned. "You've barely touched your breakfast."

"I have to get to work." I slowed as I walked past him. "If you want to replant the garden, go for it."

After all, I hadn't touched the bed that ran along the property line between my house and Marguerite's in years. I spent my days adding charm and personality to the homes of others, but I suddenly couldn't remember the last time I'd worked on my own.

I took my usual route to work, walking west on Third Street, then south on Stone Lane the two blocks to Bridge. I followed the cobblestone sidewalk until I crossed the street a half block later, where Artisan's Alley jutted off on a diagonal.

The sights and sounds of the summer morning enveloped me, soothing the melancholy I felt after my conversation with Albert. Birds sang, a pair of seagulls circled overhead, vibrant pots of impatiens lined the street, and the scents of coffee and the café mingled to create the magic that was Paris.

Manny swept the step outside his barbershop, deep in concentration.

"Great duet last night," I called out. He nodded and gave me a quick salute.

Polly Klein looked up from the chalkboard outside her Klip and Kurl to call out her congratulations. "Way to go, Destiny. I have every confidence you'll bring back the charm of the opera house."

"Thank you, Polly."

Pride welled up inside me as I made the turn down Artisan's Alley.

My father might not show an interest in my work or my latest news, but my fellow Paris residents did. They'd been my family for most of my life, not Albert Jones.

My carpentry shop sat partway down the alley, situated back from the street in an old converted two-story garage. The local florist occupied the first floor, and my work area occupied the second. There I designed and cut the pieces for my custom jobs, assembling the projects and their sections for transport to their destinations.

The building had long ago been painted a deep red—a color I'd loyally maintained over the years. I'd chosen a pop of green for the giant shutters that framed the second-floor window.

There was nothing quite like the view of Paris I enjoyed from the double-wide, floor-to-ceiling window, or the feeling of sunlight and fresh air streaming in whenever I opened the panes. There was also nothing like the sense of accomplishment I felt each time one of my creations exceeded a customer's expectations.

Restoring the ornate woodwork that had once graced the box seats and stage of the opera house would be my greatest challenge to date—a challenge I couldn't wait to meet.

I climbed the outside steps and unlocked the brilliant violet door to my shop.

Had I painted the door to match my mother's favorite color? Perhaps subconsciously. All I knew was that the door, the shutters, and this space never failed to make me smile.

The wind chimes sounded as I pushed through the door, and the smell of sawdust tickled my nose. I relaxed a notch as I stepped inside, the tension between my shoulders easing.

I'd been working on two projects prior to the opera house presentation: custom-made panel doors for Don and Nan Michaels, and kitchen cabinets for Erma Leroy's private suite in her B&B.

Both projects were nearing completion, and if I worked through the weekend I'd be able to finish one installation and schedule the other for the following week to make way for the opera house work.

I stepped to the back wall of my shop, where before-and-after photos hung beside sketches I'd completed as I planned various jobs.

Pride welled inside me. Pride for all I'd accomplished. Pride for the business I'd built on my own.

I shifted my focus to materials I'd gathered for the renovation project.

Thanks to the quality of records kept by the Paris Historical Society, I'd been able to find documentation of how the opera house had appeared prior to its last major overhaul. I'd photocopied pictures from the historical journals, and images of the original interior now hung on my shop wall, waiting hopefully for my work to begin.

I sighed happily, tracing my fingertips over the copies. Like a kid with a new toy, I wanted to start now. Wanted to measure and remeasure, sample wood selections, and run a few practice cuts on my equipment.

But not today.

Even though today and the next several days were about finishing up the old to make room for the new, they were also about creating the best cabinets and panel doors I could fashion. They were about keeping my focus on the jobs at hand.

Yet even as I turned away from the opera house photos, I couldn't help but remember how my father had once commanded that stage. Strong. Confident. Riveting.

I'd been mesmerized watching him, so proud to call him Dad.

I wanted so badly to wash away all the years since then, to go back to how things had once been, but did I dare?

If ever there was a time to listen to my head and not to my heart, this was it. For my own good.

I put on a fresh pot of coffee. Then I shut my father, the opera house, and the past out of my head, and focused on the work at hand.

CHAPTER NINE

The temperature had soared well above ninety by the time I returned home.

I watched my father from across the street, his face beet-red, his gray T-shirt drenched with sweat.

He hoisted a pile of dead weeds from the garden into a lawn-refuse bag, not realizing he was being watched.

He'd pulled out yards of dead shrubbery and overgrown weeds, and although the garden was all but bare, the property appeared transformed.

How had I not seen how overgrown and neglected the garden had become?

My grandmother had once used weekends in the garden as therapy for me, a way to help me survive grief and middle school at the same time, and I'd spent every Saturday morning trying to replicate the care and attention my mother and father had devoted to the flower bed.

At first I'd carefully tended to every plant's individual needs; then I'd shifted to merely pulling weeds. Before long, my attention and interest faded away completely. My grandmother lost her interest in the garden, too, never nagging me to resume my Saturday chore.

Perhaps the reminder of all we'd lost had been too much. Perhaps it had been easier for us both to pretend the beautiful garden had never existed.

Albert straightened, brushed his hands against his dirt-encrusted chinos, and met my gaze.

I braced myself as I crossed the street, remembering how faithfully my mother and father had tended to the annuals and perennials they'd planted.

"Looks amazing," I called out, expecting my father to say something about how badly the garden had been let go.

But he merely stood and accepted my compliment. "Now we'll plant," he said, "but I'm glad you like it so far."

He said nothing about the neglect. Nothing about the garden's sorry state, the fact that none of the original beauty remained.

The only surviving plant was the azalea, which stood untouched.

"Are you leaving that?" I pointed.

Albert shot me an incredulous look. "That was your mother's favorite."

"But it hasn't bloomed in years."

"Some plants can sit dormant for years and survive."

Picasso rounded the corner, headed straight for my father's work.

I scooped him into my arms and stepped toward Marguerite's house before the poodle and my father could start a fresh round of turf wars.

"Let me carry Picasso home," I said. "Then I'll order pizza for dinner."

"Already have a casserole in the oven," Albert answered. "Went grocery shopping."

"No kidding," I said, shaking my head in disbelief.

I followed the path to Marguerite's backyard, considering everything my father had done in a day.

Gardening. Grocery shopping. Cooking.

As much as I'd like to believe otherwise, I couldn't help but think his efforts were part of some act.

I found Marguerite painting in the middle of her backyard, her turquoise stool pulled close to her easel.

Beneath her brush, a house had taken shape. My house. Not the way it appeared now, but as it had once been. Full of life. Brightly painted shutters framed every window, and vibrant gardens trimmed every edge of the canvas.

"I remember," she said, her voice barely audible.

In the painting, lush swirls of color surrounded my house, filling the canvas with light and life. The ache inside me deepened, and I flashed on how the house had looked long ago, during the years in which my mother and father had spent their spare moments weeding, planting, trimming, singing.

I thought about how my father labored now, working to give a second life to the garden, and perhaps to us.

Second chances.

I wanted to believe this might be ours. I wanted to believe that the garden and I wouldn't return to precisely what we'd been for the past twenty years.

Forgotten.

"I can't believe you know how to make Mom's tuna casserole," I said a short while later as my father and I sat at the kitchen table. "I wish I could find her recipe cards."

I'd always wanted them and had actually searched for them weeks after her death. Grandmother had helped me, but she'd told me some losses never could be understood.

Sometimes things simply disappeared.

My father ignored my statement, and we ate in companionable silence.

I found myself remembering all the meals my mother had once made, how she'd always insisted she wasn't a good cook, when the truth was, she'd been amazing.

My mind wandered through our shared past, then veered into the years my father and I had spent apart.

Perhaps it was time to explore the mystery of the last twenty years.

"Were you successful right away when you went to New York?"

Albert choked on his mouthful of casserole. "Heavens, no, but I was lucky. By my third job I'd landed a speaking role, and by my seventh I'd landed a lead."

"On Broadway?"

He shook his head. "Off. But Broadway soon followed."

He told me stories as we ate, about his first apartment and his last. About how it had felt when he first saw his face on a Broadway poster.

I studied him as he spoke. His features had softened with age, and lines etched character around his mouth and eyes, signs of a man who'd smiled a lot.

Had he smiled a lot? I wondered.

He used to smile. He used to smile all the time.

The joy in his voice carried me back to when he'd woven stories of adventure and bravery, convincing me I could become anything I set my mind to.

"Do you remember the day I climbed Marguerite's tree?" I asked.

Albert closed his eyes and smiled, as though the scene were playing through his mind. "I'd told you that you could do anything, and you decided to fly."

He laughed, the actor's mask falling completely away. "I thought your mother might kill me. Do you remember falling?" he asked.

I shook my head. "I remember you catching me."

His smile faded, and his bright eyes dimmed.

Sadness and confusion knotted inside me. I'd never understand how he could go from that father to the father who sat before me now.

"Did you ever wonder about me?" I asked. "About my life? My work?"

"We were together every Christmas."

Christmas.

My mother's most cherished day.

I'd often wondered why he bothered to visit at all, but I suspected the real reason: somewhere in his mind, he'd convinced himself that if we were together at Christmas, he hadn't totally let her down.

The ache deepened. "But we never talked. Not like this."

He shook his head. "No. No, we didn't." He set down his fork, took a drink of water, and changed our conversation completely, apparently having had enough exploration of our family dynamic.

"Byron told me about your presentation to the opera board. Said you had some forward-thinking ideas about using the salvaged lumber from the mill for your renovation."

I narrowed my gaze, wondering why he hadn't shared this sooner. "Did he tell you I'd been selected?"

Albert shook his head. "I heard that today in town. Congratulations. You should be proud."

No, I thought, even as I said, "Thanks." *He* should be proud.

But did it matter?

I was no longer the ten-year-old who needed her father's approval. I was no longer the girl who'd climbed a tree to prove she could fly.

I'd built my business without him. I'd built my life without him. Hearing his praise now only served to remind me how long I'd survived without it.

CHAPTER TEN

My father called me back downstairs later that evening.

He'd taken a long shower while I'd cleaned up from dinner, and while I'd been changing out of my work clothes into a favorite pair of shorts and a T-shirt, I'd assumed he'd gone to his room to read or downstairs to watch television.

Instead, he'd set up a small fish tank in the kitchen.

"What is that?" I asked, feeling a fresh wave of disbelief as I scrutinized the object on my counter.

"Isn't she lovely?" he said, gazing at the smallest, most miserable-looking fish I'd ever seen. "I call her Scarlet."

"Scarlet," I repeated, stepping close to peer into the tiny tank. "Did you ever think you should ask me before adding a fish tank to my kitchen?" I asked, my tone more than a little bit annoyed.

My father straightened, his brows furrowing. "I thought you'd be pleased."

"With a fish?" I frowned. "Where did she come from?"

"Harrington's. I saw her when I was in town earlier. Kept her hidden until I had a chance to set up the tank."

Harrington's pet store had been one of my favorite stops back when my father and I would take our strolls through town. We'd peer through the window at the latest kittens or puppies, and I'd ask for a pet each time we visited.

"You always wanted a pet, and your mother and I always said no." He gestured to Scarlet as though she were the grand prize on a television game show. "Here she is."

Fatigue pushed at my incredulity. If the man was trying to win back my trust and affection, did he think he could do so with a *fish*?

"That was a long time ago."

"She's low maintenance," he explained. "She has her own plant to sleep on, you feed her only once a day, and she'll be right here"—he patted the counter—"each time you stop in the kitchen."

I rubbed my face. "I don't understand why you'd do this."

His features fell, and as much as I briefly felt bad for crushing his enthusiasm, I also realized he was an actor, capable of donning whatever facial expression he chose for the benefit of persuading others. Myself included.

Then he simply said, "I thought you'd like her."

"Well, I'm sorry." I shook my head. "I can't get excited about having a tiny aquarium in my kitchen. Can we return her?"

His eyes widened in mock horror. "She'll hear you."

We glared at each other for several seconds, during which I realized how ridiculous it was to be standing here debating the merits of a two-inch-long aquatic animal.

My father broke the silence first. "Bob Harrington said we can return her for a full refund should she pass during the next two weeks."

Pass. There was a term I'd loathed ever since my mother died, like dying were some sort of exam to be rewarded.

"Lovely."

I leaned into the counter and stared into Scarlet's tank. Then I shifted my gaze to the window. Marguerite's porch light glowed from her back patio, and I realized she must still be out there, working on one project or another.

A bit of distance from Scarlet and my father was exactly what I needed.

"I'm going next door for a while," I said. "Please leave the aquarium box where I can find it. I'll return her tomorrow on my way into work."

His features fell, and I thought about reconsidering. Instead I walked next door, desperately needing to decompress.

Five minutes later I'd brought Marguerite up-to-date on the fish, the garden, the pancakes—and the fact that I'd invited my father to stay with me temporarily.

"Sounds like you could use some art therapy," she said, firm in her belief that art was the solution to the world's problems.

She reached into one of her many supply baskets and pulled out a large, soft-backed book. Then she handed me a cup full of slender markers.

"Adult coloring books," she explained. "They're all the rage."

"*Sea Creatures*," I read before opening the cover. I shot her a look. "In honor of Scarlet?"

Marguerite smiled, but her expression had gone serious.

"I've known your father for a very long time," she said. "Since your mother and I were girls at Paris Elementary."

I sat quietly, watching her as she spoke.

Over the years she'd proven to be one of the fairest, most level-headed voices in my life. She'd also never hidden her distaste for Albert Jones, which was why her next words surprised me.

"I was friends with Albert before he and your mother fell in love." She sat back a bit, her brows lifting. "He was like a brother to me. Always was. Until your mother got sick."

"And he left," I said.

Marguerite nodded. "I know you want to believe he's here for you, Destiny. You may tell me you know better, and you may think you know better, but deep inside that heart of yours there's a little girl who still wants to believe he never meant to leave."

Her words hit their mark, rocking me.

"You can't trust him, honey," she continued. "Not yet."

I nodded. "I know that."

Marguerite leaned forward, took my hands. "I know you think you know that, but just be careful. A few meals, a neat garden, and a new pet are not enough to make up for missing out on most of your life."

Her words settled on my shoulders like a damp blanket, suffocating the seeds of hope that had taken root despite my best efforts to resist them. Yet, even though I knew intellectually that she was right, I couldn't help but hope she might be wrong.

An hour later I pushed open the door to my kitchen, hearing nothing but silence in the big old house. No doubt my father's hard physical work had taken its toll, and he'd gone to bed early.

The box from Scarlet's tank sat beside her on the counter, just as I'd requested.

I thought about boxing up the tiny red fish right then and there and banging on Harrington's door. After all, Mr. and Mrs. Harrington had lived above the shop on Bridge Street for as long as I could remember.

But when Scarlet stared back at me with her beady little eyes, something inside me softened.

My father's phone chirped from where he'd left it next to the empty box, and I glanced at the screen.

New text message. Sydney Mason.

The simple notification served as a reminder that Albert inhabited a world of people I knew nothing about.

We might be father and daughter, presently residing beneath the same roof, but we'd lived separate lives for two decades. Chances were pretty good we'd be living separate lives for decades more.

"Good night, Scarlet," I said, clicking off the kitchen light on my way toward the hall.

Whoever Sydney Mason was, she'd have to wait until morning for Albert's reply.

CHAPTER ELEVEN

I spent that weekend finishing and installing paneled French doors for Nan and Don Michaels, as well as completing Erma Leroy's cabinets.

Albert toiled in the garden, as if he craved his hands in the dirt.

I'd taken him to the garden shop several miles out of town to select several Shasta daisy and coneflower plants, along with three bushes whose names I couldn't remember, but which Albert assured me would grow with minimal care and return to full bloom each spring.

Scarlet remained where Albert had placed her on the kitchen counter. I'd put her box out for recycling, deciding one tiny fish couldn't hurt the low-maintenance nature of my life.

First thing Monday morning, as promised, I met with the full opera house board to review the proposed budget and discuss their projected completion date.

If all went well, the opera house interior would be fully renovated and restored in time for next year's spring festival.

After the meeting, I gave myself permission to indulge in something I rarely did.

I wandered.

Paris was beautiful in late summer. Honestly, Paris was beautiful year-round; I just wasn't the sort of person to walk around and notice. I preferred to work, go home, watch my neighbors and friends sing karaoke every Wednesday night at the inn, and stop off for coffee every morning at the café.

I strolled past the Bainbridge Estate, following the grassy path that marked the end of town and the start of the bike path that ran along the Delaware. I turned onto Front Street, taking note of a small line of cars at Capshaw Funeral Home.

Henrietta Baille, the town's recluse, had died a few days earlier. While I'd never met the woman, I was relieved to see that her out-of-town relatives had traveled to Paris to lay her to rest.

I had attended several services over the years, but it was my mother's funeral I remembered anytime I walked past.

The line of mourners. My hand in my father's. The faces. The condolences. The flower arrangements, their perfume heavy and haunting.

When I reached the Paris Library I hesitated, staring at the massive iron gates of the town cemetery just a few paces ahead.

During my childhood, when my grandmother had been alive, we'd visited my mother's grave every Sunday after church. We'd sit side by side in quiet reflection, leaving behind flowers and whispered prayers before we headed home for French toast and fresh-squeezed orange juice.

I rested one hand against the cold, time-worn metal.

I hadn't had French toast in a very long time.

The cemetery was fairly deserted at this time of the morning, though I imagined the funeral procession would find its way here before too long.

I skirted down two rows, turned left, and found my mother's tombstone as though I'd been on autopilot.

The side of her stone had gone a bit dark with time and weathering, and guilt blossomed inside me. A good daughter would be here more often.

It was amazing how sharply the neglect of a person's life came into focus once she stopped long enough to notice.

I brushed my fingertips against the engraved lettering of her name, tracing the dates of her birth and death.

"How was your meeting?"

Marguerite's voice sounded close, sending me reeling. She held a spray bottle in one hand and clutched a brush and folded cloth in the other.

"You scared the hell out of me." I clutched my chest, wondering just how fast a person's heart could beat.

Her auburn brows lifted. "Sorry, I was cleaning the marker three plots over." She pointed to an area behind her, then fell serious. "She was his life, you know."

Regret washed over her face instantly, evidently realizing the moment her statement hit its mark.

"He's made that abundantly clear."

She sighed softly, at an uncharacteristic loss for what to say. She held up the spray bottle. "Want to spruce up her stone?"

I frowned, confused. "Spruce up?"

She leaned past me to spray my mother's name and dates; then she handed me the brush. "Scrub," she commanded.

And so I did, working gingerly at first and adding a bit more force as the stone brightened and the darkness faded.

"Do you make this a habit?" I asked once we'd finished the stone and wiped the entire surface clean. "Showing up at graves with your spray bottle in hand?"

She smiled and gestured for me to follow. "Come on. I'll show you."

We walked silently past several rows of stones and grave markers, coming to a stop in the farthest corner of the original section of the cemetery. Here the stones dated back as far as the early 1800s, yet it was evident Marguerite had been here this morning, doing her best to brighten the marble and granite.

"I like to look after the ones who have no one else to look after them."

"Why?" I understood why Marguerite would clean the stones. She had a kind heart. Perhaps she needed something to do, but there had to be more to the story.

"One more stop," she said, waving her hand in a follow-me gesture as she headed away, back toward a more recent section of plots.

Marguerite pointed to single stone, pristine in condition, heartbreaking in information. Joseph Connors. Born 1946. Died 1967.

"Vietnam," she said softly. "He promised me he'd come back, but he never did."

I hooked my arm through hers and drew her near. "I'm so sorry."

Marguerite smiled, hesitating before she spoke. "I take care of the forgotten because it gives me hope that someday someone will do the same thing for Joseph."

"Your sweetheart?" I asked.

"My fiancé," she answered.

Her simple statement shocked me.

"I didn't know," I said slowly, staring at proof of the life I'd never known—Marguerite's life before me.

She gave my arm a squeeze. "You had enough loss in your life."

"You never met anyone else?" I asked.

She sighed, the sound a mixture of melancholy and joy. "I never met anyone else worth marrying."

A sudden possibility filled my head. Had she not married because she'd been too busy filling in for my mother?

"Was it because of me?" I asked.

She pressed a kiss to my cheek. "Absolutely not. Although I could be asking you the same question."

"What?"

"Why haven't you ever talked about getting married?"

I shook my head and laughed, wishing my mother could be right there, laughing along with me.

"Married? I've never even been in love." Hell, I could count the number of dates I'd had on one hand.

Marguerite tipped her chin and gave me a slight smile. "When you least expect it."

I shrugged. "I'm happy how I am."

"So you keep saying, dear girl. So you keep saying."

We sat together beside Joseph's grave for close to an hour. Marguerite regaled me with stories of their youth, and courtship, and life in Paris.

She fell silent after telling me about the day she learned Joseph's helicopter had gone down. Then she stood and brushed traces of dried grass from the folds of her bright turquoise skirt.

"Ready?" she asked.

"Ready," I answered.

I carried her cleaning supplies as she stopped periodically to straighten a flower arrangement or wreath.

The first of the funeral procession was pulling to the curb along Front Street as we stepped onto the cobblestone sidewalk and headed for home.

Then Marguerite stopped, faced me, and cupped my chin, the move so maternal it stole my breath.

"Sooner or later, dear girl, everyone comes home. It might not be how we wanted or when we wanted, but they do."

But as we made our way back to Third Street, I couldn't help but think how wrong Marguerite was.

Sooner or later, everyone left.

CHAPTER TWELVE

I stared at Scarlet's tank the next morning, wondering what had gone wrong.

She hadn't eaten her food, so I'd removed it using a tool that looked a lot like an old-fashioned turkey baster. I suctioned out about twenty-five percent of her now-murky water, then added fresh springwater.

The fish looked happier momentarily, if that was possible.

I stared at her, wondering how it had come to be that I was standing in my kitchen at six thirty in the morning obsessing over the health and mental status of a fish.

I'd worked late the night before, cleaning and reorganizing my shop, wanting to clear the deck to focus completely on the massive job ahead of me. Albert's bedroom door had been closed by the time I got back to the house, although I'd heard him during the night, pacing, restless.

A half-empty pot of coffee sat waiting for me on the counter, leaving me to wonder exactly how early he'd awoken and where he was now.

I headed for the front door, correctly suspecting I'd find him digging in the garden. I watched him through the sidelights, his lips moving in apparent conversation with the plants.

Perhaps I should be more concerned with his health than with Scarlet's.

"Good morning," I said, stepping outside onto the front porch. He looked pale when he turned around and my heart caught, a frisson of guilt sliding through me. Perhaps I should have checked on him when I'd heard him during the night. "You OK?"

He frowned, nodded, then shook his head, his brows furrowing.

I stepped close, laughing nervously at the sight of him, covered in dirt up to his elbows.

"What is it with you and this garden?"

He looked at me then, eyes bare of all pretense, all façade.

"Dad?" I said, dropping to my knees next to him.

His gaze brightened momentarily, and I realized what I'd called him for the first time since his return. His eyes glistened, and he dropped his chin, squeezing his eyes tight.

Fear danced through me.

Was he having a breakdown? A heart attack? Should I call Doc Malone?

"Dad?" I repeated. "Tell me what's wrong."

He shook his head before he spoke, his words barely audible. "You'll never forgive me."

My pulse quickened. "Forgive you for what?"

"Not telling you the truth."

"About?"

"The full reason I'm here."

I braced myself, my mind running through the possibilities.

He was broke. He was ill. He'd been run out of New York.

"You have a sister."

His words hit me, bounced off, failed to compute.

"She's here in Paris. I met her last night."

I scrambled backward, away from him, wanting to put space between me and the man I so wanted to trust. "What the hell are you talking about?" Then I thought about my conversation with Jackson Harding, and my voice rose to a screech. "Do you have a second family?"

"Of course not."

A buzz started in my ears, high-pitched and intense. I wondered if this was how people passed out, or had strokes, or went insane.

Albert pulled himself to his feet, brushed off his pants, and drew himself taller. Before my eyes, he transformed into his stage persona.

Rage raced through me, heating my blood. "Don't do that. Don't act with me. Don't you dare treat me like a person who paid to see you pretend to be someone you're not."

He visibly sagged beneath the weight of my words.

"Your mother and I got pregnant before we were married. Before we'd even planned to get married. Placing the baby for adoption was the best decision for everyone."

My head felt like it might explode, but I managed to say, "How long before you were married?"

"A year."

A *sister*. My mind raced in a million directions, most of them impossible, unimaginable. "You're telling me I have a sister four years older than me?"

He nodded. "She'd like to meet you. Her name's Sydney."

"Sydney Mason," I said, picturing the text that had come in the night he'd come home with Scarlet. *Sydney Mason.*

Albert didn't question how I knew her full name. He merely stood there, watching me.

"How long have you known?" I asked.

"What?"

"That she was coming"—my voice broke on my next word—"here?"

He furrowed his brow, looking guilty. "A few weeks."

"Weeks? Are you kidding me?"

He hasn't been the same lately, Jackson had said.

"Before you hit your head?" I asked.

He nodded.

Distracted.

"Where is she now?"

"Staying at the Leroy Inn." He started to say something else, but stopped short.

"What?"

"With her daughter."

I was under the impression he had a granddaughter.

Anger roared inside me—anger I'd fought to control for as long as I could remember, anger fired anew by the reality that I'd been lied to my entire life.

"She's the daughter you talked to Jackson about, isn't she? Not me."

And then it hit me, the reality of why Albert Jones had quit his job and come back to Paris. To be with her. With them. Not me.

My chest tightened, my head hurt, and panic filled me. I had to get away from him. Now.

I moved to stand, but went dizzy.

He reached for my arm to steady me, but I pushed him hard. He staggered backward, falling into my mother's azalea.

His revelation had shattered every illusion I'd held—that he'd come back to Paris for me, that he'd painted Mom's chairs for me, that he'd gardened for me, bought a fish for me—

"Was it all for *them*?"

Venom seethed through my words, and he took a backward step. He swallowed, his throat visibly working.

"I trusted you," I continued. "I let you into this house and back into my life, and you weren't even here for *me*!" I screamed, my voice shrill and unrecognizable, rage tearing through me.

Every broken piece that had begun to mend inside me shattered apart.

I turned away.

"Destiny," he said, as if he might actually try to explain himself. But I wasn't having it. I didn't want to hear another word from his lying lips.

"You bastard," I said, fighting against a wave of nausea that came out of nowhere.

And then I was walking, as fast as I could, headed anywhere but where he was.

CHAPTER THIRTEEN

Although I thought about running straight to Jessica or Marguerite, I found myself headed for Lookout Rock instead.

I needed to calm down before I could face the crowd at the café, and I had to believe Marguerite had kept the truth from me all these years as well.

She'd been my mother's closest friend since first grade. Surely she knew about the pregnancy and the adoption. And she'd never told me.

Why?

I trembled so hard I thought I must be about to collapse.

Aside from a handful of joggers, the park along Front Street was deserted. I made my way to the giant boulder and scaled the side. I sat hugging my knees to my chest, the smooth stone cool beneath the seat of my jeans. I shivered, even though the morning had dawned and the air was warming quickly.

I stared at the Delaware rushing past and tried to sort my thoughts, finding them too random, too surreal to grasp.

I had a sister—a sister my parents had placed for adoption a year before they married.

Denial battled the anger that held such a firm grip on my heart. Maybe Albert was mistaken. Maybe he'd made up the entire story. Maybe he'd lied.

Maybe he was looking for a way out of my life, and this was it.

In a town as small as Paris, surely someone would have remembered my mother's pregnancy. Someone would have told me before now if what Albert said was true.

But what if it was?

What if Sydney Mason *was* my sister?

Somewhere out there she'd lived a life I knew nothing about.

I was thinking crazy, desperate thoughts—thoughts I had to struggle to control, thoughts I needed to escape.

I slid down from the rock and headed toward the café, wanting the reassuring presence of my best friend, needing the familiar buzz of conversation and the security of the known, wanting to ease the disbelief and sadness spiraling through my mind.

A few moments later, after Jessica had poured my coffee, she leaned close across the counter. "You look like hell," she said. "Want to come in the back and tell me what's up?"

And so I did. She remained silent, her eyes going wide, then narrow, as I sat at her desk and she perched beside me, absorbing every detail of that morning's explosion with Albert.

When I ran out of words and fell silent, she took my hands in hers and held them tight.

"Your mother never told you, either. I know you were young when she died, but she and your dad must have had their reasons. Maybe they were smart enough to know they weren't ready for parenthood, and maybe they didn't want to disrupt Sydney's life once they were."

Jessica's words struck me.

I'd been so ready to place the full blame on my father I'd blocked all thought of my mother's role. The one person I'd trusted all my life had never told me the truth.

Why?

The pain in my heart became almost more than I could bear.

"Listen." Jessica tightened her grip on my hands. "I have two customers who came in a few minutes before you did. One of them was here last night. Your dad sat with her for a little bit."

"Where?" I asked, my heart rate quickening.

She took my hand and led me out of her office and into the kitchen. Together we peered through the small window in the swinging door.

"Over by the wall." Jessica pointed toward the farthest row of booths. "She's got a child with her, so take your time and think this through before you do something you might regret."

I started to argue with her, but she knew me better than most anyone else in my life.

She put her hands on my shoulders and held me back momentarily. "If that's your sister out there, Albert may not be the only one in your family looking for second chances."

Second chances.

I couldn't begin to process that now. All I could do was stare in utter disbelief at the young woman who bore such a striking resemblance to my mother, I found my head momentarily empty of thought.

Sydney Mason.

My sister.

She'd lived a completely different life somewhere else—different parents, different friends, different town. Yet there she sat.

We were part of the same, yet completely separate.

Did she have a good life? A happy childhood? Were her parents as mesmerizing as mine had been during the first ten years of my life?

I could still close my eyes and picture my parents dancing in the garden. Albert singing, my mother twirling, laughing as she held my hands and spun us as one, spinning, spinning, spinning—until we all fell down.

Had Sydney Mason known that sort of happiness? That sort of joy?

And why was she here? Why now?

I put my hand to the door to press it open, and Jessica whispered in my ear, cautioning me. "Think before you speak."

I pushed through the door and walked toward the booth, vaguely aware of several voices calling out greetings.

Reacting to the sound of my name, the woman lifted her head, recognition lighting instantly in her dark eyes.

She watched warily as I approached, as I extended my hand.

The young girl sitting across from her kept her head down, focused on some sort of drawing. Her thick hair had been tamed haphazardly in a slender headband, and I flashed on a memory of my mother attempting the same style on my hair once upon a time.

"Destiny Jones," I said to the woman. "I've heard . . . about you."

She took my hand without standing, her smile forced, her eyes nervous. "Sydney Mason," she said, her voice almost identical to my own.

Looking into her eyes was like looking into my past. Bedtime tuck-ins. Shared laughter. Long-cherished games of peekaboo.

My mother's ghost reached into my heart and squeezed tight, threatening to wring me dry.

A tremor ran through me, a combination of disbelief and anger, relief, and shock. "I just wanted to say hello," I said, barely able to speak. "Since you're here," I added awkwardly.

We stared at each other. She made no offer for me to join them, and I didn't ask.

Her dark hair fell across her shoulders, stopping just below her shoulder blades. She was as slight as I was strong. She tapped the table-top nervously after she shook my hand, her fingers long and slender. Delicate.

I could only wonder how different my life might have been if I'd grown up with a sister.

I stared at the same cheekbones and chin I saw reflected each morning in the mirror, and I knew. Albert hadn't lied.

I had never really been alone.

The woman looked nervously from me to the young girl sitting across the table from her, the child's head still dipped low as she sketched an image on the back of the place mat.

The daughter. My niece.

The girl looked up at me briefly, checking her surroundings before she returned to her art. In that split second I was transported to my past and my own young face, complete with chunky blue glasses.

"This is my daughter, Ella," Sydney said. "Ella, this is Ms. Jones."

"Nice to meet you, Ms. Jones," the girl said, a forced smile showing two crooked front teeth.

"Nice to meet you, Ella," I parroted, my knees suddenly feeling like jelly. "I . . . have to go to work . . . but I wanted to introduce myself," I said, shifting my attention back to Sydney. "Perhaps we'll see each other again."

"I'd like that," she said.

And then I bolted from the restaurant, not stopping to say good-bye to Jessica or to thank her for listening, wanting only to get outside, where I could breathe, and to my shop, where I could escape.

My father showed up with sandwiches from the café a little after noon.

"Get out." I pointed at the door as soon as he crossed the threshold.

He set the take-out containers on one of my worktables, but didn't turn to leave.

"No." His features tensed, as though he were struggling to push through a wall. "I was wrong and I should have told you, but you need to listen to me now."

"Listen to you?" I couldn't believe the man's nerve. "I don't have to listen to you ever again. And why would I? You've done nothing but cast me aside all my life."

"Let me make this up to you."

I crossed to the door, held it wide, and pointed to the stairs. "Get out. Now."

But Albert held his ground.

"I wanted to tell you years ago, but I'd made a promise to your mother."

Now he'd gone too far.

"She didn't want you to know," he continued.

"Don't you dare blame this on Mom."

He opened his mouth to speak, then hesitated, visibly composing himself.

"Your sister was well loved and well cared for. It was everything your mother had wanted. We thought it was better for everyone if you lived your separate lives."

This was unbelievable. Then I realized the ramifications of what he'd said.

"You stayed in touch?"

He shook his head. "Not really. They sent photos every now and again, but I never communicated with her until your sister reached out . . ." His voice trailed away. "Until two years ago," he finished.

"So you stopped by to see me once a year at Christmas, but became pen pals with her?"

He stared at me, his expression blank. Had he never fully thought his actions through? "I suppose I did."

I studied him, the man I'd thought I was beginning to know again, and realized I didn't know him at all. Sadness crept into my anger, but I shoved it away. I was not about to go sentimental or weak. Not now.

I grabbed my anger and held it close, knowing it was the only way to protect myself.

"All these years," I said. "I thought you couldn't possibly do anything worse than what you'd already done, but this . . . *You knew*, and you never told me."

I moved toward him swiftly, but he held his ground. "How could you do that? How could you let me think I was alone in this world when I wasn't?"

I pushed against his chest, and he faltered, taking a backward step to regain his balance.

"And now you knew she was coming here, to my town, and you still didn't tell me." I paced wildly. "Screw you, Albert Jones. You can go to hell."

He nodded, visibly swallowing. "I should go."

Moisture welled in my eyes—tears of anger, heartbreak, and frustration. I couldn't understand what the man who was supposed to be my father had been thinking.

I dropped my gaze to the floor, refusing to let him see my emotion.

I'd let him back in, and he'd done it again. He'd taken my heart and then thrown me away.

"If you'd told me before you came, even when you first got here, I might not hate you."

"But now?"

Disbelief tangled with my rage. "What do you think?"

He nodded once, stepped back outside, and closed the door.

I waited until his footfalls went silent, until he was truly gone. Then I sank to the floor of my shop and cried, letting the sorrow and the heartache and the pain of his confession wash over me.

And then I realized Albert Jones wasn't the only person who owed me an explanation.

"Did you know I had a sister?" I asked Marguerite after I found her on her patio adding touches of light to a still-life canvas.

I'd left my shop not long after Albert's visit, dropping off the lunch he'd brought with the florist downstairs before I headed for Third Street.

"I did," she said with a nod. "And based on the argument you had this morning with your father and the hum of gossip downtown, I'd say you now know too."

The bottom fell out of my stomach.

For the majority of my life, Marguerite had cushioned my blows, soothed my wounded spirit, and encouraged me to be strong.

Finding out she'd kept this secret from me during all the years I'd known her was almost more than I could fathom. I expected betrayal from Albert. I had never expected it from Marguerite.

Her features softened. "I'm sorry you found out like you did. I'm sorry Albert didn't give you a little more warning."

"I can't believe you never told me."

"The funny thing about children," she said, "is that no matter how old they become, they fail to realize their parents had lives before they were born. Your mother had dreams, and heartaches, and mistakes, and decisions bigger than any young girl should have to make."

Her stare locked with mine, and I saw the protective glint in her eyes.

"I never broke a promise to your mother. Not even this one."

Marguerite had often told me she'd loved my mother like a sister. I'd seen it in action during my mother's illness, and I saw it now in the intensity of her words.

Then I realized they must not have been the only people in my life who knew.

"Did my grandmother know?"

She nodded. "It took her a long time to accept."

"The adoption was my mother's decision?"

Marguerite nodded. "Your father was busy trying to break into acting, and they hadn't even talked about marriage. She knew he wouldn't want to be saddled with a baby, so she made plans to place your sister for adoption."

"And he agreed?"

Another nod. "He did."

"But Grandmother?"

"Did not."

I dropped my face into my palms and rubbed my hands over my face again and again. I tried to make sense of the entire last week.

But I couldn't.

I'd gone from an empty house and a routine, solitary existence to a reunion with my estranged father and the discovery of a sister and niece I'd never known existed.

"This is crazy," I said.

"Crazy," she parroted. Then she gave me the soft smile she'd been giving me all my life. The one that usually accompanied the tough questions. "What are you going to do about it?"

I splayed my hand on my chest. "Me?"

She nodded. "Seems to me you need to take a step back and think about Sydney. Think about what she might be feeling. Understand why she's come to Paris after all these years. I take it you've met her."

"Briefly."

Another soft smile. "Perhaps you should take your time and meet her again."

CHAPTER FOURTEEN

Using Mrs. Leroy as a go-between, Sydney and I agreed to meet at eight o'clock the next morning. I thought about working in the shop for an hour beforehand, but I'd be making the initial cuts on the stage paneling, and my jumbled mind wasn't in any shape to concentrate on such a vital part of the project.

Instead I left my house at seven thirty and reached the café fifteen minutes early.

Jessica nodded as I entered, then pointed to a quiet table for two near the front window. We'd talked on the phone late into the night after she'd gotten Max and Belle to bed. As usual, she'd done more listening than anything else, but she'd convinced me to give the one-on-one conversation a chance.

Sydney, apparently as anxious as I was about our meeting, arrived only a few minutes later.

Jessica poured us each a piping mug of coffee. "Bring you anything to eat, ladies?" she asked. To which Sydney and I simultaneously said, "No, thank you."

"At least we have good manners," Sydney said.

I tried to smile, but honestly, how did you smile when you were looking at the spitting image of your dead mother?

Sydney Mason so strongly resembled a younger Mary Jones that there would never be any question about Albert having a secret second family. She and my mother possessed identical cheekbones, and her eyes shone the same warm brown I could still picture as if it had been only moments, and not twenty years, since I'd seen them last.

"You look just like her, you know," I said. "It's uncanny."

Sydney took a sip of her coffee, then held the cup as if to warm her hands, even though the late-August morning had dawned warm and humid.

"That's what Albert said." She spoke without smiling. "I mean, your father."

I held up a hand to stop her. "Trust me, Albert is fine."

She pressed her lips together tightly before she asked her next question. "You had no idea?"

I laughed the same nervous laugh I'd used when Albert had first shown up unannounced. "None."

"Even your mother never told you?"

I shook my head.

She took another sip of her coffee, then splayed one hand atop the table and moved it back and forth, testing the surface. "I guess she had no reason to."

I felt sorry for Sydney, even though I was sure I shouldn't. "Maybe she would have told me when I was older," I offered. "If she'd lived."

Now it was my turn to break eye contact, to study the coffee in my mug.

"I'm sorry," Sydney said, her voice barely audible. "Sorry for your loss."

"Where is your daughter this morning?" I asked, hoping to change subjects.

"Back with Mrs. Leroy, a bag of Goldfish, and Netflix on the iPad."

An awkward hush stretched between us. Sydney spoke first. She narrowed her gaze and measured my features. "You're almost the exact mental picture I have whenever I try to imagine her grown up."

"Genes are an amazing thing, I suppose." I shrugged, hoping I didn't sound as uncomfortable as I felt.

"I suppose they are," she said, her voice trailing away.

I was an idiot. The woman had been placed for adoption by my parents. She didn't want to hear about genes. "I'm sorry."

And then she smiled, my mother's smile. Slightly crooked. Close-lipped. Forgiving.

Breathing momentarily failed me, as if I were seeing one last glimpse of all I'd lost.

"Did she look for you?" I asked.

Sydney shook her head. "I don't think so."

"What about Albert?"

Another shake of her head. "I looked for him. I wanted to know more about my background."

"So you made the first contact?" I asked, even though Albert had told me as much.

Sydney's brows lifted. "This is important to you?"

She measured me with eyes that seemed to know exactly what I was thinking.

If Sydney confirmed what my father had said, at least I'd know he hadn't been looking for her at the same time he'd been ignoring me.

"I wrote to him first," she said, pulling a fistful of dollar bills out of her pocket and setting them on the table. "Would you like to take a walk? It's a beautiful morning out there."

A walk?

The café had gone quiet. I imagined everyone there was listening to our conversation, although I knew my thoughts were more than a little irrational just then.

Getting outside in the fresh air sounded like exactly what I needed.

"Absolutely," I said, putting a few additional dollars on the table.

I waved to Jessica as we headed out, and she stopped what she'd been doing to watch us leave, concern blatant in her expression.

Sydney and I headed toward the corner, waiting for the light at Front Street to change. One lone SUV zipped past, driving far too fast for the center of town.

"You know, this road seems deserted most of the time," I explained. "Folks like to say that people who come to visit never leave, so there's not much traffic headed back across the bridge. But every now and then, there's one like that." I pointed at the receding taillights, realizing I'd begun to chat nervously. "It's always a good idea to look both ways," I added. Then I forced myself to stop babbling.

"I'll remember that."

We headed down the path toward the bike trail, and while I thought about showing her Lookout Rock, I decided not to. There were some things I wasn't ready to share.

"Want me to tell you my story?" she asked.

"Sure."

And so she did. She'd known my parents' names, but had never had the urge to seek them out. Not until her adoptive parents were killed.

"They were the best parents a girl could hope for," she said. "They never spoiled me. They'd been full of common sense right up until they bought a motorcycle and decided to turn their life into a great adventure."

Sydney headed for a bench. "Mind if we sit for a bit?"

"Not at all." I settled beside her, waiting for her to finish her story.

"Their adventure ended two years ago. On a rain-slicked road just outside Modesto, California."

The pain in her voice was still raw, even after two years, and I understood. My mother had been gone far longer, but talking about her death still brought back the heartache in a rush of memories.

"How long will you be staying in town?" I asked, and Sydney's features tensed.

"He didn't tell you?"

Familiar alarm bells began to chime deep inside my gut. "Tell me what?"

"We're not going back to Ohio. Everything from the old house is in storage." She pushed to her feet and pulled her light sweater around her. "I wanted a fresh start, so we decided to head east."

"And Paris?"

"We plan to stay for a little bit. Get to know the town." Her gaze locked with mine. "And the people." She glanced at the time on her phone. "Listen, I'd better get back to Ella. Maybe we can do this again soon."

I moved to shake her hand, but she surprised me by pulling me into a stiff hug.

Every muscle in my body tensed, my brain momentarily unable to tell the rest of me how to respond.

I returned her hug awkwardly and stood there as she walked away.

My mother's beauty had been ethereal, fragile. Much like Sydney's. Where I stomped through life, I'd always imagined my mother floated, like a luminous specter.

As I watched Sydney's stride and the way her hands swung gracefully at her sides, I realized she'd gotten the gene I hadn't. The gene that smoothed all the rough edges.

Marguerite's affirmation played through my memory.

You are enough.

And I had been. Until now.

CHAPTER FIFTEEN

That night, for the first time in years, the sights and sounds of karaoke night at the Paris Inn Pub did nothing to soothe my soul.

Albert had left a plate for me in the oven, which I'd ignored. Jessica had called twice, and Marguerite had stood in my foyer, tapping one toe of her lavender, sequined shoes, until I'd pulled on a ball cap, pushed my glasses up on my nose, and agreed to stay for one hour. No longer.

Marguerite gave my shoulder a quick squeeze as we parted just inside the pub door, and I looked for Jessica, searching our usual stretch of bar.

She waited faithfully, waving, and as I approached, Jerry set not one, but two bottles of beer in front of me.

"Probably not the night to be encouraging me to drink," I said, but took a long swallow from the first bottle just the same.

"She's here," Jessica said in lieu of a greeting.

"Here?" I tensed, knowing instantly who she meant.

Jessica nodded. "She's sitting with your father at the end of the bar."

"You need to start calling him Albert again," I said, my tone more than a little bit harsh. "Please."

She rubbed my back. "Got it. Over there."

Sydney sat beside Albert at the end of the bar, on the stool Byron Kennedy had occupied at last week's karaoke night.

She looked as unhappy as I felt. She sat stiffly, and even from this distance she appeared uneasy, obviously not a fan of the crowded space.

She caught me staring, and I waved.

She leaned to say something to my father, then excused herself, moving smoothly through groups of patrons until she reached us.

"Nice to see you," she said, when she drew near enough to be heard.

I couldn't help but notice she had her purse draped over her shoulder.

"Are you leaving?" I asked.

She nodded. "I'm afraid I don't do well with noise." She grimaced as the next act started. "Or big groups of people."

"I'll walk you out," I said, setting a ten-dollar bill on the bar.

Jessica frowned, her surprise apparent, but she said nothing.

"Not in the mood tonight," I said, by way of explanation. Then Sydney Mason and I pushed through the massive pub doors and out into the Paris night.

Silence wrapped us in its embrace, and Sydney stopped to catch her breath, pressing a hand to her side.

"You all right?" I asked.

She nodded. "Probably sat on that stool for too long. I should have gotten up and moved around."

We made our way toward the Front Street Bridge, and I couldn't help but think it was nice to walk with her again.

"Look both ways," I said as we made our way across the street and up the sidewalk to the bridge, and she laughed politely.

The river rushed beneath us as we climbed to the highest point of the crossing, and the moon hung bright in the night sky, reflecting off the water's surface in countless ripples of light.

"It's so quiet here," Sydney said. "No traffic at all."

I nodded toward the opposite end of the bridge, where the pavement disappeared on the Pennsylvania side of the river. "Most everyone who lives there stays there. Most everyone who lives here walks around town."

"Or is inside that pub." She smiled.

I nodded. "You have no idea."

"So tell me. Explain the allure of karaoke night."

I shrugged. "It's a small town. Karaoke night is one of the bright spots of our week." I leaned against the railing, staring down at the Delaware below. "It's something to do every Wednesday night." I stood silently for a moment, considering what karaoke night meant to me, crazy as that sounded. "No matter what else is going on in a person's life, they know they can walk through that door on any given Wednesday night and be surrounded by friends."

Sydney nodded, frowning. "I can't imagine."

"Karaoke?"

She shook her head. "Having this many friends. Our life back in Ohio is very different. Isolated."

"What do you do for fun?" I asked.

She wrinkled her brow. "I work a lot. Single mom."

"Ella's dad isn't around?"

"Never has been. A one-night thing."

I nodded, getting the picture. "What sort of work?"

"Nurse practitioner. You?"

"Carpenter."

Sydney nodded. "Your father said you just landed a big job. Congratulations."

"Thanks." I tamped down my annoyance that Albert had told Sydney about my life when he'd barely told me she existed. "What do you do when you're not working?"

Sydney crossed her arms to mirror mine, leaning back against the railing beside me. "I like to dance. Ballet. And I spend as much time as I can with Ella."

Silence beat between us; then she asked, "Favorite music?"

"Elvis," I answered.

"Costello?" she asked.

"Presley," I said with a grin. "How about you?"

She drew in a deep breath. "ABBA."

I groaned. "You have got to be kidding me."

Sydney shook her head and smiled. "Favorite element?" she asked.

"Element? Isn't that one step away from asking 'What's your sign?'"

We laughed easily, and I felt the knot of rage I'd held all day ease.

Sydney's laughter rolled out across the water, lighting memories inside me that had long gone dark. My mother laughing in the nighttime, long after I'd gone to bed, as she and my father sat in the garden talking softly.

I fell silent, and Sydney reached for my arm. I stared at the spot where her hand touched my skin. She withdrew her touch as if she'd felt it, too.

"Fire," I said in answer to her question. "You?"

"Water."

We walked a few steps past midspan, then stood, hands on the railing, looking down at the river.

We stood in silence, letting the night wash over our newly forged connection as the water rushed beneath us, along the riverbanks of countless towns, and homes, and lives—each with their own stories—some told, some untold, some still waiting to be revealed.

"Why now?" I asked.

"Why did I come here now?"

I nodded.

She hesitated before she answered. "Too many ghosts back in Ohio."

That, I understood.

She pushed away from the railing, touched her fingertips to my forearm. "Maybe we can keep doing this. Walking. Talking."

"I'd like that," I said, and I meant it.

She started to walk away, but hesitated. "You know, I have somewhere to be tomorrow, and Mrs. Leroy agreed to let Ella hang out, but I'm wondering if you'd like to spend some time with her?"

Her question took me by surprise. "Like babysitting?" Was that what she wanted?

But Sydney burst into laughter. "I'm sorry. I think that came out wrong. I'd like her to get to know you, if that's all right. It doesn't have to be tomorrow, and it doesn't have to be just you and Ella."

But, oddly enough, I was curious to spend time with Sydney's daughter. To talk to her.

"Sure," I said.

"Great. I'll bring her by a little before nine, if that's all right."

I gave her the address for the shop and described the building. Sydney turned to leave.

"Does she know?" I asked.

She turned back, smiled knowingly. "About the adoption?" Sydney nodded. "The kid's an old soul. She understands. You'll see."

I waited until she made the short walk down the street and around the corner to Mrs. Leroy's, smiling as she looked both ways before crossing the street, even though there wasn't a car in sight.

My sister's a quick learner, I thought.

My sister, I realized with amazement.

CHAPTER SIXTEEN

The next morning, Sydney deposited Ella at my shop.

I'd stopped for coffee and a bag of doughnuts—pink iced with sprinkles. Ella, however, wasn't interested.

"I don't eat pink things," she said without making eye contact.

She'd come prepared for a long haul, with several bags of Goldfish crackers, a bottle of water, and a gigantic Harry Potter novel.

"Which one is that?" I asked, pointing my ruler at her book.

"The seventh," she said, drawing the last two letters of the word 'seventh' into their own syllable.

"Is it good?" I asked.

"Quite," she replied.

Quite.

I laughed to myself. What a pip.

"I have to plan some cuts for today," I explained. "But I thought you might like to help me later, or design something of your own to make."

I'd planned to give her a tour of my shop and offer her everything she might need—pencils, paper, bathroom.

But Ella had already turned her attention to her book, her head buried between the pages, glasses pushed up on the top of her head, seemingly determined to interact with me as little as possible.

I understood exactly what she was doing. I'd once been a master of appearing uninterested when I was, in fact, taking in every detail.

As much as I wanted to know more about my niece, I decided to take my time. After all, she probably wasn't thrilled at the prospect of being left with a stranger for the morning.

"Are those for distance?" I asked, leaning back in the chair at my drafting table.

She looked up without moving her head, the effect borderline chilling, yet I smiled.

She could pretend all she wanted, but I had a fairly good sense that Ella Mason was as curious about me as I was about her.

"Are what for distance?" she asked.

"Your glasses."

She nodded, then dismissed me with a dropped gaze.

While I was willing to go slow, I wasn't willing to give up.

"How do you like Paris so far?" I asked.

Another lift of the eyes. "The people seem very nice," she answered. Eyes dropped.

"And Mrs. Leroy's bed-and-breakfast? Comfortable?"

"Quite."

I grinned, turning my attention down to the grid I'd drawn of the panel designs I intended to cut, piece, glue, and pin.

"Are you a loner?" Ella asked, taking me completely by surprise.

Was I? "I suppose I am." I shrugged. "Who said that?"

She sucked in her lower lip. "Nobody. Just wondered."

"Are you a loner?" I asked.

"Quite," she replied, and I smiled again.

Ella tucked her wild, dark-brown hair behind her ears as she read, the thick waves fighting her and slipping free every few minutes.

"Do you want a ball cap?" I asked.

This warranted a full lift of her chin so she could squint at me directly.

"For your hair." I pointed to my own head and the ball cap that kept my hair in a ponytail and out of my face.

Ella frowned, obviously considering my offer. Then she simply said, "No, thank you."

"OK."

I returned to my project and she to her book until a few minutes later, when my glasses slipped down my nose as I marked measurements for a test cut.

As I pushed the frames back up to the bridge of my nose, Ella's pert voice broke through the silence of the shop.

"How old were you when you started wearing glasses?"

I looked up from my work.

I remembered the day my mother took me out of school and to the eye doctor's office two towns over.

We'd stopped at a roadside stand on the way home and licked small twists of frozen custard as trails of chocolate and vanilla found their way over the waffle cones and down our hands.

This time, instead of brushing away the memory, I held it close and met Ella's waiting stare.

"Second grade," I answered. "You?"

"Same."

She smiled ever so slightly, and I wondered if we'd forged our first common bond. One tiny corner of the armor I kept anchored around my heart cracked.

By the time Sydney arrived a few hours later, Ella had watched me make test cuts to tool the scrollwork for the stage façade. I'd let her guide the saw, and I taught her how to select the necessary bits to produce the final product.

She'd warmed to me gradually, telling me anecdotes about the home and school they'd left behind.

And while I was out of practice in working alongside someone, I had to admit the nine-year-old and I made a pretty good team.

"I just need to use the ladies' room before we head home," Sydney said to Ella a short while after she'd arrived to pick her up.

Ella had proudly shown her mother our work, and Sydney had seemed pleased, although a bit distracted.

When she hadn't emerged from the restroom several minutes later, I made a show of walking toward my wall of photos to make sure there wasn't some sort of problem with the door lock or plumbing.

Ella sketched a drawing of the old suspension bridge over the Delaware, her lines precise and her strokes confident, apparently unfazed by her mother's absence.

"Sydney," I called out, next to the bathroom door. "You all right in there?"

The door popped open, and Sydney emerged, frantically scratching at the top of her head.

I frowned, curiosity dancing through me.

She made a face. "Sorry, it's driving me crazy."

I narrowed my gaze. "What?"

"This itching." She pivoted to look back to the bathroom mirror. "My head's been itching like crazy all day."

She walked out to where I stood, her eyes bracketed by frustration.

"How was your thing today?" I asked, not wanting to pry, but wondering exactly where she'd gone for three hours when she'd only been in town for a handful of days.

"Good," she answered. "It was a doctor's appointment. And it was good."

"For the itching?" I asked, knowing her health was none of my business.

But Sydney reached to the nape of her neck, hooked her fingers into her hair, and pulled her wig free. She shook the dark hair as she removed it, then ran one hand over the hair beneath.

Wavy and short, Sydney's coarse hair sat thin against her scalp.

I recognized the look, the sight tapping into one of my earliest memories, tucked away long ago into the far recesses of my mind.

In Sydney's eyes, I saw the same fatigue I remembered from my mother's eyes.

Our mother's eyes.

She said nothing as she raised her gaze to mine, watching for my reaction.

"You're sick," I said, barely able to believe what I was seeing.

Sydney nodded.

"Cancer?"

"Ovarian. Stage four."

My head spun momentarily, but I held on, fighting for composure even as I longed to sink onto a stool and press my hands over my ears.

Not cancer.

Not again.

"Second recurrence," she continued. "Before I left Ohio I made sure to lock in appointments with a new oncologist here."

"That's where you were today?" My throat had gone tight, and my calm question sounded phony and forced.

Questions scrambled for position in my mind. Was she in active treatment? Was she tired? Did she feel sick? How long would it take her hair to grow back? Was she cured? Did she need help?

Tears appeared in Sydney's dark eyes, then disappeared quickly as she corrected her response, bit down her emotions.

She waved her hand apologetically. "Yes."

My heart pounded in my chest, a fresh wave of disbelief threatening to pull me under.

"I have another appointment tomorrow," Sydney went on, oblivious. "Up in the city. New clinical trial."

I studied her, looking for heartbreak in her eyes, defeat in the set of her shoulders, but finding neither. Nothing but serenity.

Meanwhile, my new reality—the reality that included a sister and niece—shifted into one that included a sister with cancer.

Just like my mother.

Suddenly the very heartache I'd vowed to never again allow into my life stared me in the face.

"Do you need a ride into the city?" I asked, going through the motions of maintaining normalcy, when there was nothing normal about the moment at all.

"Ella, honey," Sydney called out. "We should get going. I'm sure Miss Destiny's got a lot of work to do." Then to me, "I'm OK, but thanks. Albert's going to drive me in my car." Then she cut a look to where Ella still sat sketching. "I don't suppose you could take Ella for another day? It shouldn't take long."

"Of course," I said. Then, even though my mind was reeling from the bombshell she'd dropped, I added, "My pleasure."

CHAPTER SEVENTEEN

Albert and I walked together to the Leroy Inn the next morning. He, to pick up Sydney and her car. Me, to pick up Ella.

He'd been at a garden-club meeting the night before, and I'd gone back to my shop after eating a quick dinner. I'd worked until well after midnight, and Albert's closed bedroom door had shown no sign of light by the time I'd returned home.

Even though I was still hurt and angry, I took full advantage of our time together that morning to ease my curiosity.

"Did you know she has cancer?" I asked.

My father nodded. "That's why she reached out to me. To find out about the family medical history."

My mother had died of cervical cancer, and I wondered if there might not be some genetic link.

"And you suggested she come to Paris?"

He rolled his neck, as if he could deflect my line of questioning. "She mentioned how alone she was, and I thought this town might do her good."

"Did you ever think, at any point there, that perhaps you should have filled me in or sought my opinion?"

"Sorry." He spoke so softly, I barely heard him.

"Is there anything you *have* been up-front with me about since you moved back to Paris?"

He studied me for a moment, his eyes sad. Then we walked the rest of the way to our destination in silence.

A short while later, Sydney and Albert were on their way to New York, and nine-year-old Ella Mason and I were strolling through Paris almost as though we'd done so countless times before.

I'd worked late the night before so that I could show her around town today, perhaps stopping by the house and introducing her to Marguerite.

We looped down Artisan's Alley, then past the opera house. I pointed out the river and the park that ran along its banks as she hopped from cobblestone to cobblestone, doing her best to avoid the cracks.

She told me about their home back in Akron, but for the most part remained reserved.

I'd brought her a Trenton Thunder baseball cap, and this time she'd expertly pulled her ponytail through the opening in the back of it and started walking beside me, peak pulled low.

We stopped at Jessica's café for bagels to go, then, instead of heading for my shop, we headed for Third Street and my home.

She'd seen where I worked. I thought she might like to see where I lived.

I waited for her on the top step of the house as she lollygagged by Albert's garden, commenting on the azalea and asking specifics about what had been planted.

I shrugged. "You'll have to ask Albert when he and your mother get back." Then I added, "Do you like gardening?"

She mimicked my shrug, then climbed the stairs.

She was lanky, with legs like a colt, and slender, as though the rest of her body hadn't caught up to her height. Just the sight of her inside my house seemed unbelievable, a mirage that could vanish without warning.

She cut her eyes at me periodically as she roamed from room to room, corner to corner, trailing her fingertips along table edges and the backs of chairs.

"Did you grow up in this house?" she asked.

"All my life."

"Lucky."

I felt sorry for her then, wondering how it must feel to be uprooted from your childhood home. "Were you always in the same house in Akron?"

Ella pulled a face. "We moved a lot. Apartments. We lived with my grandparents for a little while." She smiled slightly, sadly. "That was nice."

She stepped into the sitting room and came to a standstill in front of my favorite pictures of my mother and grandmother.

She pointed to the photo of my mother. "Is this her?" she asked, her voice going soft.

"My mother, yes," I said. "Your mom said she explained everything to you?"

Ella nodded. "Your mother placed my mother for adoption."

She spoke the words as if her mother's adoption had been a good thing, and I realized I wasn't sure why a person would expect anything different. I'd imagine adoption into a loving family was just about the best thing that could happen to a baby, and for all I knew, Sydney's childhood had been far happier than my own.

Ella faced me, tearing her gaze from my mother's beautiful smile. "You never met my Mom-Mom Rose, but she was the best. She always smelled like lemons."

I worked to maintain eye contact when I wanted nothing more than to look away from the child's intense brown gaze, suddenly uncomfortable with my thoughts and questions about what it might have been like to have been raised by a mother, a father, and grandparents.

"She was cool," Ella said. "So was Pop-Pop."

The kid had a certain something that came solely from being raised with confidence and love. Sydney and her parents had obviously done their job well.

"They died in a motorcycle accident."

She spoke the words as though she'd said them countless times before, flatly and without emotion.

"I'm sorry."

"Me, too," she said.

She hesitated for a moment, her unrelenting stare never leaving my own. I feared she might broach the subject of her mother's health, but she turned away to resume her meandering exploration of my home, slowing only when she came to the bookshelves that lined the hall between my dining room and kitchen.

"Do you like to read?" I asked, wondering how in the hell anyone carried on a conversation with a kid.

Ella exhaled and rolled her eyes, and I remembered the tome she'd brought with her the day before.

I had to laugh. "Right. Dumb question. Follow me," I said, stepping toward the kitchen. "Did you know Mr. Albert got you a fish?" I asked, stealing my father's thunder and not caring in the least.

"Grandpa Albert?"

Grandpa Albert.

The phrase took me by surprise, but I shook off the reaction I wanted to have, the one where I raised my voice and shouted, "Are you kidding me?"

Instead, I plastered on a smile and said, "Yes. Grandpa Albert." I held out a hand. "Want to see her?"

"My momma used to have hair like yours," Ella said as we cleared the bottom step and headed for the kitchen. "She even had a stripe like yours, except hers was blue." She wrinkled her nose.

"But now she has shorter hair," I said, one of those statements adults make to children when they really can't think of anything but the obvious to say.

But Ella's attention had been captured by the fish tank on the kitchen counter. "Scarlet," she breathed on a gasp. "How did you get here?" Then she spun on me. "Is this Scarlet?"

Albert's words bounced through my brain. *She looks like a Scarlet, don't you think?*

I nodded, at a loss to say anything more for fear I might blurt out the truth: that this was some random red fish her grandfather had brought home—zero relation to whatever fish she'd had back in Ohio.

Ella pressed her nose close to the aquarium wall, her cobalt-blue glasses brushing against the plastic. "I came home from camp and she was gone. Momma said sometimes the people we love have to go away, but here she is." She tipped her head. "Though she looks a little different. Her water looks weird."

"Maybe that's it," I said, pressing my palm to the small of her back. "New Jersey water is weird. Let's go to the back patio and see if Marguerite is outside."

"Who's Marguerite?" she asked as we stepped out onto the patio. Then she said, "Whoa," as she took in the fence and long expanse of yard.

I pointed over the fence. "There she is."

Marguerite sat on a stool in one corner of her yard. Before her sat a blank canvas on an easel, and she stared at the stand of trees in the opposite corner of her yard, appearing to expect them to perform a miraculous trick. On a small table to her side sat a glass of lemonade, a bowl full of crayons, and a small dish of cookies.

"What is she doing?" Ella asked in a whisper so loud neighbors two blocks away must have heard her.

"She's waiting for someone to come draw these trees," Marguerite answered.

Ella gasped in surprise and I smiled, remembering what it felt like to be on the receiving end of Marguerite's special brand of kindness.

"Do you think you might be able to help me?" Marguerite left her stool and sauntered over to where we stood, caught red-handed, peeking over the top of the fence.

"Me?" Ella asked, her voice climbing in hopeful expectation.

I hoisted her into my arms. She stiffened, but wrapped one arm around my neck.

"I don't think she's talking about me," I said. "You ready?"

Ella nodded and I lifted her clear of the fence, setting her down on the other side.

"This is Miss Marguerite. Miss Marguerite, this is Ella."

Marguerite folded one arm around her waist and hoisted the other in the air as she bowed dramatically. "The pleasure is all mine, Miss Ella, and please, simply call me Marguerite." Ella giggled, and somewhere deep inside me, a jagged edge mended. I remembered Marguerite saying the exact line to me back when I'd been even younger than Ella.

"What do I call you?" Ella said, turning her attention to me.

"What do you want to call me?" I asked.

She drew her dark brows tightly together. "Auntie D? I've never had an aunt before."

My breath caught, and emotion knotted in my throat. "I'd love that." Then I shrugged, doing my best to keep my voice from cracking. "I've never had a niece before."

I'd filled Marguerite in on Sydney's cancer, and her expression now was a mixture of pride and sadness, obviously hoping Ella and I might find our way to friendship together, even though heartbreak threatened down the road.

"Auntie D it is," I said, and then I added, "I'll be right over. I just have to walk around."

Ella nodded as she pointed to the table. "Who are the cookies for?"

"Well, they're for the visiting artist, of course," Marguerite answered.

"And the lemonade?"

I was still grinning as I headed back through my house and out the front door. Albert had planted three new azalea bushes along the property line, and I had to give him credit for making the property look homier than it had in years, even though every addition he'd made—right down to the fish—had been for Sydney and Ella.

I hesitated before I stepped through Marguerite's gate, wanting a moment to simply watch Ella in action. She chomped on a cookie while Marguerite gestured wildly to the trees.

I remembered many an afternoon spent sitting in almost the same spot, painting or coloring with Marguerite while my parents tended to the garden.

After Mom died and Dad left, I'd continued to sit in the same spot, coloring, yet somehow the moments were never again so magical as they had been before my world had shifted.

"These crayons are broken," Ella said, her voice full of disappointment as she fished four fractured pieces out of the bowl on Marguerite's table.

"Ah," Marguerite said, giving a wiggle of her eyebrows, "that's the funny thing about crayons." She leaned close and met Ella's gaze head-on. "Even the broken ones still color."

CHAPTER EIGHTEEN

That evening, my father readied burgers and hot dogs for an impromptu cookout, and I couldn't deny the resentment I felt. Were any of these efforts for me? Or were they purely for Sydney and Ella's benefit?

While Ella stayed busy creating broken-crayon masterpieces with Marguerite, Sydney and I took our walk.

Albert had been quiet upon their return from New York, but Sydney had been downright subdued.

"Do you want to talk about it?" I asked as we headed toward the Bainbridge Estate and the bike trail.

"The question should be, do you want to hear about it?" Sydney answered, waggling her brows as if she were about to deliver humorous news and not an update that might concern her chances of survival.

We turned onto the gravel path that circled the huge old estate home, and I touched her arm lightly. "Yes." I nodded. "I do."

Each time I saw Sydney and interacted with her, I became more and more amazed at how comfortable I felt. The sensation was almost as though we'd known each other all our lives, even though those lives had been spent separately.

"The thing about cancer," she said, silencing my internal monologue, "is that everyone wants you to fight. They expect you to fight."

We turned down the path that cut through the estate's garden and disappeared between towering hedges of butterfly bushes.

"Your friends, your family, your children, your doctors," she continued. "Fight." She fisted her hands and took a mock swing at the air. "I've seen patients fight. I've seen them survive. I've seen them die. I've seen the treatments kill them before the cancer has a chance."

She came to a stop, so I paused, taking a step back to where she stood, arms wrapped around her waist, features tense.

I flashed back on my mother's fight—the days she put on a brave face and kept up appearances, the days she stayed in bed, the way the light had faded from her eyes a little more each day.

"The drug for the clinical trial has been shown to extend life for a decent percentage of women," Sydney explained.

"Extend life?" I questioned.

"Time." She shrugged. "Isn't that what we all want?"

Was it? Didn't we all want a cure instead?

We turned around and headed for home, realizing we'd gone farther into the estate grounds than we'd intended.

"So I said yes," Sydney continued, her voice tired and defeated. "'New hope, Ms. Mason. New roller coaster. New paperwork. New side effects.'"

She bit down on her lip in an attempt to hide the depths of her emotions, but failed miserably.

"You're allowed to cry, you know."

But Sydney only shook her head. "Ah, that's not what fighters do."

So I did the only thing I could think to do. I took her hand and held it tight the entire way back to the house.

A short while later we dined around the table on Marguerite's back patio. Ella bounced between the table and the yard, ducking in and out of the perennials that had lined the border of Marguerite's property for as long as I could remember.

Vibrant violet bushes sat beside fully blooming hydrangeas, their lush pink and blue flowers all but shimmering in the late-August sun. I remembered their name because they'd been one of my mother's favorites, and I realized they'd become one of my favorites, too, somewhere along the way.

The humidity had broken with a late storm the night before, and although condensation gathered on our tall, hand-painted glasses, it didn't pool in circles on the table as it tended to do all summer long.

Sydney made polite conversation, glossing over her day, keeping her eyes bright and her smile wide as Ella switched from dancing to presenting a parade of her new artwork, showcasing one crayon drawing after another.

I watched Sydney as a person might watch a dream—partially detached, partially awed. Then I realized Sydney *was* a dream. She was part of what I'd longed for all my life. Family.

"You should stay here," I blurted, wishing I could take back the words as quickly as I'd spoken them.

Was I crazy? What was I thinking? That she and Ella would simply pack up their things and move in like we were one big, happy family?

Then, while everyone studied me, their expressions stunned, I realized that what I'd said made perfect sense.

There was a good chance the new clinical trial would make Sydney sick, and there was no sense in her staying in a bed-and-breakfast when I had plenty of room here. Here, where Albert, Marguerite, and I could help her with anything she might need.

I grew more sure of what I'd proposed than I'd been of most things since Albert's return to town.

"I never thought about moving Sydney and Ella in here too," Albert said as he wiped a napkin across his mouth. He did his best to appear surprised, but an undeniable relief slid across his features.

I glared at him, my pent-up anger boiling inside me. "You really are incapable of telling the truth, aren't you?"

My truth was that even though I knew my father had moved back to Paris intent on opening my home to Sydney and Ella, it was still the best choice.

"You're not working." I pointed at him. "You can help during the day, take Sydney to appointments, and cook your healthy dinners."

"And I'm just next door," Marguerite said, squeezing Sydney's hand as Ella danced from one side of the backyard to the other, apparently sensing our conversation had turned serious and she was safer keeping her distance.

Albert stared at Ella as he spoke, and I wondered whether he might be remembering another young girl dancing around the backyard, trying to pretend her world wasn't falling apart.

Sydney lowered her face to her hands and shook her head. Then she lifted her gaze to mine. "I can't ask you to do this."

"You didn't ask me to do this. I asked you."

"Destiny's right," my father said. "This is where you belong." He patted the tabletop. "Where we can all help. Whatever you need."

This from the man who'd done the opposite when I'd needed him. Then I realized this second chance might be less about his relationship with me and more about redeeming himself for how he'd faltered during my mother's illness.

Could the mighty Albert Jones be feeling remorse?

"This is too much," Sydney said. "This wasn't my intent when we came here."

"I know that." A sense of calm washed over me as I spoke, and I grew more sure of what I was doing with each second that passed. "You were planning to stay in Paris during treatment, right?"

Sydney went a bit pale, unmistakably blindsided by my question. "I wasn't sure, but yes, I'd thought about it," she said.

"Then why don't we give this a try?" I shrugged. "If it doesn't work out, it doesn't work out."

But what if it did? I thought. What if combining all our efforts was exactly what Sydney needed?

Hope slid through me.

Sydney shook her head. "I still say it's too much."

Marguerite gave Sydney's hand another squeeze. "Not true." Then she flashed the smile that had set my heart at ease for as long as I could remember. "Not true at all."

Ella danced back to the table, stopping to lean against Sydney, who reflexively looped one arm around her daughter's waist.

"Are we going to live with Grandpa Albert and Auntie D?" she asked.

Sydney visibly relaxed and fell quiet before she met my waiting stare, her expression growing determined.

"OK." She nodded. "But the minute this doesn't make sense anymore, we leave."

After dinner, I drove Sydney and Ella back to Mrs. Leroy's bed-and-breakfast. We loaded their belongings into their car and stopped for groceries at the Paris Market on our way back.

By the time we pulled back into the drive and burst through the front door, Marguerite had changed the linens in my parents' old bedroom and the smaller bedroom that had once served as my grandmother's office.

Sydney sat on the end of the bed that had once been my parents', and I shivered, shaking off the sensation of watching my mother's ghost.

Ella bounced through the upstairs, peering into one room after the other, until she stepped inside the old office.

Both rooms still boasted the same paint they'd had in my youth: my parents' room a pale blue, Grandmother's office a sensible ecru.

Stiff, brightly patterned curtains hung from the large original windows. The curtains were not much to look at, but effective on cold winter nights.

And beneath them sat large panes of glass, perfect for throwing open once the cool autumn breezes arrived, or peering through on a clear, starry night.

"Look at this," I said to Ella, as I remembered one of my favorite hiding places from my youth and stepped into the smaller room behind her.

I crossed to the large closet door and cracked it open. The interior sat bare, much like the two rooms. Stripped clean of all signs anyone had ever lived here.

"Great place to hide," I said, and then I shrugged. "Or put your clothes."

Then, much to my amazement, Ella moved to stand beside me. She graced me with a wide, bright smile and slipped her hand inside mine.

Suddenly I saw how forgotten these spaces had become.

I'd lived my life around them, ignoring them, much like my memories.

Perhaps now, with the arrival of Ella and Sydney, these old spaces would get their second chance to live.

"What about school?" Marguerite asked quietly, as Ella settled in upstairs with Albert's help, and we three women put away groceries and warmed the kettle for tea. "The end of summer's just around the corner."

"I thought I might homeschool," Sydney said. "Until we know where we'll end up permanently."

"Nonsense." Marguerite shook her head. "Why not have her attend Paris Elementary so you can rest, even if it's only temporary? I'll call Mary Beth Brooks first thing tomorrow."

Mrs. Brooks had been the principal longer than I could remember. I had no doubt she and Marguerite would have Ella enrolled and ready to go long before the first day of school rolled around.

Sydney fell silent, her expression a tangle of surprise and confusion.

"Are you all right?" I asked, feeling concern. Was she dizzy? In pain? Feeling ill?

"I never expected you to be so generous," she said. "Not to someone you barely know."

Marguerite laughed. "That's the thing about Destiny. She talks a good game, but deep inside, she's got the same soft heart her mother had."

Later that night, still mulling over Albert's reaction to my decision, I found him in the kitchen, dishing out a bowl of ice cream.

"You did a good thing today," he said.

I answered tightly. "That's what I came down here to talk to you about."

He pulled out a chair to sit down, but I remained standing. I had no plans to make this conversation any longer than it needed to be.

We'd coexisted in strained silence for days, and I wasn't sure I'd ever be able to forgive him for what he'd done. This latest betrayal had cut me to the core.

"I didn't ask them to stay because you wanted me to," I said. "I asked them to stay because I wanted to."

He'd raised a spoonful of ice cream to his mouth, but set the spoon back in the dish untouched. The lines around his eyes deepened as he tried to wrap his brain around my words.

"I'm glad Sydney and Ella are here, and yes, I owe that to you, but you need to stop and realize that you've lied to me over and over again."

"I'm sorry." He spoke the words so softly I could barely hear him.

"Then start telling me the truth."

He swallowed visibly. "I am proud of you," he said, "for opening your home. Your mother would be proud."

The mention of my mother brought a wave of emotion, but I tamped it down. I wasn't about to give him the satisfaction of seeing me react to his praise.

The amazing thing was that I didn't care what he thought. Not anymore.

I'd asked Sydney and Ella to stay because I wanted to help. I wanted to be part of their journey.

I'd done this for me. Not Albert.

"Good night," I said, leaving Albert behind as I headed for the hall, finally silencing the ten-year-old girl who'd wondered for so long why her father hadn't come back.

CHAPTER NINETEEN

A few nights later, six of us gathered around the old kitchen table in my parents' kitchen, in the space where I'd eaten more meals alone than I cared to think about.

Jackson Harding had driven over from New York to check on my father, who had invited him to stay for dinner.

He looked exactly as he had the two previous times we'd met. Faded jeans. Tweed jacket. Plain T-shirt.

He chatted easily with Sydney and Marguerite, did his best to engage Ella, and listened patiently as Albert described his plans for the garden.

Jackson had hung his jacket over the back of his chair as we ate. I couldn't help but notice how relaxed he looked.

I also couldn't help but notice how often I glanced in his direction, a disconcerting observation about myself.

Conversation filled the small space, silverware clinked and clattered, and I sat taking it in. Watching. Listening. Wondering what it might have been like to grow up in a house full of people.

Like this.

Sydney made conversation easily, while Ella had been a bit reserved since Jackson's arrival.

Jackson, much to his credit, appeared even more at ease here, tossed into the middle of our unconventional family, than he did back in the New York City park where we'd shared hot dogs.

He explained how foreign opening night at the Manchester had seemed without having Albert onstage. When all trace of emotion vanished from my father's face, Jackson switched gears, regaling us with stories and descriptions of the many sights found in Times Square.

"Why would a cowboy want to be naked?" Ella asked, and we fell into peals of laughter, the warm notes rising in the small space, filling every crevice that had formerly gone silent.

After everyone finished eating, Albert and Ella disappeared to go check the garden for rogue weeds. Marguerite headed next door to put together a plate of cookies, and Sydney and I moved to clear the dishes.

Jackson, much to my surprise, gathered three place settings before I'd cleared my first.

He nodded toward Scarlet's tiny tank as he set the dishes in the sink.

"Your fish is trying to tell you something."

I'd changed the water again and again, and still the fish was barely visible inside the dingy tank.

"I'm obviously doing something wrong," I said.

The truth was that if I'd let her die to begin with, I could have returned her. But I didn't want to imagine a person who could do such a thing. Scarlet had become a fixture in the kitchen, Ella loved her, and I was determined to keep Ella's fish alive and happy.

I carried a second stack of dishes to the sink and peered into the tank. "I don't even see her."

But Jackson was already in motion. "Do you have a large bowl?"

I set the dishes in the sink and reached for one of my mother's old Pyrex mixing bowls in a lower cabinet.

Jackson grabbed the container of springwater I kept on the counter for tank changes and poured quickly, filling the bowl sloppily and splashing water onto the counter.

"Hey—" I started to complain, but he was reaching for the lid to the tank, setting it aside.

Scarlet had jumped out of the water and onto a leaf, where she sprawled, sides heaving.

"Net?" he asked.

"No." I shook my head.

He gently dipped the leaf into the water long enough to cup Scarlet in his hands and transfer her to the bowl of clean water. She sprang into action, swimming with abandon in frantic circles around the edge of the bowl.

Jackson pointed to the tank. "Something went wrong with her environment. Is there a pet store nearby?"

"Harrington's," I said, glancing at the time on the wall. Eight fifteen. "But I think they've already closed for the night."

"How about a chain store?" he asked.

That, we could find.

"Big one." I nodded. "Just outside of town."

"Do you do this often?" I asked a few minutes later, as Jackson, Ella, and I drove out of town, headed for the large pet store ten miles away in the nearest strip mall.

Jackson smiled. "Rescue small aquatic animals?" He grinned. "Only when their demise is imminent."

"You're like a fish superhero," Ella gushed from the back seat, all shyness forgotten. "Did you see the way Scarlet was swimming around that bowl? Who knew she even liked to swim? She never does anything."

"Because I think she was half-dead," Jackson said as he pulled the car into the parking lot. "But we're going to fix that."

Inside the store, I headed for the first employee I spotted in the aquatic section, but when I glanced behind me, Ella and Jackson had disappeared.

Adrenaline rushed through my veins. "Ella?" Surely I hadn't misplaced the nine-year-old the second we walked through the door.

Jackson's reassuring voice called out a split second later. "She's with me. We'll be right there."

I breathed a sigh of relief, then rattled through Scarlet's list of symptoms, watching as the young clerk's perfectly made-up features settled into a frown.

"Did you rinse the gravel?" she asked.

Did Albert? "I don't know," I answered. "I wasn't the one who set up the tank."

The young clerk nodded. "That's important. You want to rinse off any dust or dirt. Are you feeding her every other day?" she asked brightly.

I frowned. "The food says two to three times daily."

She blew out a sigh. "Overfeeding. I'm surprised she didn't jump out of her tank sooner. Her water's probably full of ammonia. Maybe fungus."

Fungus? Ammonia? Who knew taking care of a fish would be so complicated?

Jackson and Ella had still not appeared, but I could hear the rumble of his deep voice in the next aisle over, followed by Ella's giggle.

I smiled, relieved to hear her laugh.

"I'd go with a bigger tank, maybe a five-gallon. Add a filter, a heater, and a thermometer," the clerk said. "She's probably constipated."

"You have got to be kidding me."

She shook her head.

I thought about the murky fog spreading upward from Scarlet's gravel. "What about the gunk in the tank? Will that happen again?"

"If you feed her less, keep the filter running, and rinse your new gravel, no."

She stared at me as a voice over the loudspeaker sounded. "Candace to small reptiles. Candace to small reptiles."

I glanced at the girl's name tag. *Candace.*

"I have to go," she said. Then she counted off on her fingers. "Filter. Water conditioner. Heater. Thermometer. Less food."

I waited until she was out of sight; then I studied the shelves for some of the items she'd mentioned.

Jackson and Ella came around the corner behind me, pushing a cart.

Ella rode on the side, her hand in a salute, a wide smile plastered across her face. "Reporting for duty, Auntie D," she said.

Behind her, Jackson shot me a wink, and inside the cart sat a glass tank five times the size of the one Scarlet had now, a bag of black gravel, a purple silk plant, a resin pirate ship, a heater, a thermometer, a filter, and a bottle of water conditioner.

Jackson plucked one small container from the bottom of the cart and gave it a shake. "Blood worms. She'll love these."

Ella wrinkled her nose.

After Jackson insisted on paying our ninety-eight-dollar-and-seventy-two-cent tab, we loaded the car and headed back to Paris.

Two hours later Scarlet had acclimated to her new home, and Jackson stood in the kitchen sliding his arms back into his jacket. Ella appeared beside him, holding out a crayon drawing of Scarlet in her tank. I grinned when I realized she'd drawn a pirate's patch over one of Scarlet's eyes.

"Thanks for helping Scarlet. She's been a little stressed out."

Jackson laughed, running his hand lightly over the top of Ella's head. The gentle move did something odd to my heart, and I had to blink myself back into focus.

Ella, however, was staring into Scarlet's tank. She frowned, then dropped her voice to a whisper.

"I know it's not really my Scarlet," she said, wrinkling her nose, "but I sure do appreciate Grandpa Albert trying to make me feel at home."

Emotion fisted in my throat, and I pulled her into a hug. "You're a good kid, know that?"

Jackson gave me a quick smile and turned for the door.

"Maybe I'll stop by again sometime," he said. "To check on Scarlet."

"We'd like that," I said.

Ella and I watched his car pull away from the curb out front, and I replayed his words through my mind.

Maybe I'll stop by again sometime.

I hoped he wouldn't wait too long.

CHAPTER TWENTY

One and a half weeks later, Ella started fourth grade at Paris Elementary.

I'd lingered at home in order to see her off, watching nervously as she and Sydney headed down the street toward the center of town.

New school. New friends. New opportunities.

Later that morning I'd stopped off at the opera house to take some additional photos of the stage frame and double-check my final measurements for the panels—step one of the three-part renovation.

But when I emerged from the opera house to head to my shop, I spotted Sydney sitting across the street on a park bench, her body language defeated, her facial expression vacant.

Worry exploded inside me. Was she sick? Had something gone wrong at school?

"Hey," I yelled out, trying to make light of what looked like anything but a light moment. "Did you look both ways?"

She blinked, clearly pulling herself back, then laughed, the sound taking the edge off my fears.

"How did you get out of gardening?" I glanced to my left and right before I jogged across the street to where she sat.

Albert had made a great show that morning about sacrificing his gardening partner to formal education, and Sydney had vowed to take Ella's place. Yet here she sat, a block from school, apparently lost in thought.

She wore an Ohio State cap instead of her wig, and I looped my arm through hers as I sat beside her. Although she held herself upright, she radiated fatigue.

"Ella's first day of school," she said.

"Pretty exciting."

But Sydney looked broken. "She didn't give me so much as a glance over her shoulder."

"And you?"

"Having a moment." Tears welled in her eyes, and I pulled her close. "What if I don't see her grow up?" she asked softly, and my heart broke in two.

I wanted to answer her, wanted to say something wise or comforting, but I wasn't capable.

I managed a simple "I'm sorry," then realized I'd rarely stopped to think about what cancer had been like for my mother. I was intimately familiar with what it had been like for me, her survivor. But what had my mom felt and thought as her prognosis grew bleak?

Had she sat in this same spot staring at the same school, wondering if she'd see me grow up?

"Know what you need?" I asked.

Sydney shook her head, and I pulled her to her feet.

"A large to-go cup of Jessica's magic coffee, and physical labor."

"Physical labor?" She made a face, and I spotted the slightest glimpse of a smile. "Have you heard about the chemo?"

She'd started the sixteen daily capsules required by the new trial and had completed her first infusion of the second drug in the protocol last Friday.

"Chemo, shmemo." I pulled her toward the curb. "Let's go pound some nails."

I stepped off the curb just as a small white car zipped past, and Sydney tugged me backward in one smooth motion.

"Son of a bitch," I said, and then we laughed until we both held our sides.

We looked to our left, to our right, and to our left again. Then we headed toward the Paris Café, arms linked, as if we'd walked beside each other, just like this, countless times before.

The walk from the café to my shop wasn't a long one, but Sydney labored over each step.

Although the sun shone brightly and the early air all but crackled with the promise of cooler fall weather to come, I couldn't help but worry about why she seemed so tired. Her fatigue was always apparent, but today seemed different. Today seemed more.

"Would you rather go home?" I asked.

Sydney shook her head. "This new drug's kicking my ass, but no."

"We can."

"No," she said, her tone sharp.

We rounded the corner onto Artisan's Alley, and shop window after shop window glistened in the sun. Behind their glass panes sat antiques, elaborate sun catchers, furniture, framed paintings, and more.

"Any of this yours?" she asked.

I pointed, and her features brightened. "Rocking chair. See it?"

"The white one?"

The shopkeeper had carefully draped a patriotic quilt over the chair's back, and while the effect was eye-catching, it hid some of the shaping I'd done on the chair's back and arms.

"That one was a pet project. I keep thinking I'm going to take it back if it doesn't sell."

We continued down the block, and the two-story garage that housed my shop appeared a few buildings later.

"You going to be all right with the steps?" I asked, but Sydney only nodded, saying not a word as she climbed the wooden boards one at a time, her concentration never wavering.

I unlocked the door and we pushed inside.

"It's a mess now," I said. "Bit different than the last time you saw it."

Every inch of drafting table, worktable, counter, and wall space was covered with photos, sketches, grids, and diagrams of the opera house interior. I'd embraced the renovation wholeheartedly, focusing solely on the project and letting it consume my shop and my creative mind.

"Amazing," Sydney said. "You can feel the creativity in this space."

A frisson of pride wound through me. "Thanks, I guess. Unless that's your way of saying it's chaos."

She graced me with the smile that brought my mother back to life. "Creative chaos."

I swallowed against the knot of emotion in my throat and looped my arm through hers.

"Come on," I said. "I'll show you the project."

I carefully maneuvered her through the now-crowded space, detailed the workings of every machine, and explained the sketches and progress photos from the opera house. Then I flipped through my brag book—photographs from every job I'd ever completed.

I stopped myself when I realized I was acting like a kid trying too hard to please a new friend.

"Sorry. I'm probably boring you."

"Never. I love how passionate you are about what you do."

"Don't you feel that way about nursing?"

She shook her head. "Not anymore. Now I'm just tired."

Tired.

"Let's sit you down. I have the perfect project to take your mind off Ella starting school."

I handed her a mask and a pair of safety goggles, then held up a narrow strip of wood, carefully explaining how I planned to feed it through my favorite saw four times, using a different bit each time to create the lovely scroll molding I'd glue and pin to each section of the opera house stage frame. Her job would be to apply the molding, following my careful design grid, after I'd made sure the wood had been cut and mitered to fit.

She looked at me like I was crazy.

"Are you out of your mind?" she asked. "I can take your temperature, diagnose your appendicitis, or set your broken fingers, but I am not about to screw up your opera house work."

I held up a pencil drawing of the vertical view of the molding design, proudly showing Sydney each measured angle and cut.

Then I fed a piece of wood through the saw exactly as I'd explained. Four careful passes.

When I was finished, I held up one long, beautifully trimmed piece of molding. Then I explained the measurements for turning the strip into mitered pieces that would perfectly fit each panel of the stage façade.

Sydney's eyes had gone vacant, and I realized I'd been rambling on for quite a while.

"Earth to Sydney. Did I lose you?"

"Just for a second." She shook her head, noticeably trying to wake herself up. "Sorry."

"Don't be silly. Sometimes I bore myself when I get going about corners and measurements and angles."

I pulled a precut section of stage panel and set it on the worktable beside her. "Ready for the fun stuff?"

Sydney nodded, even though I could read the trepidation in her eyes.

"Don't worry. I've got plenty of materials, but I have a feeling you'll be a natural.

"We glue first," I explained. "Plenty of time to catch any mistakes before we pin."

"Pin?" she asked.

I held up a jar of tiny nails and one small hammer. "Pin. Holds the molding in place for good. Then our last step is staining, but we'll hold off on that until all the sections are complete."

"How long will this take?" she asked.

"I'm thinking the panels will take the better part of two months. The box seats and stage trim will take longer. Completion's expected next spring."

"Wow." She narrowed her gaze behind her safety glasses. "Impressive."

"Thanks."

A short while later I used the saw to cut trim for a second section, while Sydney meticulously tapped pins into place on the first piece. She had managed not only to glue the entire panel herself, but finished the pinning without my supervision.

A ridiculously satisfying sense of pride welled up inside me. I threw open the floor-to-ceiling windows to let in fresh air, sawdust dancing in the beams of sunlight, and I laughed through my mask. Then my eyes met Sydney's beyond my safety goggles.

"Thank you," she said.

I gave her a quick shrug. "For what?"

"For this." She gestured to the shop, the saws, and the wood scraps on the floor. "For all of this."

I could see it in her eyes. *Relief.*

For just a few hours, in the buzz of my saw and the smell of freshly cut wood, she'd been able to escape her reality.

For that, I was grateful.

CHAPTER TWENTY-ONE

Not long after seven o'clock on Saturday morning, I heard movement in the house and pushed out of bed to investigate.

Sydney's bedroom door sat tightly closed, and Albert had fallen asleep in his favorite chair downstairs, a half-full cup of coffee by his side and a crossword puzzle on his lap.

During the days since Sydney and Ella had moved in, he'd been cooking meals, helping with chores, and spending quality time with Ella. And yet I couldn't bring myself to forgive him.

I studied him for a few moments, thinking of the handful of times he'd tried to bridge the gap between us. Perhaps I was being too stubborn. Perhaps I should at least agree to talk to him. But maybe some walls were too high to knock down.

A flash of color out the front window captured my attention.

Ella's mop of dark hair was tousled, her natural waves having exploded overnight, and as I realized what she was doing I found myself mesmerized and more than a little amused.

One by one she gathered the large river rocks her grandfather had used to edge the restored flower bed. Picasso danced around her heels, stopping only to hike his leg on a brilliant yellow chrysanthemum. I bit back my laugh so as not to wake Albert and reignite the short-lived Albert-Picasso turf war.

When Ella's arms were full and she visibly sagged beneath the weight of her haul, she disappeared around the fence, headed toward Marguerite's house. Picasso followed close on her heels.

She worked intently and moved purposefully. As far as I was concerned, if the kid wanted to run an early morning rock raid, I wasn't going to stop her.

I could, however, keep an eye on her.

I headed back through the house, carefully opening the kitchen door to avoid its customary squeak. The morning air hung crisp and cool, the sky barely light. Dew glistened on the lawn and patio, leaving the table and the violet bistro chairs visibly damp.

Voices sounded from Marguerite's yard, and I realized Ella wasn't alone.

"Did you get them?" Marguerite asked.

"As many as I could carry."

I smiled at the excited tone of her voice. She'd come a long way from the cautious child who'd first studied me inside my workshop.

Marguerite, of course, still had a way of breaking down a child's walls through her love of art and her warm, welcoming spirit.

I moved stealthily across the patio to steal a peek through the fence.

Marguerite helped Ella set the stones on her worktable; then she ruffled Ella's dark hair. "I'll get the hot chocolate." She pointed to a line of colorful bottles. "You start picking paint."

I sank lower and watched. Marguerite disappeared back into the house, and Ella carefully selected a small group of bottles. She squeezed globs of color onto some sort of palette and then began the task of choosing rocks. She lifted first one and then another, studying a third, turning a fourth, setting a fifth upside down, until she'd chosen what appeared to be the smallest of the bunch.

Marguerite reappeared, her fluffy lime-green robe billowing in the cool breeze that had picked up from the river. I realized my cover had been blown the moment I spotted three mugs on her serving tray.

"I already added cream to your coffee, Destiny," she said, making no effort to conceal her grin.

I frowned and stood. "I just wanted to see what Ella was up to."

"Well"—Marguerite shrugged—"you can't squat there forever."

To my relief, Ella giggled, then waved at me to come around the fence. For a moment I'd been afraid she'd resent my intrusion.

"What *are* you doing?" I asked a few moments later.

"Painting smiles," Ella answered.

I pointed to a bare rock. "I hate to break it to you, but that's a rock."

"Ah," Marguerite said. "But is it?"

As I sipped my coffee and watched, Ella methodically painted hearts on the surface of the rock until it was transformed from pale stone to an explosion of bright colors.

A blue heart nestled against a red heart. Two purple hearts framed a teal heart. A yellow heart topped them all, like a heart-shaped sun at the rock's upper edge.

"A smile," Ella said softly when she'd finished.

"I love it, but I'm still confused," I said.

Ella looked to Marguerite, and Marguerite shook her head. "This is your project; you explain it to your aunt."

Your aunt. My attention hung on my new reality, but I quickly shifted back to what Ella was saying.

". . . then I'm going to put them places, like in someone's garden, or down by the river, maybe outside a shop." Her deep-brown eyes glimmered with pride. "When someone sees them, they'll smile."

"So, you're painting these for strangers?"

Ella nodded. "I got to thinking that Momma and I probably aren't the only people in town with problems. Maybe somebody else could use a smile."

"Smile rocks," I said, my heart expanding.

"Everyone deserves a smile." Ella's voice faltered as she chose her next rock.

And although I was filled with the sudden urge to pull her into a hug and never let her go, I resisted, instead drinking my coffee and watching, proud beyond words, while Ella painted smiles.

That afternoon, I headed to the opera house to work on additional design sketches.

Albert sat waiting across the street when I emerged. He stood as soon as he spotted me, waving as if I might not notice him there.

I thought about pretending I didn't see him. I thought about running in the opposite direction. Instead, I crossed the street to where he stood.

"Do you remember standing here?" he asked. "Watching the last renovation?"

He kept his eyes on the opera house, and I couldn't decide if he was avoiding meeting my gaze or if he was picturing our past.

Ella had given me one of her smaller smile rocks as a gift. One stone. Painted with a simple purple heart. I'd carried it in my pocket all day, and I reached for it now.

"I do," I answered, wrapping my fingers around Ella's smile even as I missed *that* Albert, the dad who would have never left my side.

"I should have known right then you'd work on this building one day." He turned to look at me, and for a moment there was no filter. There was only *that* dad, and my traitorous heart cried out for more.

"I work on a lot of buildings." I fought to keep the emotion I felt out of my voice as I looked away, pulling the rock from my pocket, fisting my fingers around the smooth surface.

He shook his head. "No. This building meant something to you back then."

"It means something to me now. It's the biggest job I've ever had." I spoke the words too quickly, defensively.

When our eyes met again, his told me he knew this job was more than simply another project to be completed.

"I always loved it here," he said.

I thought he might mention Mom, might reminisce about the last time we'd all been here together. I thought he might wish me well or ask me how my work was going. He did neither.

Instead he simply said, "My favorite memories are of you and me standing right here, staring over there."

His words reached deep into my heart and squeezed, and in the moment when I shifted away from him to fight the tears that threatened, I dropped Ella's rock.

He plucked it from the sidewalk, studying it in his palm. "What's this?"

I reached for the stone with the painted purple heart, resisting the urge to snatch it out of his hand. "Ella painted it this morning."

Albert stared without saying a word, by all appearances forgetting how children could turn just about anything into something magical.

"You were right when you accused me of coming back to Paris for Sydney and Ella and not for you."

The words stung more deeply that I'd imagined they would, and I flinched inwardly.

"You deserve that truth," he continued. "The thing is, the moment you opened your front door that first night, everything I lost hit me full in the face."

"Mom?" I asked.

"No." He folded my fingers over Ella's rock, and then closed his hand over mine. "You," he said. "I lost you."

I swallowed against the tightness in my throat, but my tears beat wet paths down my cheeks.

He reached to dry my cheeks, but I dodged his touch.

"When you and I went back to the theater, and I stayed for rehearsal while you left to go back to Paris, I realized I'd stayed for enough rehearsals. I've done enough shows."

I moved to free my hand from his, but he tightened his grip.

"I'm not going anywhere, Destiny." He shrugged, the same shrug I'd been making all my life. "Whether you believe me or not."

Then he released my hand.

I opened my fist, rolling Ella's rock in my palm.

Was he telling the truth?

"What did she paint?" he asked. "A heart?"

I shook my head, feeling a chunk of my anger slide away.

"No," I said. "It's a smile."

"A smile?"

I nodded. "She calls them smile rocks." I laughed softly. "Imagine that."

When I looked from Ella's smile to my father, his focus sat not on the rock, but on me. He smiled the wide, welcoming smile I remembered from my childhood.

And he repeated simply, "Imagine that."

CHAPTER
TWENTY-TWO

I had never had the slightest urge to salute the sun, but since Sydney had learned to pin trim for the opera house stage panels, when she asked me to try yoga early the following week, I said yes.

Now that we stood inside a dimly lit studio, candles burning, surrounded by obviously well-practiced yoga enthusiasts waiting for the class to begin, I started to question my decision.

I had never considered myself either coordinated or graceful, and I was feeling nervous.

"You need to relax," Sydney said, and then she giggled, a sound I hadn't heard before. "But then, I suppose that's why I brought you here."

"You're right," I said. "And you should laugh more."

Her expression grew defensive. "I laugh."

The instructor entered the room and started the session before we had a chance to say anything more to each other.

"Let's warm up. Focus your breathing," she said.

Focus your breathing? I was a person who pounded nails and ran lengths of wood through monster saws for a living. I wasn't someone who focused her breathing.

"Sun salutation," the instructor called out, and everybody reached their arms overhead, appearing to have been preprogrammed for the class.

"I can't do this," I whispered to Sydney.

"Yes," she said between breaths, "you can. Just follow along."

When we bent at the waist, I tried to press my palms to the mat, like Sydney did. When we raised up to a flat back, I seized the opportunity to twist around to see what the instructor and everyone else was doing. I succeeded in losing my balance just as they all shot their feet backward into a lunge, and by the time they'd lowered themselves into the plank position, I was flat-out on my belly.

"Nicely done," Sydney whispered.

"You have got to be kidding."

"Ladies," the instructor said in our direction. "More breathing, less speaking."

Sydney giggled again, and I smiled. Twisting my body into impossible poses was a small price to pay to see her this relaxed.

Five minutes later I'd completely rethought my position. We'd moved through the sun salutation into something called a chair pose, and my thighs and butt shook as if I'd never used a muscle in my life. When we broadened our stance into something called a crescent pose, I wobbled, staggered, then fell over, picking myself up as quickly as I could. Mortified.

"Use a modification if necessary," the instructor called out. "Lovely work, everyone."

"What the hell is a modification?" I asked Sydney, wobbling off my mat for a second time.

The instructor moved the class into balance pose, then tree pose, which Sydney navigated beautifully, tucking the sole of one foot up along the inside of her opposite thigh, standing tall, balancing like a majestic tree.

"Put your foot down by your ankle," she whispered. "Or keep your toe touching."

"Touching what?"

"Ladies," the instructor gently called out again. "More breathing, less speaking."

This time I wobbled off my mat just as she spoke, and Sydney's laugh burst from between her lips.

I shot her a glare, twisting my features into my best terrifying face. She responded in kind, adding a snarl.

After that, class went more smoothly. Oh sure, I fell three more times, but for every impossible pose, I had Sydney beside me, her subtle laughter and not-so-subtle faces urging me on.

Somewhere between warrior one and warrior two, a flash of color from Sydney's toes captured my attention, and I couldn't believe I hadn't noticed the brilliant polish when we'd first slipped off our shoes.

"Your toes are teal," I said.

Sydney smiled as she flawlessly followed the yoga instructor into an angle pose. "Teal warrior," she answered.

I shot her a quizzical look as I desperately tried to hold my balance.

"You know how the ribbon color for breast cancer awareness is pink?" Sydney whispered.

I nodded, panting.

"Everyone does," she said. "But not many people know teal is the color for ovarian cancer awareness."

"More breathing, less speaking," the instructor repeated. Then she said, "One more sun salutation, everyone."

Sydney wiggled her brows, and I grinned.

"I wear teal to raise awareness," she whispered, even more softly. "If I can help just one person know more about recognizing the symptoms and getting treatment earlier than I did, then I'll wear teal toes forever."

A few minutes later, as the instructor led us through a final series of stretches, every muscle in my body screamed in protest.

"I'm going to hurt in places I never knew I had," I said.

Sydney stretched and twisted, meeting my gaze, a measure of joy slipping from her expression. "I think that's how you know you're alive."

Her words haunted me as we rolled our mats and headed for the car. "Think I could pull off teal toes?"

A smile pushed away the sadness that had edged into Sydney's eyes. "Most definitely. And I'm just the girl to paint them."

We took the long way home from the yoga studio, making most of the trip in silence, simply enjoying each other's company and our—though I hated to admit it—relaxed states of mind.

"Ready to take on the world?" Sydney asked as we climbed the steps to the front door.

"Or take a nap." I grinned.

"You secretly liked it."

I shrugged. "I'll never tell."

"Let's sit out back," she said. "I'll go grab my polish."

Teal toes. So she'd taken me seriously.

Clearly sensing my thoughts, she hesitated, one foot on the center stairs. "You meant what you said, right?"

"Well"—I wrinkled my nose—"I was under the influence of that warrior pose, but yes. Go get your polish."

A few minutes later we'd settled outside, basking in the mid-September warmth.

We'd passed Albert, working in the garden out front.

"How was yoga?" he'd asked, to which Sydney had said, "Wonderful," while I'd merely groaned.

His latest project was replacing the river rocks Ella had borrowed, and I couldn't help but notice he'd added an extra pile.

I pointed to them. "For?"

And he'd answered, "Future smiles."

Now, as Sydney and I sat out back, I wriggled my toes self-consciously as she shook the polish bottle. While I was constantly barefoot unless I was working, I had never once in my life indulged in a pedicure.

"Relax," Sydney said. "We're painting your toes, not lopping them off."

"Tell me more about the teal toes," I said. "You really think this helps somehow?"

She nodded. "Half the battle"—she hesitated—"probably more than half the battle, is awareness. The thing about ovarian cancer is that everyone thinks it's silent, but it's really not. It whispers."

She slicked polish onto my big toe, then sat back to study her work.

"Your job"—she looked up at me and smiled—"now that you're going to have teal toes, is to know the symptoms so you can educate people."

"And they are?"

"Bloating, abdominal pain, more indigestion than usual, feeling full quickly."

"Those aren't that abnormal," I said, suddenly wondering what had led to Sydney's diagnosis.

"They are if they last for more than two weeks," she said, brushing polish on one, two, three more toes.

I studied my feet, amazed at how much difference a little polish made.

"Wonder if you would have done this if we'd been kids together?"

Silence beat between us, and I regretted ever uttering the words.

"I wonder," she said softly.

And then I asked, "How did you find out?"

"About the cancer? I had the symptoms." She capped the polish and gave it a quick shake before setting down my left foot and reaching for my right. "You have to remember, I've had patients with ovarian cancer; I've just never had any as young as me.

"My first surgery was my debulking, where they remove everything they can get their hands on. That left me with a colostomy. Then I got this." She pulled aside her shirt to expose a small area of her chest where something had been set beneath the skin.

"What is it?"

"My very own port," she explained. "For chemo, blood draws . . . It's quite handy, actually."

She smoothed her shirt back into place, hiding the port. "My chemo left me with no hair, no eyelashes, no nothing."

She smiled, and I wondered how many times she'd forced the same smile during the past four years.

"Then I had a year off. My hair grew back. I had a few eyelashes. I even had some eyebrows, and they were able to reverse my colostomy." She blew out a sigh. "Then I got headaches. I felt confused, and I backed my car into a wall."

"Your brain?"

Sydney nodded. "Seven lesions." She patted the base of her skull. "Most tiny. All in one area. I did what they called whole-brain radiation, and I spent almost three weeks in the hospital."

"Ella?"

"My parents took good care of her, and they took good care of me. My hair fell out again, but my lesions died."

"And now?"

"Now my parents are gone, and it's trying to sneak back. One lesion started to grow a few months ago, and I had what they call gamma knife radiation." She pointed her fingers like she was shooting. "Zap. Right to the tumor. Dead."

"So that's good."

She nodded. "Better than the alternative, as my dad always said."

Sydney concentrated then, carefully painting the toes on my other foot. I said nothing as I watched her work, thinking about all she'd been through, all I wished I could have helped her with, been there for.

She related her story casually, as if recounting the details didn't affect her, but I suspected it did. How could it not? For each step of her journey, I imagined there had to be a million what-ifs. What if she'd done something differently? Found something sooner? Tried a different drug? What if?

Or maybe I was completely wrong. Maybe there weren't a million what-ifs. Maybe there was only one.

What if she didn't survive?

I watched her with different eyes. Eyes that appreciated all the moments I'd missed in not knowing her. All the moments she'd had with Ella. All the moments she still had, taking nothing for granted. Then I let my mind wander to all the moments she might never have.

I remembered my mother reading to me even as her energy and voice failed, and I realized I'd been too young to understand just how hard she'd fought to be with me, to stay with me.

"Why do you think it'll come back again?"

"Because that's what ovarian cancer does."

She brushed on polish expertly, one toe at a time, and I savored the touch of her hand, the warmth of her thigh beneath my heel.

"The trial I just started is designed to kill any circulating cells. Some patients have seen success."

"And you?"

"They're worried about a new spot in my brain, and my tumor marker's been climbing." She shrugged, obviously trying to put me at ease.

I asked the question then that we'd not yet discussed, even though we'd danced around the topic.

"What about Ella?"

Sydney sat back, replaced the brush in the polish, and tightened the cap.

"Did you come here to ask Albert to raise her?" I asked.

She furrowed her brow. "You have to understand that I have no one in Ohio. No one at all." Sadness seeped through her words.

"So, Albert," I said flatly. "And Paris."

Sydney nodded. "Paris, yes. Just being here for these past weeks gives me a sense of what a wonderful place this must have been to grow up."

Yes, I thought. *A family, where I had none.*

Sydney continued. "I see how she looks at you, Destiny. She doesn't let many people in. She's a lot like me in that respect, but you and she . . ."

"Are alike," I said, finishing her sentence.

"She misses her grandparents," Sydney said, her voice going soft. "I'm not sure how she'll survive when I'm gone."

But I knew. She'd adjust to her new normal, her motherless world, compartmentalizing her grief until it was merely a part of her, to be carried forever.

"You've been there," she said. "I see how you watch her."

"That's because she's a great kid."

"Thanks."

Then I realized where Sydney was headed, and a shiver slid across the back of my neck.

The ramifications of her words were serious—more serious than anything I'd encountered in my adult life.

"Are you asking me to raise her? If something happens to you?"

Sydney nodded.

The shadows of my past rose before me—echoes of heartache and loss—but as we sat together, saying nothing, I measured the risk. I weighed the benefits.

Sydney had already found her way into my heart. If she lost her battle, no amount of protective walls would ease the pain of losing her. Not for me. Certainly not for Ella.

But I could be there.

I could be there for Ella, could help her pick up the pieces, navigate her new normal, and remind her of the good in life—the laughter, the adventure, the hope.

"I'd be honored," I said, pushing the words past the knot in my throat.

She stared at me, her gaze crowded with gratitude, trust, and fear. Then she uncapped the polish and turned her attention back to my toes. "Thank you," she said, brushing on one flawless stroke after another.

"I'll never let you down," I said.

Sydney spoke, so softly I could barely hear, her words quavering with emotion.

"Hold still," she said. "I'm not done yet."

CHAPTER
TWENTY-THREE

I was elbow-deep in salvaged maple lengths on Friday afternoon when my cell rang. I'd hired two laborers to help me transport the wood from the mill to my shop, and the last thing I needed was an interruption when I had assistants on the clock.

I glanced at my phone, not recognizing the incoming number.

"Destiny Jones."

"It's Doris over at the school," a familiar voice said.

The Paris Elementary office manager. I'd installed custom wall units in her family room just last March.

"I'm calling about Ella," she said, and my inner alarm began to chime.

What time was it? I'd been so engrossed, I'd lost all track.

I glanced at the old clock I kept mounted on the wall. Five minutes after three. Twenty minutes after school let out.

Ella.

I'll never let you down, I'd told Sydney.

And now, the very first day I'd agreed to walk Ella home from school, I'd forgotten her.

Sydney had an MRI and an infusion scheduled in the city, and Albert had driven her. Marguerite was tied up all day setting up for an art exhibit a few towns over.

My job—*my only job*—was to pick up Ella after school.

I glanced at the two men, who had at least another hour of work ahead of them.

"Shit," I shouted far too loudly into the phone. "I'll be right there. Tell her I'll be right there. Five minutes."

"Please hurry," Doris said, then dropped her voice low. "The poor kid's sitting in the lobby trying not to cry."

Trying not to cry? When I'd been just a little older than Ella, I'd walked home from school with my friends every day. Even if I'd been by myself, I'd known everyone in town.

But Ella barely knew anyone, and there she sat.

I knew her well enough to know she'd already run the on-her-own-in-life scenario through her brain countless times, wondering what it would be like if her mother died. She was too much like I'd been not to have done so.

Sitting alone in the lobby of her brand-new school wasn't doing a thing to chase those demons out of her sweet mind.

I'd worked with the two guys hauling maple up the steps previously, so I trusted them. Truth was, I didn't have much choice. The wood had to be unloaded, and Ella had to be picked up from school.

How did people juggle kids and work every day?

I turned over my shop keys and made them promise to lock up and leave the keys with the bakery downstairs when they were through. Then I grabbed my backpack and raced for the school.

I sprinted up the length of Artisan's Alley, slowing only to cross Bridge Street.

While I might not have any parenting experience, I did have first-hand knowledge of what it felt like to watch your mother battle a faceless disease. I remembered what it felt like to be in a constant state of limbo, waiting for the next *thing* to happen.

Ella knew where Sydney had gone today, and I'd left her alone with those fears.

I scrambled up the front steps of the school just a few minutes later. Doris was standing by the door, waiting to buzz me in.

"I am so sorry," I said as I brushed past her.

Ella sat in a standard-issue school chair, her back to the wall, her gaze on the floor.

I knelt in front of her, reaching for her chin. "Hey, I am so sorry. So sorry."

But Ella said nothing, refusing to meet my gaze.

Had one screwup sent us back to round one, and no more eye contact?

"Momma promised you'd be here to pick me up."

Her heartbroken tone and her words gutted me. I'd let her down. I'd let Sydney down. No doubt about it.

"Please look at me," I said.

Ella begrudgingly met my gaze, but kept her scowl firmly in place behind her blue glasses.

"I messed up," I said. "I have no excuse. I was working and cutting and measuring, and I didn't pay attention to the time."

"Isn't that an excuse?" She twisted up her mouth.

"You're right. Duly noted." I took her hands in mine and held on tight. "This won't happen again."

Ella stared at me, unmistakably not fully convinced.

"I'll get an alarm clock for the shop," I continued. "Heck, I'll wear it around my neck."

Her lips twitched, but she held firm.

"You have my word, Ella. Forgive me?"

She let me sweat before she gave me her answer, but eventually she nodded.

Then we headed for the exit. "Thank you, Doris," I said as Ella and I made our way outside.

That night, before dinner, my father pulled me aside. "Marguerite told me what happened. Are you all right?"

Was *I* all right? "Sure," I said. "Ella's the one you should be worried about."

Recognition flashed in his eyes, but he shook his head. "I'm talking about the job. Your work. I know how difficult it is to manage a family illness like this and a career."

While I imagined he'd intended his words to provide comfort, they actually did the opposite, making me realize he was speaking from experience, remembering the days he'd had to choose between taking a role and staying home.

The familiar anger simmered inside me.

"I'm all right," I muttered, although I wasn't sure I was.

If I'd screwed up the first time I needed to be somewhere for Ella, how would I juggle the opera house renovation and her needs?

Maybe I was no different than Albert had been, and that realization shook me to the core.

After dinner, Sydney and I took our usual walk.

She said nothing until we got to the corner of Stone Lane and Bridge Street.

"Got a call from school when we were driving back from the city."

I winced. "I should have told you right away. I'm sorry. I lost track of time, but it won't happen again."

Tension crackled off her as we crossed the street. "You're talking about my daughter, the daughter I just asked you to *raise* when I die, and you lost track of time?"

Remorse welled up inside me.

"They told me she was sitting there crying, Destiny. Crying."

"I'm sorry. I won't let you down again."

"Again," she said sharply. "Which means you've already let me down once."

I was wrong. I knew that. And I was sorry, but something told me there was more to Sydney's anger than me being late to pick up Ella today.

"Want to tell me what else is going on?"

She turned on me sharply, her gaze burning with a fury I hadn't yet seen in her. "What else? Do you think there needs to be something else?"

Her voice cracked on the last word, and she sank onto the next bench we reached.

By the time I sat beside her, tears were streaming down her cheeks.

"Don't you think if I had anyone back home, I'd be there instead of here?" she said. "I never asked to be here."

Her words cut more deeply than those of someone I'd only known a month should.

"Do you think I wanted to be here, Destiny? In Paris? Dying?"

"You're not dying." I took one of her slender hands between both of mine and squeezed.

"That's the thing," she said, dragging her free hand across her face, trying to eradicate all evidence of her outburst. "I found out today that I am."

For a split second, I felt as though my heart stopped beating. The world around us fell silent, and the only sound I could hear was the echo of her words.

I am.

She swallowed, squeezing her eyes shut tightly before she continued.

"My tumor marker's still climbing, my MRI shows a new inflammation in my brain, and the rest of my blood work indicates I'm a total treatment failure on this clinical trial."

Fresh tears slid down her cheeks, and I fought my own as I held on to her hand, not knowing what to do or say.

"I'm so sorry."

She nodded. "Me, too."

"Options?" I asked.

She shook her head. "More steroids, which I hate, and we continue the clinical trial so they can track their precious numbers."

"Continue chemo?" I asked.

"Only to buy me some time."

We sat side by side, letting the world pass by as Sydney's new reality sank in.

My mind traveled to nights spent listening to my parents talk behind closed doors, the sound of my mother's tears, and my father's insistent voice.

"Hey," my father said, startling me from my thoughts. I struggled momentarily to figure out whether his voice was in my head or real, but there he stood, hands shoved into his pockets, worry painted across his features.

"Marguerite said she'd get Ella ready for bed so I could check on you two."

I looked at Sydney, narrowed my eyes.

She nodded. "He knows about my news."

He settled at the other side of the bench, taking Sydney's hand, his move the mirrored image of my own.

We sat together, staring into the future, as life in Paris passed by and the song of late-summer crickets chirped to life.

I couldn't help but wonder if their thoughts were carbon copies of my own, one word repeating over and over, on an endless loop.

Why?

CHAPTER TWENTY-FOUR

The next morning, at the first sign of light, I tiptoed into Ella's bedroom.

While I realized it was somewhat unfair to wake a nine-year-old so early on a Saturday morning, I also knew the payoff would be worth the effort.

I wanted to make up for yesterday, and I was pretty sure I'd hit on a perfect solution.

Sydney had helped me pack for our excursion late the night before, but had encouraged me to make our trip without her.

"Hey, sleepyhead." I gave the lump beneath my niece's giant pile of covers and quilts a shake. "Let's go hide some rocks."

We made our first smile-distribution excursion down by the river. The final traces of summer clung to the riverbanks in gardens of withering daisies and impatiens. The Paris Garden Club's chrysanthemum beds had bloomed in all their glory, like a carpet of yellow and white, edging the walkways and circling century-old oak trees that seemed to disappear into the brilliant blue September sky.

Ella gasped as we stopped on the opposite side of Front Street before crossing.

I instinctively grabbed for her hand, suddenly filled with images of her racing into traffic in her excitement.

Ella, however, was far less concerned with traffic than she was with sport.

"Do people ever swim there, Auntie D?"

Did they ever.

I nodded. "There's a huge river festival every July, and there's a place farther down where you can rent tubes and float out on the river. It might be getting too cold now, but we could plan on it for next year."

Next year, I thought wishfully, hoping she and Sydney would both still be here in Paris with me.

Back in high school, my girlfriends and I had spent most every summer afternoon along these banks, talking, lazing about, swimming. Summer had been my favorite season, and September had always made me a bit sad. It was a reminder that everything faded. Leaves. Flowers. Even the warmth of the Delaware.

I'd long since stopped noticing the river, much as I hated to admit that to myself. But the unfiltered amazement in Ella's eyes was enough to pull me back, and when I looked across the street for a second time, I tried to see the park and riverbank through her eyes—imagining I were the one seeing this part of town for the first time.

Magic.

This had once been mine.

I spent most of my time in downtown Paris. Which, given that the town was the size of a postage stamp, wasn't what anyone from a real city would call much of a downtown.

There were a handful of antique shops for tourists, one very narrow toy shop housed inside the oldest building in town, a hardware store, several restaurants, two hotels, Mrs. Leroy's bed-and-breakfast, Jessica's café, and Artisan's Alley.

I walked to work every morning. I walked home every night. And on the occasional night when I couldn't sleep, work was only three blocks away.

But now, standing on the edge of town, with the expanse of the Delaware River before me, I remembered how I had once explored every inch of Paris.

I let my mind wander to the possibility of Ella growing up here, just as I had. She'd paddle and swim in the river all summer long. Explore the bike trails in spring and fall. Camp out beneath star-filled skies. Perhaps get a summer job downtown when she was old enough, either with me in the shop or with Jessica in the café.

Life in Paris had been good for me. It would be good for Ella, too. Wouldn't it?

"Looks like we're clear," I said, refocusing on the here and now and Ella's mission. I checked for traffic to our left, to our right, and to our left again.

"Want to see my favorite place?"

She nodded eagerly, so I took her hand and led her down the path, then over to Lookout Rock.

"Whoa," she yelled out as she dropped her pillowcase full of rocks to climb the massive boulder beside the river. She stood at the top, hands fisted on hips like an explorer who'd just discovered the Delaware and planned to claim this territory as her own.

I scrambled up beside her, taking in the view. "This is where I used to do all my thinking when I was your age."

"Your momma let you come here by yourself?" she asked, excitement in her voice.

"She did," I answered simply, leaving out the part about how my mother had been too weak to notice. "Sometimes I came with my dad."

"Lucky," she said, and I kept myself from telling her the truth about what most of my life had been like with her Grandpa Albert.

A moment later I decided we needed less introspection and more action. "Ready to hide some smiles?"

I climbed down, caught Ella when she jumped, then hoisted her pillowcase full of rocks into the air.

She pulled ahead of me once we reached the path, racing toward the water farther up the bank. My heart caught, but as quickly as she'd sprinted away, she returned, her cheeks flushed with color and excitement.

She held out her hand, reaching for the pillowcase. "I can carry them."

"OK."

And she was gone again, moving from tree to tree, garden to garden. She hadn't yet reached for a single rock, but seemed to be taking in every inch of the park, studying the spaces, reveling in the solitude. I sank to my knees and then sat cross-legged in the damp grass, tipping my chin to the sky and shutting my eyes. Just listening. Stopping.

For a moment I could almost pretend my life hadn't shifted in ways I could have never imagined.

I could pretend Albert Jones was still a Broadway fixture, that he'd never come home.

I could pretend Sydney and Ella didn't exist, or that they did exist somewhere out in Akron, Ohio, and I lived my life without ever knowing them.

"Auntie D," Ella's voice called out from a distance, and my thoughts scattered.

I didn't want to pretend any of those things. The surety of that realization spread through me, enveloping me even as I pushed to my feet and jogged to where Ella stood, frantically waving her arms over her head.

My anger toward my father had loosened its grip, and Sydney and Ella had filled a part of my life that had long been empty.

"Are you all right?" I asked.

She nodded, eyes bright. "What do you think?"

She'd picked a group of three trees planted together near the riverbank. The garden club hadn't added any mums or daisies or impatiens, yet the barren ground and exposed roots had been transformed by Ella's rocks. Smiles and hearts and whimsical faces peered up from the ground, flashes of vivid color woven between dirt and root and grass.

I laughed, emotion welling up inside me, pure joy.

"See?" Ella asked, excitedly pulling at my hand. "It works. Come on. Your turn."

She fished inside the pillowcase and pulled out the rock I'd painted, the saddest attempt at a smiley face I'd ever seen.

"Sweetie, I don't think that's going to make anyone smile," I said. "He looks demented."

Ella rolled her eyes, and I had to wonder who it had been back in our bloodline that first rolled their eyes. She orchestrated the move so perfectly, I had to believe the skill was innate rather than learned.

"He's awesome, Auntie D."

She reached for my hand and placed the rock squarely in my palm, folding my fingers over its edges, as though my pathetic smiley face were precious treasure.

"Go." She nodded excitedly, then burst into giggles. "Pick any spot you like."

So I did.

I headed for the center flower beds, intending to set the rock deep inside the plants, where my less than stellar work of art could hide, but Ella was onto me.

"Not there," she said, just as I reached my arm behind the mums and beneath a bed of daisies.

I grinned. "I thought you said I could pick any spot I liked?"

Another eye roll. "You can't *hide* him."

"I thought that was the point."

She pressed her lips together and shook her head, clearly dismayed she had to explain this to me *again*.

"You hide him in plain sight," she explained.

I wasn't through giving her a hard time. "Did you ever wonder who came up with that saying? Hide in plain sight. I mean, seriously. It makes no sense. Right?"

Ella planted one hand on her hip, still holding the pillowcase in the other. "*Auntie D.*"

Just then laughter sounded from down near the river, where Ella had left her first batch of stones.

Two small children squatted beneath the trees, pointing to each rock, chattering excitedly as their mother looked on, her face lit by her smile.

"See?" Ella said. "Smiles."

"Hidden in plain sight," I added.

I plucked the smiley-face rock from where I'd stashed it and brought it to the front of the garden, leaving it tucked behind the garden edge, yet in an open space between plants.

Ella nodded approvingly.

I looked over to where the two children were still admiring Ella's rocks. "Are you going to tell them you put them there?"

"Not the point." Ella shook her head. "Come on," she said, headed off in the opposite direction. "Let's find places for these."

I studied her as she walked away, humbled by the kid's wisdom.

"What's the hurry?" I asked.

Then she looked back over her shoulder, grinning hard, dimples peeking from both cheeks. Alive. Happy. "I want to get home to paint more rocks." And then she added, "Next time we hide smiles, let's bring Momma and Grandpa Albert."

And I thought, *Let's.*

CHAPTER
TWENTY-FIVE

The next week, Sydney withdrew.

Marguerite and I kept Ella busy every day after school, and Albert put her to work in the garden, but Sydney barely left her room.

I knew the chemotherapy had taken a toll, but my gut told me her grim prognosis had taken much more.

Saturday morning, after Ella had escaped to Marguerite's and the promise of chocolate-chip pancakes, I sat in the sitting room and stared at the framed photo of my mother.

There had been a time in my life when I'd slept with the picture tucked inside my pillowcase. My grandmother had never said a word, pretending she didn't know.

I'd realized she'd found the frame the first time she'd stripped and changed my bed.

Sure, the frame had been tucked neatly inside the pillowcase that night when I'd collapsed onto the pillow, but my fingertips hadn't touched metal when I'd slid my arm inside. And they always touched. Just perfectly.

I hadn't been able to sleep for weeks after Mom died and my father left, not unless my grandmother sat beside me, rubbing my back until I fell asleep.

Then one night, instead of kissing my mother's picture good night and setting it back on the nightstand, I'd tucked it inside my pillow. That had been enough. It had to be.

Now I couldn't remember when I'd moved the picture back downstairs.

Perhaps it had been once I reached middle school and the age of sleepovers, the age when I started having to explain why I found so much comfort in a framed photograph of my dead mother.

My grandmother had died three days after my twentieth birthday. After her death, I'd placed my high school graduation picture beside my mother's photograph. In it, my grandmother's love and pride shone brightly. She'd even smiled, the moment captured for eternity.

I liked that two of the most important women in my life stood together once more, where I could see and remember them every day.

I took a backward step and sighed. What I wouldn't give to talk to them now. To ask them what I should do. To find out all about Sydney and why neither of them had ever told me the truth. To ask them if they believed I had what it took to raise a child.

I felt my father's presence behind me before he spoke.

"That picture was taken four years before you were born," he said.

His words startled me, and I willed my heart rate to steady as I turned to face him, struggling to comprehend his statement. "What did you say?"

He looked around me, past me, to the photographs.

Instead of slowing, my pulse quickened. I saw the words in his eyes before he spoke them.

"The baby in that picture." He shook his head. "She wasn't holding you."

My heart pounded in my ears. Thump. Thump. Thump.

"What the hell are you talking about?" I sounded hysterical, even to myself.

His features fell. "She wanted to hold the baby. Even though she'd made her decision, she wanted to hold her."

Moisture swam in his eyes. "After she died, you found this photograph in our bedroom, and you thought it was you." He shook his head, the skin around his eyes crumpling, as if he felt my pain and wanted to help bear the burden of his words.

All I could wonder was how much of his visible emotion was real, if any.

"Now you know." He shrugged, as if he had done me a favor. "That was my last secret. Now you have your truth. All of it."

I said nothing for several long moments, fighting against my urge to scream at him, to accuse him of lying.

I lifted the framed photo from the end table and stared at the baby, looking for my eyes, my nose, and finding Sydney's. Then I studied my mother's expression—the expression of pure love I'd clung to all my life as being meant for me.

"You son of a bitch." I clutched the frame to my chest and crossed to where he stood. "You cared more when you were up on those stages in front of hundreds of people you never even knew than you've ever cared about me. You stand there and dump this on me like you're doing me a favor?

"Where are your emotions now?" I waved my hand at the carefully positioned set of his features. "What is this? Part of the act you've perfected?"

He kept his expression calm, his jaw stiff, yet in his eyes I saw that I'd hit home with my final words.

The truth was, Albert Jones hadn't forgotten how to act. He'd forgotten how to live.

"What is wrong with you?" I asked.

I pushed the frame into his hands, shoving a bit harder than necessary before I headed for the front door.

I hit the sidewalk in a full sprint, wanting to be as far away as possible before I broke.

I made it as far as Bridge Street before I realized I wasn't the one who should be running. So I gathered myself, focused my anger on thinking through all the things I wanted to say to Albert, and headed back toward the house.

When I stepped through the still-open front door, however, it was Sydney, not Albert, who knelt in the middle of the sitting room.

"Where is he?" I asked, but then I realized she cradled the frame in her lap and sobs racked her shoulders.

"Why?" she said softly. "Why?"

I hesitated, thinking momentarily that I should leave. I should let her have this moment to work through everything she must be feeling.

Of course she'd overheard Albert and me arguing. How could she not? Her bedroom was directly overhead.

But instead of leaving I stepped toward her, gently calling her name, not wanting to startle her any more than she'd already been startled.

"Sydney?"

She dragged a hand across her face quickly, her complexion blotchy and pale.

"I should never have come back here." Her words were awash with loss and shock and grief. "I've stolen this from you."

I moved quickly to her side, sinking to the floor beside her, enveloping her in my embrace.

"No. He stole this from me. He stole this by never telling me the truth."

But Sydney remained staring at the captured image of my mother's face in the moments after her birth.

"Look how much she loved you," I said. "So much." I choked on my words and tears flooded my vision.

"I had a great life," Sydney said softly. "Somehow, seeing this helps as much as it hurts."

"She kept it in her room, tucked in the drawer of her nightstand. That's where I found it after she died. I slept with this inside my pillowcase, thinking I was keeping her near." A path of moisture trailed down one cheek. "Who knew I was keeping you near, too?"

Then Sydney turned to hug me, and we clung to each other for several long moments, both of us at an apparent loss for words.

As betrayed as I felt by my father's latest truth, I kept my thoughts in this moment, with Sydney.

"Would you change things?" I asked her a few minutes later, after we'd dried our tears and set our mother's picture back in its place.

Her answer appeared to come easily. Perhaps she'd given the topic plenty of thought during the weeks since she'd arrived in Paris.

She shook her head. "I loved my parents."

"Is that why you waited until you were sick to look for us?"

Her gaze went dark, sad. "I'm not going to beat this."

"And you wanted a family for Ella?"

She took my hands and held on tight. "That, and I didn't want to die without knowing you."

Jessica called me not long after Sydney went upstairs to rest to tell me Albert had been sitting at the counter, drinking coffee, and talking to other customers.

"You might want to get down here," she said. "Otherwise I don't think he's ever going to leave."

"Keep him," I said. Then I filled her in on the picture and our argument.

"I'm so sorry. Wow."

"Yeah, wow."

The reality of the photograph had started to sink in, and I'd begun to realize what I thought had been a treasured moment was simply a moment lost.

My mother had kept the photo, hidden the photo, undoubtedly cherished the photo. A piece of her life I'd known nothing about. Her life with Albert. Before me.

Marguerite's words ran through my mind. *Your mother had dreams, and heartaches, and mistakes, and decisions bigger than any young girl should have to make.*

The truth was that once upon a time, she and my father had loved me more than any little girl could ever hope to be loved. The fact they'd lived before me and kept Sydney's picture hidden in the nightstand did nothing to lessen what the three of us had shared as a family.

"Well." Jessica's tone lifted sharply. "That explains this, then."

"Explains what?" My all-too-familiar internal alarm bells began clanging. "What has he done?"

Jessica laughed. "I can't complain, but he's buying coffee and a doughnut for anyone who'll sit down and tell him one thing about you."

I said nothing for a moment, letting her words sink in. While I wanted to be amused or touched or feel some sense of forgiveness toward my father, I couldn't quite trust that his intentions were pure.

I could only think he was doing this for show.

"Maybe you should come talk to him," Jessica said. "Second chances, remember?"

I pushed through the door of Jessica's café less than fifteen minutes later.

I spotted my father immediately, cozied up to the counter sharing coffee with Millie Carmichael. Her eyes widened as I approached.

"Destiny," she called out. "I was just telling your father what a genius you are when it comes to carpentry."

"Thank you, Millie. You're too kind."

I glared at my father, and Millie took note, gathering up her purse and plopping the last piece of her doughnut into her mouth. "Lovely to chat with you, Albert. See you soon, Destiny."

Then she was gone, leaving me alone with my father.

"What are you doing?" I asked. "Haven't you wreaked enough havoc in my life for one day?"

But my father, instead of becoming defensive or argumentative, simply signaled to Jessica, who poured a fresh cup of coffee and placed it in front of me.

"Your turn," he said. "Tell me one thing about you I should know."

One thing? Disbelief welled up inside me.

How about twenty years' worth of things?

How about that no matter how much I tried to let him back into my heart, he kept giving me reason to slam the door shut?

I shook my head. "No. *You* tell *me* one thing. Explain today. Explain why you never came clean about that picture."

"I never told you because I didn't want to break your heart."

"And breaking my heart was acceptable today?"

He waved a finger at me. "Risking this was acceptable today. Your anger. I wanted there to be no more secrets between us."

I started to push away from the counter, not interested in another excuse, but my father reached for my arm to hold me back.

He lowered his voice, and that was when I realized none of this was for show.

"Yes, I came back here because I knew Sydney was sick, and I knew she needed a place to go, a place for Ella, but I want to stay here because I realize how much I screwed up my relationship with you."

He leaned close, pulling me in. "The thought of raising you alone terrified me, and I took the coward's way out. But if you'd let me, I'd like to be part of your life now. A permanent part. I can help you raise Ella when the time comes."

I couldn't do it. I couldn't stand there and listen to him make empty promises about staying, about raising Ella. I couldn't stand there and picture the future, a future without Sydney.

"Are you done?"

He nodded, easing his grip on my arm enough that I could slip free. I leaned close enough to speak directly into his ear.

"You may want to think that your being absent from my life damaged me somehow, but I did just fine without you. As a matter of fact, I thrived without you. I had Grandmother and Marguerite. I had this town. Turns out, I didn't need you.

"So thanks, but no thanks, on your offer to stay. I got over waiting for that a long time ago."

He called out to me as I headed for the exit. I became aware that all conversation inside the café had stopped, but I didn't care.

As lovely as his words might have sounded, the sting of the photo was too fresh, too sharp for me to listen to anything else he had to say.

CHAPTER
TWENTY-SIX

I found Marguerite and Ella huddled on the patio, painting a second supply of rocks.

Sydney had joined them and sat wrapped in an afghan.

"Couldn't sleep," she said as I pulled up the chair beside her. She gestured to the table full of painted rocks. "I found this. Aren't they beautiful?"

Beside Marguerite sat a collection of rocks painted with intricate circles of dots. Concentric circles spiraled out from the center in alternating colors. A white center dot sat surrounded by dots of red, then orange, then yellow. The circles grew larger as they stretched for the rock's edge. Lime green, bright green, ivy green, turquoise, cobalt blue, royal blue, then gray and white.

The stones were amazing, and I found myself dumbfounded that such beauty could be created using a rock and simple, painted shapes.

Ella had graduated from hearts and rainbows to people, characters in all shapes and sizes, smiling, frowning, laughing. Each one different. Each one emotive. All spectacular.

"You two should join us," Marguerite said.

And so we did.

I worked to set aside my tangled thoughts regarding Albert, doing my best to savor every second of this moment, painting smiles.

Inspired by Ella's changing style, I tried my hand at painting fish. Sydney studied me after I painted my third stone, this one embellished with a bright red fish, complete with metallic stripes and one navy-blue eye.

"I think Ella's right," she said, amusement dancing in her tone. "You do have fish issues."

I studied my row of completed fish—red, yellow, and purple—and grinned. "Either that or I'm just excited to find something I can paint."

Sydney, on the other hand, added careful brushstrokes to an intricate ladybug. She'd made her first by painting a large rock red, then adding the head, antennae, spots, and black base. She was now working on her second. This one teal.

Where my fish were painted quickly—simple shapes with basic lines—Sydney's ladybugs were works of art, intricate in their designs, their details sharp and proportioned.

"Why ladybugs?" I asked.

"Hope," she answered.

She went back to work, the tip of her paintbrush expertly shaping the ladybug's body.

Hope.

I let her word settle over me as I shifted my gaze from her teal rock to the teal scarf she'd wrapped around her neck.

I couldn't help but notice that her eyes had dimmed, much as my mother's eyes had years earlier. While I didn't remember all the details of my mother's illness and death, I remembered the fading. I remembered how much it hurt, how much it had frightened me.

I glanced back to Ella, who sat, head down, tongue sticking out between her lips, lost in concentration as she perfected another figure, this one a young girl with dark wavy hair and glasses.

Sydney's hair had gone even thinner, and yet she hadn't worn her wig today. Instead she'd embraced what short, wavy strands she had left.

I glanced again at her scarf and wondered if she tired of wearing teal. I'd thought about asking her on several occasions but had always kept my mouth shut, just like I was doing now.

I cleaned off my brush and reached for another rock, this one larger, its surface smooth and round. I tapped the plate on which she'd squeezed out a generous dollop of teal paint.

"Mind if I share?"

She smiled, the move restoring a measure of light to her eyes.

Yet her smile faded as she refocused on her work, and the recent, seemingly permanent touch of sadness returned to her face.

I wondered if she was thinking about the photograph of my mother, or perhaps about Ella and their future.

I watched her for several moments, wishing with every fiber of my being that teal was simply a color she loved instead of a representation of the beast she fought, even now, as she sat beside us painting rocks.

A few hours later we set out on a family excursion to place Ella's second batch of rocks—Ella, Sydney, Albert, and I.

Ella had insisted that Grandpa Albert join us, and he'd agreed. I'd kept my mouth shut, not about to quiet Ella's excitement simply because I'd been hurt earlier.

We walked first toward town square; then we headed for the river and the wide expanse of green lawn. The foliage had turned, and the skyline was rimmed in golds and ambers, oranges and vibrant reds.

Albert carried the pillowcase full of smiles, his steps sure, his mood upbeat. Our conversation from the café looped through my mind.

Had I been unfair? Perhaps he'd been sincere about staying, sincere about becoming a permanent part of my life.

He slowed as we neared the path toward Lookout Rock, setting down the pillowcase and reaching for Ella's hand. They veered off on their mini-adventure, and Sydney and I continued several yards until we reached the next bench.

Her steps faltered a time or two, but I pretended not to notice, even though worry wound its way through my brain.

Was she more off-balance than she'd been the day before? Had we made a mistake in walking so far?

We sat in silence, hands clasped, as Albert hoisted Ella up onto Lookout Rock, then sat beside her. The autumn days were growing shorter and the afternoon sun had begun to drop, silhouetting their figures where they perched along the river.

In their images I saw the past I'd so fervently missed and the future stretching out before me, whether I believed myself ready or not.

Theirs was the shadow of what I'd lost and what I'd wanted, my family intact, my father's great love. While I'd never have that family again, I could have this one, if I let myself believe in the possibility.

As I watched them I felt a shift inside me, and the wall I'd so carefully guarded cracked.

I remained by Sydney's side while my father and Ella hid smiles. They raced each other, chased each other, scrutinized locations, and worked until the pillowcase hung limp, empty.

They waved to us, gesturing for us to join them at the base of the hill, on the flat expanse of lawn that ran the length of the park.

My father and I stood watching as Sydney took both of Ella's hands in hers. They spun together in a tight, slow circle, lost in the moment.

My heart caught, and for a split second, I saw my own mother, and me, and Albert, spinning. Always spinning.

I could hear my father's laugh, smell my mother's perfume.

And then I realized . . . I owed this to Albert. Sydney's presence. Her friendship. My growing love for Ella. Without him, none of this might have happened.

Watching Sydney and Ella together was like capturing a memory. They spun with abandon, their laughter rising on the crisp autumn air. Ella smiled, a grin so wide I couldn't help but smile myself. I couldn't help but laugh.

They spun and spun, Sydney not caring about her new bald patches—side effects of her latest chemotherapy infusions—or her occasional misstep.

They looked for all the world like a mother and daughter full of life, untouched by illness.

Then they slowed long enough to break their circle and reach for me and Albert, their hands outstretched.

"Auntie D, Grandpa Albert," Ella yelled. "Dance with us."

I studied the distant look on his face and wondered if he'd been thinking the same thoughts, remembering the same joyful moments.

Sydney and Ella continued to move, circling, hands outstretched, faces hopeful.

"Destiny?" My father reached for my hand, offering me an olive branch I desperately wanted to grab.

I thought about turning away and retreating, afraid of the heartbreak that waited months or years down the road.

But instead I stepped forward, reaching for his hand. And then we ran, awkwardly, toward Sydney and Ella, and the four of us spun together, hands clasped, laughing, in a sloppy, lopsided circle.

We danced beneath the perfect September sky as I let old memories slide aside to make room for the new.

CHAPTER
TWENTY-SEVEN

As wonderful as our weekend had been, Ella came home from school on Monday in a mood that suggested either her hormones had gone wild or she'd had a really bad day. Based on what little I knew about nine-year-olds, I went with the latter.

Sydney had spent much of the day in bed, after a long night battling nausea. She slept now, and I did my best to keep Ella and her mood contained to the sitting room.

"I wish we never came here," she said, keeping her voice low, but angry, in a manner that suggested she'd had plenty of practice not waking up her mother. "She was fine before we came here. Fine."

Tears streamed down her face, her cheeks flushed a deep red. "Now she's tired all the time, and her hair's falling out again." She pointed her finger at me. "It's your fault. You didn't even want us here, and now she's sick."

Ella's every word hit me like a slap, spot-on in her accusations.

Her mother was sick. Just like my mother had been.

She was tired all the time. Just like mine had been.

I understood the anger and remembered the heartbreak, but instead of trying to soothe Ella, I unleashed the hurt and the sorrow and the disbelief I'd buried for most of my life.

"You'd better stop and think about who you're talking to. I opened my home to you, Ella. I can't control your mother's illness any more than I could control my mom's. Do you honestly think I want to go through this again? Do you?"

Guilt slammed me as soon as I spoke the words, but they were true. I didn't want to go through this again—the hell of watching someone I loved dying.

She narrowed her eyes on me, hitting me with a glare that chilled me to the core. "You probably wish she was dead already so you could send me away."

"No," I said, suddenly realizing how I'd sounded. "Don't ever say that again."

"Why?" Her eyes blazed. "Because it's true? You don't care about us. You invited us here because you felt sorry for us, and now you're probably just waiting to get back to your opera house work, right?"

Yes! I screamed internally. *Yes, I did invite you here because I felt sorry for you, and yes, I'd love to run to the opera house or my shop and simply hide.*

Instead I said, "Stop it. Stop it right now."

But was she right? Was I as bad as my father had been, back when he'd disappear to New York or to a regional dinner-theater performance as my mother lay fighting for her life?

His job had come first.

His wife had been dying, and his job had come first.

No, I assured myself. I had to work, and I thought I'd done a pretty decent job of keeping all my balls in the air.

"You're not being fair," I said, thinking I could reason with an angry, emotional child.

Ella picked up a pillow and hurled it at me. When I ducked, the pillow missed its mark, sending the photos of my mother and grandmother crashing to the floor. Glass shattered, shards flying in every direction. Slivers glistened in the carpet, beneath the end table, in the far corners of the room.

Ella ran, racing away from me and the echoes of our argument.

"Get back here right now and clean this up," I shouted. But she'd gone, vanishing up the stairs.

Her bedroom door slammed, and I wrapped my arms around my waist, hot tears stinging at the back of my eyes.

You don't love us at all.

Her words screamed through my mind.

I did love them, even though I'd once vowed to never love anyone again.

I'd let Sydney and Ella into my heart. They were part of me now.

My family.

That realization slammed me to my knees.

I could hear her in the distance, sobbing, the sound a knife to my heart.

What the hell was wrong with me? How had I come to this place of anger? Even worse, how had I let myself direct that anger at Ella, a frightened nine-year-old carbon copy of the kid I'd once been?

Was I so damaged that I was incapable of showing her kindness? Or listening to her fears? If so, how could I possibly help her survive the seemingly unsurvivable?

I'd failed to separate my pain from her pain, and I'd let my broken spirit rain all over hers. How dare I?

I'd lived through my nightmare, and I'd made it to the other side. Now it was my turn to protect Ella as she lived through her nightmare. Only, the difference was, if Sydney died . . . when Sydney died . . . Ella needed to know I'd never desert her.

"Destiny." My father's voice interrupted my thoughts as he placed a hand on my shoulder.

I broke emotionally, dropping my head, letting the sadness and the anger and the frustration win.

"How do I do this?" I asked, and then I thought of Jessica's words when I'd asked her how she managed work and motherhood.

I just do.

Then I saw it in his eyes. He didn't know. My father had no answer for me.

He gave my shoulder a squeeze. "I'll check on Sydney; then I'll help clean this up." He nodded toward the shards of glass strewn across the floor.

I followed the sound of Ella's sobbing, making my way up the steps to the landing, then to her closed bedroom door.

I knocked, and her sobs grew quiet, but she said nothing.

"I'm coming in," I said as I turned the knob, grateful to find it unlocked.

Inside the bedroom she was nowhere to be found, but her closet was closed.

I tapped lightly against the paneled door. "Ella?"

Silence.

"I'm opening the door, honey. I had no right to yell at you. None. I'm coming in. Ready?"

She shrank back into one dark corner as I peered inside.

"I'm so sorry, Auntie D," she sobbed. "I didn't mean to break it. Please don't be mad at me."

I saw her then, the little girl terrified of losing her mother, terrified of disappointing me, terrified of being left alone.

Twenty years of grief and betrayal and loneliness welled up inside me, threatening to pull me under, but I steadied myself and focused on Ella. Just Ella.

I hesitated before I answered, working to keep my voice calm, steady. "Oh, honey, I'm the one who should be apologizing to you. I'm sorry I yelled. I never meant to frighten you."

"But I broke your picture."

The fear in her voice hurt my heart, the thought that I'd value a picture over her feelings. "You're more important than a picture." I pulled the door open wide. "Let's be honest, it was the pillow's fault."

Her sweet, scared face looked up at me, and I pointed to the empty floor beside her in the closet. "May I?"

She nodded, pulling her knees to her chest and making herself appear even smaller than she had seemed a moment before. I crawled beside her, careful to give her plenty of space.

"I think sometimes we get so angry we don't know what to do, so we act out." I stole a glance and spotted the drop of her chin.

"You're angry at me," she said.

"Never. I'm not angry at you."

"Not even for the picture?"

"Especially not for the picture."

"At Momma?"

I shook my head. "No way."

She frowned.

"I'm angry at the cancer. I'm guessing that's what you're angry at, too."

She nodded.

"You know, when my mom had cancer, I once tried to punch my fist through a wall."

"You did?" Her voice climbed three octaves, curiosity pulling her ever so slowly out of her shell.

"I did." I rotated my right hand until I found the spot where the silvery scar still showed. "Three stitches."

She winced.

"You'd think that would have taught me to cool it, but sometimes I'd do things before I even realized I was doing them."

"Like what?"

"Like one time I threw a baseball through Marguerite's window."

"Was she mad at you?"

I nodded. "For about a minute, and then she handed me a bucket of broken crayons."

That got a smile.

"Because she loved me," I said. "She still loves me. Just like I love you."

I loved her—this wonderful little kid with the clunky glasses and the huge heart. The realization bolstered my resolve to get through to her, to make her hear what I was saying.

"And," I continued, "she had room in her heart to be sad about my mom—who was her best friend—and still have patience with me."

Ella's focus dropped to her lap, where she worried the edge of her shirt between her fingers. "How old were you when your mom died?"

"Ten."

Silence beat between us.

"And it sucked," I added.

She snapped her attention to me, eyes wide.

"Worst thing that ever happened to me," I said. "I'm not going to lie to you. But I survived."

She swallowed visibly, then opened her mouth as if she had another question, but she remained silent.

I'd been in her place, though. I'd lived her fears.

"No matter what happens, you'll survive, too," I said.

"Sometimes I just get angry," she said, her voice barely more than a whisper.

"Honey, if you weren't angry, you wouldn't be human. Maybe the trick is to find words to use instead of actions."

"Sorry," she said again, sniffling.

I anchored my arm around her shoulder and pulled her close. "No more apologizing. Let's figure out how to get through this together. Want to?"

Ella nodded.

"Any ideas?" I asked.

"Stop throwing pillows?" she answered.

I gave her shoulders a squeeze. "Good one." Then I added, "How about we both stop yelling?"

She patted my knee. "Another good one."

I pulled her up onto my lap and to my surprise she curled into me, tucking her head beneath my chin. I breathed in the citrus scent of her shampoo, suddenly filled with the urge to hide with her there forever, in her closet, where the real world couldn't touch either one of us.

"So what else can we do?" I asked, having trouble forcing my words through the knot in my throat, the knot of fear and grief that didn't want Sydney to die, didn't want Ella to grow up without her mother.

"We could get a password," Ella said.

"Password?"

I felt her nod beneath my chin. "Momma and I have a password for when I'm scared."

"Want to tell me?"

Another nod. "Rainbows."

"Rainbows?" I screwed up my features, but she couldn't see me. "Doesn't exactly sound scared."

"That's the whole point," Ella explained. "Momma says it's to make us stop and talk about whatever the bad thing is. It makes us remember the good stuff."

I hugged her tight, love welling up inside me for this child I hadn't even known a few months earlier. "Your momma's pretty smart."

"The smartest."

She was correct, of course. Wasn't every little girl's momma the smartest? Mine had been.

"Any ideas for an angry word?" I asked.

Ella sat quietly, but offered no suggestions.

"Can we stay with rainbows?" she asked finally.

I shifted from one butt cheek to the other, wishing Ella's closet had a padded floor. "I don't see why not. Think your momma would mind?"

Ella shook her head.

"We should ask her anyway."

"OK."

"So whenever one of us feels angry—"

"Or scared," she added.

"Or scared," I corrected myself, "we say rainbows."

"And then we talk it out," Ella said.

"Want to tell me what happened today to make you so angry?"

She hesitated momentarily, then spoke slowly. "A girl at school said you'll probably send me away after Momma dies because I'm not your kid."

I flinched, wondering how another kid could be so cruel. But she was right—Ella wasn't my kid.

Could I do this? Parent her? Day in and day out?

For the briefest moment, I understood why my father had run. But I wasn't my father.

"That kid's a jerk," I said. Then I waved my hand in the air. "Rainbows. That wasn't cool. I should have said, you tell that kid that you're my niece, and you're not going anywhere. Not now. Not in the future. Not ever."

I wondered then if Sydney had shared her decision with Ella. Had she told her what we'd discussed?

"Has your momma told you what she and I talked about? That if someday she can't take care of you, you're going to stay with me?"

She nodded.

"What do you think about that?" Nerves built inside me, and I realized I was worried about what Ella would say.

"I think I'd like that."

With those five words, Ella released a flood of relief inside me, feelings so intense I realized I'd kidded myself about how anxious I'd been.

I took a moment to settle on what I could do to show her how I felt in addition to telling her.

"Listen," I said. "I know it may seem like I spend a lot of time on the opera house project. Want to come with me sometime? When you're not in school."

"To your shop?"

I nodded. "Maybe I could teach you how to sand the cut lengths of wood, apply finish, maybe even hit some nails."

Beside me, Ella straightened. "And I can stop worrying about what that girl at school thinks."

I kissed the top of her head. "Know something?"

She shook her head.

"I think you just might be even smarter than your momma."

"No way." She laughed, pushed free of my embrace, then stood up inside the closet.

A sudden idea hit me, the image appearing fully formed in my mind's eye.

She fit this space. Her safe space. Here, inside the closet.

Padding for the floor. A built-in seat. Throw pillows. Shelves. Books. Art supplies.

Escape.

"Ella?"

She stopped, one foot outside of the closet, one foot still inside.

"I think I have an amazing idea."

My father and I spent each evening that week fabricating the pieces we'd need to build a reading nook inside Ella's closet.

I removed the door during my initial measurements, but Ella asked to keep it, loving the silence she found when she was closed inside.

Who was I to argue? I understood the love of silence, even if the only solitude I found these days was during the hours I worked alone at my shop.

Truth was, even though I missed the quiet, I'd grown fond of the sounds of life inside my once silent home.

Although Sydney had wanted to come to the shop to help with Ella's project, she'd struggled with nausea and fatigue since her two days of respite over the weekend.

So I'd asked my father to help, taking my turn to extend an olive branch.

I worked feverishly all day on building the trim pieces for the opera house stage, and at night Albert and I sanded, finished, and painted pieces for Ella's nook.

Some nights, we worked in silence. Other nights, we reminisced about the past, about how we'd once explored every inch of Paris, even though the memories we treasured the most were the ones we'd made on Third Street, in our own backyard.

Although I still hadn't been able to forget the fact he'd known about the photo all my life, I began to forgive him, understanding his not wanting to shatter a little girl's heart.

By the end of the week, we were ready to transform Ella's closet. Not only were the component pieces cut, painted, and labeled for assembly, but the residents of Paris had been dropping off books at Jessica's café with an overabundance of generosity.

Such was life in Paris. Word spread. Sometimes that was an annoying thing. On most occasions, like this one, it was a wonderful thing.

My father and I drove to the shop after dinner to transport the shelving pieces back home, and at one point, as we joked over how long it took us to load my car, he laughed, pure joy dancing in his eyes.

In that moment I saw the man he'd been, the father I'd loved so deeply, and I realized that somewhere along the way I'd started believing we'd find our way out of our damaged past and into our new future.

Soon we were sitting elbow to elbow inside Ella's room, fitting pieces, securing mitered edges, and sinking nails.

Sydney sat back and watched as Ella excitedly read title after title from the boxes of books she'd gathered.

Marguerite had headed downstairs to retrieve the set of four padded floor cushions she'd sewn when the doorbell rang.

"Jackson," I heard her say.

My heart flipped inexplicably, and I kept my focus down, afraid my father or Sydney would spot my reaction.

"What a lovely surprise," Marguerite's voice continued. "Everyone's upstairs in Ella's room."

The stairs squeaked, and Ella sprang to her feet and ran to the landing.

"Mr. Jackson," she called out. "What are you doing here?"

"The last time we spoke on the phone, your Grandpa Albert told me you were building a reading nook." His deep voice reverberated in the hallway. "So I brought you some books."

Ella squealed. "*Percy Jackson*. Is he your cousin?"

"No." Jackson laughed, obviously amused. "But they're autographed."

"Thank you so much," Ella exclaimed as she burst through the door. "Look what Mr. Jackson brought me." She foisted the hard-backs onto Sydney's lap. "They're *autographed*." She enunciated each syllable deliberately and carefully, as though she'd been handed priceless treasure.

"Lovely," Sydney said, just as Jackson appeared in the doorway.

"I heard this was where the volunteers report to build the reading nook?" His voice boomed into the small space.

My father crossed to greet him, and the two men embraced warmly, patting each other's backs.

"So glad you could stop by," Albert said, and I found myself wondering when the two had spoken—and why.

Jackson's hair had grown a little longer, the look softening his previous intensity. He wore blue jeans and a long-sleeved gray Henley, the sleeves pushed up casually.

His gaze found mine and held for a fraction of a second.

"That depends on how handy you are with a fistful of nails and a hammer," Sydney replied, extending her hand. But instead of shaking it, Jackson bent to wrap her in a gentle hug.

His show of affection left my sister visibly affected, and something deep inside my heart softened.

Then he crossed to where I stood and shook my hand. And although we'd never done more than that, part of me had hoped he would surprise me with a hug also.

"I was passing through," he said with a grin. "Thought maybe you could use some help. That, and I promised to check on Scarlet."

Scarlet, I thought. Thank goodness for Scarlet.

For the next hour he worked beside Albert and me, fastening pieces, fitting sections into the spacious closet, and anchoring each unit into the interior walls.

Occasionally Jackson's hand would brush against mine, our eyes would meet, and we'd smile.

I knew that in the midst of everything else I had going on in my life, an attraction to the man was ridiculous, but for that shared time in that small space, I let myself simply enjoy the possibility that he might feel the same.

Later, after the shelving was in place and Marguerite and Albert had fit the padded cushions into the floor space, Jackson worked beside Ella to build her library.

He hung on her every word and direction as if there were nowhere on earth he'd rather be, helping her shelve titles from Dahl, Bloom, Rowling, and Gutman. The kid had received enough books to fill her nook with hours of adventure, fantasy, and escape, thanks to the kindness of Paris.

I'd spent my whole life in the small town, and I'd taken part in numerous acts of kindness, and now the friends and neighbors I loved had welcomed my new family as warmly as they'd always embraced me.

I might be nervous about the idea of raising a child alone, but the truth was I'd never actually be alone. Not here. Not in Paris.

CHAPTER
TWENTY-EIGHT

Sydney's energy returned the next week, and she helped me in the shop for a few hours each morning before she headed home to rest in the afternoons.

Albert drove Sydney to the shop each morning, and together they worked beside me to assemble the façade pieces for the stage.

Sydney had become an expert at gluing and pinning the ornate façade woodwork, and I loved the way she beamed with confidence each time she helped me finish a new section.

My father had mastered the hard work of making sure the pieces would fit, fixing the scrolls and ornate cuts to each section before I readied them for transport to the opera house.

My subcontractors were scheduled to help with the actual installation during the coming weeks, but here, in my shop, the tradeoff of silence for family was one I was growing to count on.

Sydney returned to New York at the end of the week for one more MRI, this one to determine whether she'd continue chemo.

I picked up Ella after school, and she worked beside me in the shop, staining trim while we waited. My father had promised to drop off Sydney as soon as they returned from the city.

The late-September sun had partially set, casting long rays of violet and melon through the windows by the time Sydney walked through the door. She wore a careful smile as she hugged Ella, yet her eyes told me everything I needed to know.

A deep ache grew inside me as I watched them, mother and daughter, denial pushing at the tiny voice at the back of my brain telling me we were running out of time.

"How was your day, Momma?" Ella asked, her voice light with hope and innocence.

"OK," Sydney said. "Hey"—she shifted Ella's attention by pointing to a half-stained section of paneling—"is that your work?"

Ella nodded proudly. "Auntie D taught me how to stain."

"She's a natural," I said, ruffling Ella's hair. "What do you say we head over to Jessica's for dinner? You've got to be starving."

Dread slid through me, and I wished for a moment that we were alone, just the two of us, so that Sydney could let her hopes and fears and news pour forth.

"I'm actually not that hungry," she said. "But I'd love to go along."

Ella growled like a lion. "I could eat a horse."

"Let's go." I sealed the stain, dropped our brushes in the work sink to soak, and reached for the keys. "I think I have the best crew in town, don't you?"

I took Sydney's hand to steady her as we headed down the steps. She squeezed my fingers, letting loose a shaky sigh. "Maybe a cup of tea," I said.

"Maybe."

We headed up Artisan's Alley to Bridge Street. Pumpkins and scarecrows had begun appearing in shop windows and doorways, and Ella stopped to ooh and aah at the window of the gift shop, which overflowed with skulls and bats and broomsticks.

When Ella skipped ahead, Sydney and I took our time. I matched my steps to hers, never letting go of her hand, sadness building inside me as I wondered how much longer she'd be able to walk without some sort of assistance.

"I can't thank you enough for the time you're spending with Ella." Moisture welled in her eyes. "She's blossoming right in front of us."

"She's had a great role model."

She hesitated a few moments before she said, "When you're diagnosed with cancer, your world shrinks. For a while everyone rallies around you. They bring you meals. They take your kid on playdates. They offer to bring you groceries. They bring you coffee, and they sit and chat. But as the weeks and months stretch on, they get tired. Tired of the bake and take. They fade away. I get that. I don't blame them.

"After my parents died and the cancer came back," Sydney continued, "most people stopped meeting my gaze in the grocery store and at church, and I needed to go somewhere where I wasn't defined by my disease."

I grabbed her arm, pulling her around to face me. "I can't believe you were ever defined by your disease."

Moisture shimmered along her lower lashes. "That's because you're my sister. You have to say that."

"I think you know me better than that."

But I understood what she meant. I remembered the sad looks, the pitying stares. I hated being the girl whose mother had died.

Sydney's lips trembled and her voice broke. "How will I ever tell her nothing's working?"

A wall of grief built inside me, waiting to fall.

"The inflamed area's gotten larger."

"I . . ." I fell silent, unable to push a single word past the anger that flooded every inch of my body. Sydney didn't deserve this. Ella didn't deserve this. None of this. "I'm sorry," I said finally, my voice barely audible.

"Hurry up," Ella called out from up ahead, where she'd dutifully stopped at the curb to wait for us. "I'm starving." She grabbed her stomach dramatically and rocked back and forth, her smile huge, her eyes bright.

Beside me, Sydney cleared her throat. "Smile," she said. "She's watching."

But even as I plastered on the best smile I could muster, a little piece inside of me fractured, and I held tightly to Sydney's arm, wanting to never, ever let go.

CHAPTER
TWENTY-NINE

A few days later I sat at the counter inside the Paris River Café and watched Jessica work her magic. Customers chatted, sipped her fabulous coffee, and dined on their made-to-order breakfasts.

I played with the pieces I'd broken off my chocolate-glazed doughnut without ever taking a bite. My coffee sat untouched, and my mind raced with the various scenarios the future might hold.

I remembered my mother's last weeks and how I'd vacillated between wanting to hide and wanting to be by her side. My father had kept me away at the very end, in her final hours, and I'd never quite gotten over the guilt of not being there as she took her final breath.

I didn't want the same guilt for Ella. Not if she and Sydney were OK with her being there.

I wanted to do whatever it took to make sure Ella would have no regrets looking back.

"Hey." Jessica tapped the counter beside the plate with my mangled doughnut. "You're still going to have to pay for that, you know."

Even though I knew she'd intended to make me smile, I felt myself sag, the effort to eat simply more than I had in me.

"I should just go," I said. "Maybe I'll feel better if I get to work. Stay busy. You know?"

"Or maybe you should try to eat something more than a doughnut and coffee," she said. "You can't afford to get sick. You've got a lot of people depending on you."

Her words landed with a heavy dose of reality.

My days of skimming through life as one were over.

Jessica tapped the table again, like she'd had a brainstorm. "I'll grab you some fruit and a large orange juice."

I groaned. "Please. Just let me mangle my doughnut, and I promise I'll drink my coffee at work."

She studied me, sighing deeply. "I'm worried about you."

"Don't be."

"How can I not be? You're my friend, and I love you." She dropped her voice before her next question. "How is she?"

"Fading, I'm afraid."

Fading. There was a word that should only apply to paint or curtains or a crayon picture taped to a wall. It shouldn't apply to people, especially people you loved.

People shouldn't fade, and yet they did.

"Anything I can do?"

I started to say no, but then realized there was something Jessica could do.

"Would you bring the kids over sometime? Ella could use some kid time."

"Of course. They'd love to see Ella."

"Maybe after work one night soon?"

She gave my hand a quick squeeze. "You bet."

Another customer called to her from the end of the counter, but she held up a finger, then leaned quite close. "Hospice?"

"Not yet."

Jessica's features tensed, and I knew she wanted to ask me something, something she wasn't comfortable with.

"What?" I asked.

"Am I that obvious?"

I nodded. "For as long as I can remember."

She drew in a slow breath, then exhaled before she spoke. "I know you weren't there when your mom died, but I can't imagine you want Ella seeing her mother die, either. Right?"

Some of the warmth I'd felt a moment earlier cooled.

I'd spent the last two nights before my mother's death sleeping at Marguerite's, sort of a phony slumber party while my life crumbled in the house next door.

"You're not going to let Ella stay there, are you?" she asked.

I shot her a warning glare. "What if I am? More important, what if Sydney is? It's her choice."

Color flared in Jessica's cheeks. "What if she reaches a point where she's not able to make that choice? Will you step in and protect Ella?"

"From what? Her mother's going to die. Don't you think that's about as bad as things get for a nine-year-old girl?"

Jessica's customer called out again, and she excused herself, attending to his bill and returning quickly.

"Look," she said, "I'm not trying to second-guess you, or tell you what to do, but I don't want you to do something that might scar Ella just to ease the guilt you feel over not being there with your mom at the end."

Her words pushed every button I'd tried to bury for twenty years. I hadn't been there when Mom died, and I'd wanted to be. In the eyes of a child, I'd failed her, and I had no plans to let Ella carry similar regrets into the rest of her life.

"I know you mean well, Jessica, but how Sydney dies and whether or not her daughter is by her side during that entire process is up to Sydney."

I pulled out my wallet, but Jessica pressed her hand across my arm. "This one's on me. After all, you're walking out of here with the same empty stomach you walked in with."

"Thanks."

I moved to stand, but Jessica tightened her grip on my arm.

"I'm just trying to help," she said.

"I know," I said. Then I turned and headed out the door, leaving my battered doughnut and untouched coffee behind.

That day I worked alone, my hands going through the motions of my job while my head and heart weighed Jessica's concerns.

Sydney wasn't ready to die, but she was growing quite weak. I knew Jessica had stated her concern out of love and friendship, and I understood. I also understood that the question of whether Ella stayed with her mother in her final hours was a personal one.

Even that day, Ella had chosen being with Sydney over coming to my shop after school. My dad had agreed to meet her after school to walk her home.

While he still spent an hour or two with me in the shop each morning while Marguerite visited with Sydney, his attention had shifted to home, to staying as close to Sydney as possible.

I couldn't help but contrast the way he'd dug in to help now with the way he'd vanished to do a show or make an audition when the going had gotten tough decades earlier.

So when I found him late that afternoon sitting beside the garden, his hands in the dirt, surprise flickered through me.

"Hey," I called out. "What are you doing out here?"

"Marguerite and Ella are painting her nails," he answered.

I sat down on the grass beside him, not quite ready to go inside, suddenly craving a moment alone with him, just us two, as I'd once imagined our life would have been.

"Not in the mood for a manicure?"

"No." He shook his head and smiled, even though his momentary amusement couldn't quite edge out the worry that bracketed his eyes.

"How's Sydney?" I asked.

"She slept a lot today."

He pulled the remains of a stubborn vine from between the branches of my mother's azalea as he spoke. I studied the way he worked gently, tenderly, careful to extract every rogue tendril and root. I thought of how he'd sacrificed his time here, in the garden he loved, to help me in the shop, and I pushed up the sleeves of the heavy sweatshirt I'd worn for my walk home.

"Can I help you?"

His hands stilled, and his gaze met mine, surprise flashing in the depths of his pale eyes.

I shrugged. "Can't a girl help her dad?"

A small laugh slipped between his lips. "Of course. Yes. That would be nice."

We worked together, side by side, hands in the dirt, until it was time to go inside. And I realized that if my father believed this garden might one day bloom, so could I.

That night, not long after Ella had fallen asleep, I heard stairs creak. I turned, expecting Ella. Instead Sydney stood at the bottom of the steps, clutching the railing.

"Do you have a pair of clippers?" she asked.

"Clippers?"

She ran a hand over the clumps of hair that remained intact. "It's time. I'd feel better with it gone."

Manny, who'd been the only barber in Paris for as long as I could remember, walked through our front door a half hour later, just moments after nine o'clock.

"I can't thank you enough," I said as I led him back into the kitchen.

Sydney sat at the table with my father, sipping on the cup of tea he'd made her. Even in her visibly fragile state, she held out her hand to Manny, greeted him warmly, and thanked him for coming.

Then she sat, spine straight, stoic, as Manny buzzed the remaining strands of her hair. They fell on the towel I'd anchored around her neck and onto the floor, as if she were shedding her last vestiges of hope.

She'd been beautiful with them, and she was beautiful without them. I looked at the cape around her shoulders, and I knew. I knew exactly who she was.

"Superhero," I said.

But even as my dad kissed her cheek and Manny brushed the loose hairs from her neck, she shook her head slightly. Because in Sydney's eyes, she was no stronger than anyone else fighting a battle.

In my eyes, however, she was the bravest person I knew.

An hour later, after Sydney had gone to bed, and my father, Manny, and I finished a snack of milk and cookies, I thought of Sydney and her hair, and made a decision.

"I know it's late, but before you head home, do you think you'd have time to do the same thing to my hair?" I asked.

"You sure?" Manny asked as I pulled off my ball cap.

"I'm sure."

My father's eyes went wide, and confusion danced across his tired face.

"Why?" he asked.

I shrugged. "Why not?"

I wanted to give Sydney some tangible sign of my support. She wasn't defined by her disease or her hair. I could match her in that.

"I have my shears," Manny said. "We can braid the length before we cut it."

"Wigs and Wishes," I said, thinking of a regional charity event that helped children and women who were going through treatment.

Manny took one last bite of his cookie. "Perfect," he said.

I waved my hand over my head. "Let's do this."

"One more thing," my father said, as he reached for the towel that had been around Sydney's neck.

He smiled as he wrapped it around my neck, knotting it lightly in front, and I wondered if he remembered all the times he'd done this in my youth.

Then he looked at me, his stare locking with mine, and he simply said, "My girl."

And I knew.

CHAPTER THIRTY

I found Ella at the kitchen table the next morning, armed with a lineup of rocks and a set of new permanent markers Jackson had sent her from New York.

I wondered how he'd been; my father hadn't mentioned him lately. The markers, however, had made Ella's entire week.

Waves of dark hair hung across her face as she worked, and the tip of her tongue pushed between her lips.

She finished decorating a rock, then slid it across the table to join a group of five others.

"Do you want to see?" she asked.

"I do," I said as I stepped into the room and leaned down to study her work.

Ella's attention shifted instantly to my shorn hair. "You're not sick, are you?" she asked, eyes wide.

"No, no, no." I wrapped my arm around her shoulder. "I just wanted to do something to surprise your mom."

"Wow," she said, unable to take her gaze away from my head.

"Show me." I tapped the table, wanting to shift focus back to what she'd created.

On each rock she'd drawn a person, cartoon-character style. A woman. A girl. A man. Another woman. A boy. Each figure wore a mask, like a superhero. At least, I hoped they were superheroes and not a group of bandits ready to hold up the Paris Market.

I thought of Sydney and how much she'd looked like a superhero the night before, draped in her towel cape as Manny had shorn her hair.

I realized she wasn't just the bravest person I knew, she was also the bravest person Ella knew, just as my mom had been for me.

"What's with the masks?" I asked, my voice thick with emotion.

"You'll see," Ella answered, putting the finishing touches on another female face.

When she lifted her gaze to mine, I realized her joy magically reappeared whenever she was doing something creative. I gave silent thanks for Marguerite, her bowl of broken crayons, and the way she'd given Ella an escape from the sadness in her life.

"Color them in, Auntie D."

I twisted up my features. "Kid, I was never good at coloring between the lines."

Then I measured the happy expectation plastered across her sweet face, and I sank onto the chair beside her and reached for a red marker. "OK. I'll try."

Ella pressed her hand over mine. "Not that one." She reached for a teal marker and slid it toward me. "This one. Just the mask," she instructed.

A frisson of nervousness rippled through me. Hand me a hammer and I was good to go, but a fine-tipped teal marker on the kid's carefully drawn creation? Terrifying.

The corners of Ella's mouth pulled into a grin. "You can do this, Auntie D."

In her tone I heard Sydney's quiet confidence, and sudden tears welled in my eyes. Tears for the years we'd never had, for the years Ella was about to lose.

My family.

And then I concentrated, filling in the space between the lines of one superhero mask after another. Teal here. Teal there. Until they were complete, a set of rocks transformed into warriors, just like Ella's momma.

Beside me, Ella uttered a slight gasp.

Sydney stood at the doorway, her favorite gray shawl drawn tightly around her shoulders as she leaned heavily against the frame.

"What have you done to your hair?" she asked softly.

"Solidarity for my sis," I answered. "You like?"

Color rose in her cheeks, and I wondered if she might be embarrassed by such a public display. "I love," she answered, stepping close enough to touch my head.

Her fingertips felt slender and cool, and I closed my eyes, doing my best to capture this moment and the gentleness of her touch, wanting to lock both away in my permanent memory banks.

"What are you making?" she asked, shifting her attention to her daughter's creations.

Ella said nothing, transfixed by the sight of her mother up and around.

"Superheroes," I answered, filling the void. "She's made the most amazing set of superheroes ever."

Sydney took one careful step after another toward the table, then quietly studied Ella's work. Her face, swollen from her steroids, softened as she smiled. Moisture glistened in her eyes, yet she didn't cry.

I realized I'd never seen her cry in front of Ella. Not once.

"Oh, sweetie." She held out one arm as she leaned against the back of a chair. Ella jumped to her feet and moved to her mother's side, letting herself be wrapped in Sydney's embrace. "They're amazing." She looked at Ella, beaming. "Teal warriors, yes?"

Ella nodded. "Just like you, Momma."

Sydney looked up, and our gazes met and held. "Just like me." Then she cupped Ella's chin. "I thought I might make pancakes for breakfast."

Ella let out a whoop, but I couldn't deny the worry that slid through me.

"You sure you're up to that?"

Annoyance flashed in Sydney's eyes, and I held up my hands in a gesture of surrender.

She laughed. "Sorry. Thanks for your concern, but I can do this, and I make the meanest pancakes around."

Ella and I helped her gather ingredients and tools, then I headed upstairs to get dressed while they set about making breakfast.

Ella came tearing up the stairs several minutes later, screaming my name.

I found Sydney on the kitchen floor, fighting to pull herself upright, half-propped against the cabinet beneath the kitchen sink.

Superhero rocks lay scattered across the floor, having apparently fallen with the tablecloth.

"I couldn't catch myself," Sydney said, her voice weak, frightened.

"Get Grandpa," I told Ella as calmly as possible as I rushed to Sydney and pulled her against me. "Steady. I've got you."

"Can't feel anything," she said, her voice trembling. "My face. My side."

I swallowed against the fear that clawed its way up my throat. I fought the tears that threatened, and I focused on Sydney, on staying strong, on being as brave as she was.

The color drained from my dad's face as he rounded the kitchen door. He moved to where we sat and squatted down, pressing a palm to each of our faces. Then he pushed to his feet and raced for his phone.

CHAPTER THIRTY-ONE

Sydney grimaced as the ambulance made its way toward Hunterdon Medical Center, and I tried to ignore the churning cauldron of fear and shock that threatened to make me ill.

"Ella?" she asked.

"Safe with Albert," I answered.

I didn't need to tell her Ella had been hiding inside her closet when the ambulance came. I'd left Albert gently talking through the door, assuring her everything would be all right, when both of us knew nothing could probably be farther from the truth.

Sydney mouthed the words, "Thank you," then softly said, "Your work?"

I laughed nervously. "Seriously?"

She reached for my arm, wrapping her fingers around my wrist. I covered her hand with my opposite hand, and we rode in silence for several minutes, holding on to each other as if neither of us intended to ever let go.

I stared at her teal nails, defiant in the face of the odds stacked against her.

"I'm more upset about not getting those pancakes you promised," I teased, and a smile pushed at the lines of worry and fear on her beautiful face.

Then a lone tear slid from the corner of her eye. I wiped it away with a quick brush of my fingertip, settling my hand back into place over hers.

"Scared," she said.

"Me, too."

"Thought you didn't get scared." Another weak smile.

I drew in a deep breath, then sighed. "Apparently, I do."

There was a reason I hadn't been scared for most of my life. It was simple: I hadn't lived. From fifth grade on I'd been smart enough to know that if I never let myself love anyone the way I'd once loved my mother—and my father—I'd never again suffer a broken heart when they left.

Then Albert had showed up at my door, and Sydney had driven into town with Ella, and everything had changed.

The girl who had once vowed to stay alone and protect her heart now sat in the back of an ambulance holding on to her newly found sister, ready to fight anyone and anything that might take her away.

And even though I knew deep inside my soul that this moment might be the one that changed everything—the moment that catapulted us toward the unthinkable—I wasn't about to let go, wasn't about to shield my heart or walk away.

I was in this for the long haul—whatever that might mean—today, tomorrow, or next week.

Sydney had found her way under my skin and into my heart, as though she'd been missing all along. Part of me. A missing piece slipped back into place.

I dipped my forehead to hers and held on tight.

And then we rode together in silence, clinging firmly to our belief that maybe, just maybe, fate still had one last miracle in store for us.

Late that night, after several long hours of waiting, a CT scan, a brain MRI, and a spinal tap, Sydney's doctor stood at the foot of her bed and delivered the news.

I wondered how my father had felt in moments like this with my mother, back when I'd been too young to realize what a roller coaster her battle must have been.

I was afraid, plain and simple. As I sat beside my sister and waited for the doctor to look up from the chart and deliver his news, fear and dread wrapped themselves around my insides and squeezed so hard I could barely breathe.

"While it's often difficult to know for sure whether an area like this is new disease or necrosis, we're fairly confident this is the latter," he said finally.

His words made no sense. "I don't understand. Isn't that a good thing? That it's not disease."

The oncologist's brows furrowed. "It's dying tissue," he explained. "A side effect we see sometimes after multiple rounds of radiation treatment."

The bottom fell out of my stomach, and I reached for Sydney's hand. She stared at the doctor, dumbfounded.

Then she laughed, the sound a mixture of shock and disbelief. I tightened my grip on her hand.

"I'd imagine that when you underwent your radiation treatments, one of the risks explained to you was this," the doctor said. "Radiation necrosis." He paused, giving Sydney time to digest what he was saying. I was thankful for that small kindness. For everything else, I wanted to strangle him with my bare hands.

"The area of your brain where your lesions were is now dying," he explained.

"A side effect." Sydney drew in a slow, steady breath and turned, looking me straight in the eye. "Son of a bitch."

"Does it go away?" I asked, not wanting to overstep my bounds, but frantic for answers. How could this have happened? Why did it happen? How quickly could we fix it?

The doctor took a backward step, the move subtle. "The drug combination typically administered is the same combo you're currently using."

"That's not working," Sydney said flatly.

He flipped through her chart. "Evidently not. And based on the increase in affected area between today's scan and your last, I'd say your necrosis is spreading."

"But it's not cancer?" I asked.

He blew out a breath, clearly anxious to get out of Sydney's room. "Not in her brain."

Sydney nodded, pressing a hand to her lips. A single tear ran down her cheek. I let go of her hand long enough to wipe it away before I interlaced our fingers once more.

"As for the paralysis," he said, "we'll increase your steroid dosage to get the inflammation down as much as possible."

"Can she go home?" I asked, suddenly desperate to get her out of this place, away from the doctor and his chart and his words that sounded hopeful but were undoubtedly anything but.

"Let's see what the morning brings," he answered. "I want the results of that spinal tap." Then he was gone.

The next morning a different doctor explained that Sydney's spinal tap had been inconclusive. Based on her symptoms, however, the team felt the cancer had spread to her central nervous system.

I dropped my face to my palms, wanting to reverse time, wanting to undo the doctor's words and this new reality.

"Prognosis?" Sydney asked, her voice steady, strong, amazing.

"A month or two."

He might as well have kicked me. Based on the way Sydney grimaced, she felt the same. Although I was certain her pain resonated far more deeply.

Neither of us said a word until he was out of the room and the door swung shut.

"Let's go home," Sydney said.

"What about treatment?" I asked, desperate for something, anything that might change her apparent fate. "Surely there's something we can try."

She gave me a gentle look, her expression one of total resignation. "I'm done, Destiny. It's over."

"Not yet," I said, grabbing on to my denial and squeezing tight.

But Sydney merely nodded. "Time's up. I want to go home."

"What if they're wrong?" I asked, full of a hope so desperate it stole my breath.

Sydney only shook her head, knowing exactly what I meant. "It's science," she said. "As much as I hate it, it's just science."

"Not good enough. They can still be wrong."

My ten-year-old self came back to life, clawing at any possibility of hope, any possibility of saving the person I loved.

I moved to Sydney's side and grabbed her hands.

She breathed slowly, calmly. "I've been fighting this battle for four years. You've been fighting for two months. It's enough. We live our lives, and we never stop to think how quickly things can change." She lifted her tired gaze to mine. "Until they do."

And then something shifted inside me. My desperation gave way, and my defeat took over.

"I don't know how to watch you die," I said softly. After all, I hadn't watched my mother die.

This time, however, I wasn't going anywhere. I'd stay by Sydney's side and hold her hand, no matter how much my heart might hurt.

"Me, either," Sydney answered.

Then I thought of Ella and how devastated she'd be by today's news.

I thought of Ella and my promise to Sydney, the parallels between my life and my dad's, and I understood how terrified he must have been.

"I don't know how to raise an amazing kid like Ella."

"Who does?" Sydney asked. "But I know you'll do just fine." Then she drove her last nail home. "I know you want to fix this." She patted her chest. "Fix me. But maybe some things are just meant to stay broken."

CHAPTER THIRTY-TWO

Our days began to run one into the next.

Sydney's condition and strength deteriorated until, two weeks later, she could no longer use the walker we'd purchased. Ted Miller, our local pharmacist, used his medical-device connections to find a wheelchair, which we kept by our front door. I'd installed a simple ramp, and when he wasn't sitting by Sydney's side, reading to her, my father spent every waking moment in the garden, as though he believed planting new bulbs might somehow change the future.

Sydney had experienced a difficult night, and I sat with Ella the next morning, outside on Marguerite's patio. The weather was unseasonably warm for October, even though the morning air nipped at our cheeks.

Ella had grown withdrawn in recent days, and Marguerite spent much of her weekends drawing my niece out of her reading nook and into the fresh air for art lessons and conversation, much as she'd done for me so many years ago.

Marguerite now sat cradling a cigar box in her lap. Ella knelt patiently at her feet, and I nursed my second cup of coffee.

Marguerite lifted the box's lid, and a pale yellow card winked out from inside. A single line of words had been written on it in ink.

"What does it say?" Ella asked, her voice an excited whisper.

"'Happy is the heart that still feels pain,'" Marguerite read.

"Who said that?" I asked.

Marguerite's lips curved into a sly smile. "I have no idea."

"Well"—I took another sip of coffee—"he was an idiot."

Marguerite pulled out a stack of letters neatly tied with a green ribbon. She sighed.

"From Joseph?" I asked.

Marguerite nodded as she carefully slid the ribbon from the stack, leaving its bow intact. "I thought you might like to see them."

"Who's Joseph?" Ella asked, brows furrowed.

Marguerite held out the letters, and Ella held up her palms. "He was my one true love," Marguerite answered. "We were going to be married, but he was killed in a war a long time ago."

Ella tensed, holding the letters as if they might break or explode or vaporize.

"Did you write letters to him?" Ella asked.

"I did."

"What happened to them?"

Sadness washed across Marguerite's features, but she caught herself, quickly recovering. "I'm not sure, sweetie, but I know he got them, because he kept writing me back." She pointed to the letters on Ella's palms.

"Can we read one?" Ella's tone brightened. "Are there secret messages? Codes?"

Marguerite laughed, gathering the letters into a careful pile before she slid the ribbon into place. "No codes. No secrets. Just a lot of private mushy talk about love and marriage and family."

Ella's face fell. "Will you keep them forever?"

Marguerite nodded.

"Why?"

"Because, even though I can't see Joseph anymore, I'll always have a piece of him here"—she tapped the envelopes—"and here." She tapped her temple. "In my memories."

"Will I have letters from Momma?"

Marguerite and I exchanged looks, and I locked on to what she'd said just before Ella's question.

Her letters from Joseph gave her something to hold on to, something she'd have forever, just like letters from Sydney could do for Ella.

I thought of Jessica and her desire to help, and I realized that if we worked together, if we helped Sydney, there was no reason we couldn't give Ella something she'd have forever as well.

"We'll see," I said, not wanting to raise her hopes before I'd shared my idea with Sydney.

Ella sighed loudly. "That means *no*. 'We'll see' always means no."

"Except when it doesn't," Marguerite said with a gleam in her eyes, her thoughts apparently following the same route mine had.

"Will I be able to write Momma letters if she dies?" Ella asked.

I opened my mouth to protest, to tell her we could still win the battle. She wouldn't need letters. Something. Anything. But Marguerite beat me to the truth.

"Of course you can," she said, her voice gentle. "You'll be able to talk to Momma, pray to Momma, remember her, and write her letters."

And although her words felt like a betrayal of any hope for a miracle we might have left, I knew Marguerite was right. Sydney wasn't going to live forever. None of us were. It was better to prepare Ella with the truth than with placating words.

"How do we survive this?" I asked Marguerite, dropping my voice low after Ella jumped up to dance around the yard.

Marguerite took my hand and held it tight. "With hearts broken but chins up."

The sound of small feet racing through fallen leaves mixed with happy laughter in the late October air. Paris youth made their way from door to door, street to street, bringing the town's Halloween tradition to life for yet another year. Residents sat on front steps, fire pits glowed, and neighbors talked animatedly about life and costumes and candy.

"Ella," I called up the stairs as I waved good-bye to two three-foot-tall salt and pepper shakers and their parents. "We'd better get going before the candy's all gone."

The evening was unseasonably mild for late October in New Jersey, and Albert stood outside on the front step.

He laughed at costumes, cowered from ghouls, and handed out treats exactly as he'd done back when I'd been Ella's age.

I caught myself watching him, remembering, wishing we could freeze this moment forever—this moment when laughter filled the air and the costumes and masks gave us all a chance to hide from reality for just one night.

"Auntie D," Ella admonished as she rounded the top of the stairs, "stop teasing."

I shrugged. Teasing the kid had become one of my favorite pastimes. "Momma?" I asked.

Ella shook her head, her smile fading. "Too tired."

I patted her shoulder as she reached me. "Sit tight; I'll be right back."

She'd picked a costume based on a character she'd fallen in love with in one of her books, a steampunk heroine, complete with velour top hat and brass goggles. I straightened her hat and then headed for her mother's room.

I found Sydney sitting in the white rocking chair beside her window. Not long after the day she and I had walked along Artisan's Alley, I'd purchased the chair back from the store owner. Then I'd placed it in Sydney's room. The rocker had become her favorite seat, where she spent hours resting with her shawl pulled tightly around her shoulders.

She stared through the glass panes as the town trick-or-treated past, her expression one of utter heartbreak. "This is my last Halloween," she said softly, and although I heard her, I pretended she'd said nothing.

"If you're strong enough to sit in that chair," I said, "you're strong enough to sit in the wheelchair."

She turned to face me, anger flashing through her dark eyes. "Ella doesn't need her momma in a wheelchair, slowing her down."

"Bullshit." I reached for her, anchoring one arm around her back as I helped her push to her feet. "You get down those stairs, and I'll take care of everything else."

"I hate that chair," she said.

"Tough."

"I don't have a costume."

"I'll tie a towel around your neck and draw a mask on your face," I said as we walked side by side down the hall. "I think there's a Sharpie in the junk drawer. That'll work."

The defeat on her face softened, and a smile played at the corners of her eyes. "You're a real pain in the ass," she said. "Has anyone ever told you that?"

"Who hasn't?" I stopped our forward progress long enough to tighten my arm around her shoulder in a hug. My mind flashed through all the possibilities of shared experiences we might have had. Bikes. Books. Muddy feet. Skinned knees. Halloween.

"Thank you," Sydney said softly, and my heart twisted inside my chest.

"Ella," I called out, determined to make this Halloween work. "Get Grandpa Albert, please. Tell him we need your momma's chair at the bottom of the stairs."

Sydney steeled herself on the top step, drawing in a long, slow breath, like a warrior headed into battle. I saw her then, in flashes of images through my mind. Diagnosis. Denial. Anger. Acceptance. Battle.

I hadn't been there for any of it. Hadn't even known she existed. But I could be here now, for however long we had. "You hold the railing, and I'll hold you."

Sydney nodded, then stepped forward and down. One step at a time. Two feet planted. One foot forward.

"You could always sit down on your behind and slide," I said, trying to lighten the mood.

Even though perspiration beaded on her forehead, she smiled. "Now, there's a mental image for you."

Ella waited at the bottom of the steps, her brows pinched with concern and fear—too much fear for a nine-year-old's face. My dad appeared with the wheelchair, moving toward us, hands outstretched to help, but he knew better than to touch Sydney when she was fully determined to make it on her own.

At the bottom of the steps, she eased herself into the chair and exhaled, as if she'd held her breath during her entire descent.

I gave Ella's shoulders a squeeze, then turned to Sydney. "I'll get you some water."

A moment later I was back. My father had opened the front door and stood ready.

He rolled Sydney's chair down the ramp, then stood back as we started to move away. I could see the longing in his eyes, how much he wanted to join us.

"Leave the bowl," I said. "We can write a note, tell everyone to take one piece."

But he shook his head, his features going serious. "You girls go. I'll man the fort."

So we made our way down Third Street—Ella, Sydney, and me—but when I glanced back my dad was still watching, by all appearances trying to capture the moment so he'd remember every detail.

We worked one side of the street and then the other, laughing as Ella raced from front step to front step, wielding her pleases and thank-yous like a champ.

She wished everyone a happy Halloween—other trick-or-treaters, neighbors in doorways, parents standing at the curb.

"She's lovely," I said, and Sydney nodded. "You've done an amazing job."

"I had help," she answered.

"Your parents?"

Another nod.

"I'm sorry. You must miss them terribly."

She nodded again, this time with eyes glistening, and I let the silence stretch between us. I'd learned at a very young age that platitudes meant nothing. *Time heals. She's in a better place. She'd want you to be happy.*

None of those meant a thing.

So I did the only thing I could do. I stood beside her and gave her grief the space it needed.

By the time Ella had hit the last house on Third Street and we turned the corner onto Front Street, Sydney had regained her composure. We trick-or-treated until Ella's bucket was nearly too heavy to carry, and then we headed for the river, and the town's annual bonfire.

Ghosts, goblins, princesses, and superheroes raced and played, laughing, shouting, and dancing as families gathered. We settled at a picnic table beside Jessica and her children; then Ella, Max, and Belle dashed off to join a spontaneous limbo competition.

Jessica and I hadn't spoken again about the issue of hospice and where Sydney would spend her last days. She looked at me now, sliding her hand across the table to cover mine.

"About that thing," she said, as Sydney stared off at the children dancing. "I was out of line."

But she had been trying to help, and I understood that. Hell, I appreciated that. Jessica had been there for me every step of my journey, and I knew she only wanted to be there for me now.

I nodded. "I know."

Then I reached for Sydney's hand, and we sat surrounded by children's laughter.

I broached the subject of Marguerite's letters. Sydney's expression grew somber as I explained how Marguerite had lost her fiancé, and how she'd saved every letter he'd written, priceless keepsakes of the love they'd shared.

Jessica, to her credit, remained silent, waiting for Sydney to make the first response.

"I've thought about leaving something for Ella." She spoke slowly, searching for her words even as she worked to say them. "But I'm not terribly creative, and now . . ." She hesitated, took a slow breath in and out. "I don't have the stamina for much of anything."

"That's where we come in." I gave her hand a slight shake. "Me and Jessica. You talk and we'll write."

Sydney's eyes lifted to mine, searching.

"Letters," I continued. "Love notes. From you to Ella. Words she'll cherish for the rest of her life."

Jessica's features crumpled.

I could read her like a book. Always had.

I was certain her mind had gone immediately to her children, and what it would be like to know she was leaving them forever. Then I imagined her thoughts had traveled to the past and my mother, a woman Jessica had once loved like a second mom.

"I'll help," she said. "Anything for you."

Sydney's expression brightened, then a slight smile curved her lips.

"So it's settled," I said. "We have a plan."

Ella bounded to Sydney's side, her face full of innocent hope. "Dance with me, Momma."

Sydney's features fell, and Jessica grimaced.

"Oh, sweetie," Sydney said. "I'm afraid I spent all my energy walking down the steps."

But instead of frowning or pouting or complaining, Ella grinned, her smile wide and bright. "What about your chair?"

Sydney frowned and smiled simultaneously. "My chair?"

Ella nodded, excitement radiating from beneath her purple wig. "You can dance in your chair."

The three adults—Sydney, Jessica, and myself—sat motionless for several moments, stunned by the simplicity of Ella's reasoning; then Jessica and I launched ourselves into motion.

"What are you doing?" Sydney asked, as we pushed her across the grass, toward the fire.

"I'll get the kids," Jessica said, once we'd reached an area of packed dirt and the wheels of Sydney's chair moved smoothly, almost effortlessly.

"Destiny," Sydney said, uncertainty heavy in her voice.

I leaned down to place my lips to her ears. "You're going to dance with your daughter, and I'm going to help."

I only wished my father were with us, so we could all dance together one more time.

Jessica, Max, and Belle returned, and we danced along the banks of the Delaware under a harvest moon, with the sparks of the bonfire floating up into the darkening sky.

CHAPTER
THIRTY-THREE

A cold front moved through early that next week, and yellow and orange leaves blasted down Third Street. A gust buffeted the house, and the eaves creaked. Leaves tapped against the window, countless points of contact, begging to be let inside, out of the cold.

I sat beside Sydney's bed, my head in my hands.

Tuesday may have dawned as a new day, but in this room—this space—I couldn't help but feel every moment brought me closer to losing what I'd only just found.

She'd asked for hospice on Friday, and again over the weekend. The pain in her head had intensified and had spread down into the back of her neck. Although my dad and I had done our best to keep pillows fluffed and ice bags full, we'd had to call the emergency number twice over the weekend to help us navigate her pain relief.

The hospice staff had spent most of Monday ensuring we had everything we needed. The guest bed had been taken apart and stowed in the closet. A hospital bed had been installed, complete with height and tilt adjustments available at the push of a button.

A steady infusion of Dilaudid held the monsters at bay, and we sat, waiting.

I'd sent Ella to school and Dad to the market. I'd taken the day off from the shop and wanted to focus on Sydney.

She stirred and reached for her ginger ale, smiling. Always smiling.

"You comfy?" she asked.

Who cares? I wanted to scream, but instead I nodded. "Absolutely. You?"

She pushed herself up to sitting. "Would you open the window?"

I pointed at the swirling, gray sky outside. "Do you hear that wind?"

She nodded, a smile teasing at her lips.

I shook my head and patted her hand. "It's too cold."

Her sly, stubborn grin widened. "You afraid I'll catch my death of cold?"

"Not funny," I said, while I thought, *truthfully, yes.* "Too cold," I repeated.

"Open the window," she insisted.

"No." I made a show of checking her ginger ale, pretending I might need to run to the kitchen at any moment.

"Open. The. Window." She spoke clearly and distinctly, each word its own declarative statement.

And although we'd spent the first thirty years of my life apart, she was still my big sister. I pushed to standing. "You sure?"

She nodded. "I want to smell the air."

I gave her hand a squeeze and moved to the old original casement windows. Neither my parents nor I had ever installed screens, and when I unlocked the panes and pushed the windows open, cold air rushed into the room, sending the sheer cotton curtains fluttering wildly.

Sydney inhaled sharply, and I pulled the panes back toward me, afraid the sudden drop in room temperature might shock her system.

"Open," she said, more forcefully than I'd heard her speak in days. I pushed the windows completely open and turned to face her.

"Do you smell that?" she asked, looking at the ceiling, and I wondered if she might be hallucinating. "Oh, my, that's lovely."

She spoke in barely more than a whisper, and I found myself frozen, captivated by the simple beauty of her words.

A sudden burst of wind hit the front of the house, sending a swirl of leaves through the open window and into the room. They danced above Sydney's bed—flashes of amber, scarlet, and gold—and we laughed, awkwardly trying to catch them in our hands.

Sydney shivered, a smile on her lips, and I pulled the windows close together, leaving only a crack between panes.

"Enough," I said softly, taking note of the way her lids drooped after a hum from her pump and a fresh infusion of pain medication.

"OK." She nodded, grasping a large yellow maple leaf between her fingers.

For that moment, we were just two sisters sitting side by side, until sleep claimed her once more. Then I sat, staring at the leaf that rose and fell with her inhales and exhales, wondering how much time we had left.

Ella continued her withdrawal after Sydney went on hospice. The more we tried to engage her, the more she disappeared into her silent world. She spent hours inside her reading nook, went to school and back, and barely spoke to Marguerite, Albert, or me. She'd fall asleep each night beside her momma, one arm across Sydney's waist, her head on the side of Sydney's bed. Then my dad or I would carry her back to her room, where we'd tuck her into bed.

She ate little. She played little. She stopped painting rocks.

My dad and I huddled in the violet bistro chairs late one afternoon as Sydney and Ella spent time together upstairs.

"I don't know how to reach her," I said. "Any advice?"

His features softened, then fell. "I'm afraid Marguerite was always better at drawing you out of your shell than I was."

The memories came crashing back, and I said nothing, tired of the past, tired of the present.

"I'm sorry," he said.

I squeezed my eyes shut for a brief moment, then snapped them open to look at him. "You've already apologized, and I think I finally understand."

I opened the floodgate of fears I'd guarded so tightly.

"What if I'm no good at this?" I asked. "What if I panic and leave? What if I'm not cut out to be her stand-in mother? I don't know anything about guiding her through grief and tween years and life."

But my father only smiled; then he reached over to gently set his hand on top of my arm.

A short while later I stood inside the kitchen, staring out the window over the sink.

Marguerite slipped through the kitchen door to drop off a loaf of homemade bread. She pulled me into a hug, sensing instantly how much I needed her. She'd never hesitated to treat me like her own, and as far back as I could remember—back as far as losing Mom—she'd loved me, and I'd rested secure in that knowledge.

Could I do the same for Ella? *Would* I do the same for Ella?

"I wish I could be more like you," I whispered against her shoulder.

"That's funny"—she pushed me out to arm's length—"I wish I could be more like you."

A laugh slipped between my lips. "Like what?"

Her expression softened, yet her gaze grew intense. "Strong. Sure. Confident."

I shook my head, sighing. "I'm not strong, and I'm certainly no more confident than you."

Marguerite cupped my chin. "Yes, my dear, you are."

Her simple statement soothed my spirit, and when she turned to leave, I patted the loaf of bread. "Thanks for this. Maybe she'll finally eat something."

"Mac and cheese." She smiled, presumably remembering. "That always worked for you." And then she was gone, slipping out the back door as quickly as she'd slipped in.

"Was that Marguerite?" My father's voice sounded from behind me. He'd gone upstairs to check on Sydney and Ella.

"How are they?" I asked.

"Quiet," he answered.

I held up the loaf of bread. "Marguerite suggested we try macaroni and cheese for Ella." I wrinkled my nose. "I don't suppose you know how to make it?"

The light in my father's eyes shifted, and curiosity slid through me.

He held up one finger, gesturing for me to stay put. "I'll be right back."

When he returned a few moments later, he handed me a large plastic index-card box, and my breath caught.

A tiny, battered silk rose sat glued to the center front of the lid, just as I'd remembered it. The ivory petals had darkened with age.

"You had Mom's recipes?"

He nodded, watching as I set the box on the kitchen counter. I opened the lid as though the world's most precious treasure lay inside, waiting for my discovery.

"Grandmother and I looked everywhere for these after you left."

"I should have told you years ago." He tensed, hearing himself. "Or when I first came back, but somehow I couldn't let go of her . . . of these. They were all I had left." His pale gaze lifted to mine, the remorse I saw there genuine. "I'm sorry."

For the briefest moment I thought about getting angry, thought about telling him that this was just one more truth he'd kept from me. But then I stopped to think about the man—the father—he'd proven himself to be since his return.

I thought about Marguerite's letters from Joseph and the letters Sydney had been dictating for Ella.

Perhaps he'd simply wanted a tangible piece of Mom to keep with him forever, and I couldn't fault him for that. Her recipes. Cards she'd written and touched, ingredients she'd listed and tested, meals she'd prepared.

Countless index cards and scraps of paper sat tucked inside, their edges worn, bent, some corners missing, evidence they'd once been greatly loved.

I pulled out a single card and traced my finger across the faded ink of her handwriting.

Cinnamon Rolls.

I could still smell the yeast rising in her glass dish, covered by her favorite turquoise tea towel.

"She was like no one else," he said.

In his eyes I saw mirrored the pain and fear I'd known my entire life. He'd shut out the world—our world—when he'd lost her, but he'd taken this personal reminder with him, and he'd held on to it.

The old sadness rose inside me. He'd held on to this box. He just hadn't held on to me.

I searched for the recipe that had led to this moment.

"Macaroni and cheese," I said as I pulled the card free.

"Your favorite," he said.

He remembered.

My father's abandonment had colored my life perhaps even more than my mother's death. If my father had stayed and raised me like I knew she'd wanted him to do, my life would have turned out differently, surely.

But perhaps, after all the years and all the time spent apart, it wasn't too late to move forward. And while part of me wanted to explode and accuse him of keeping the cards hidden in his room because he'd never planned to stay this time, either, I said nothing of the sort.

We'd brokered a fragile peace, and in the grand scheme of all we'd been through, I could forgive this secret. I could forgive this box of memories kept to himself.

"You should keep the cards," he said. "She would have wanted you to have them."

"They're here now," I said. "You're here now."

He fell silent, and the exhaustion that had bracketed his eyes for days seemed a little bit lighter.

I leaned the macaroni and cheese recipe against a set of cobalt-blue canisters and ran my fingers over the top of the box's contents one more time.

My fingers stopped when they hit the last visible edge, this one thicker than the rest.

I pulled free a photo, a faded snapshot.

I remembered the costume—a sky-blue ballerina dress, brocade down the front, the tulle skirt lovingly stitched by my mother's hand. I'd worn a tiara, back when tiaras were sewn with beads and sequins, not pressed from plastic. The knees of my blue tights sagged, darkened by a tumble through wet leaves before my mother could snap the picture.

In the photo my father stood tall beside me, holding my hand. He smiled—not at the camera, but down at me, looking at the top of my head with so much love it rendered me weak in the knees.

Myriad questions raced through my brain, all starting with the same word.

Why?

He'd already apologized for leaving. Already apologized for the way he came back. He'd already promised to stay.

But why had he left in the first place?

He'd loved me enough to carry my picture with him for twenty years, but he hadn't loved me enough to stay.

"You looked just like her." My father's voice. "Too much like her."

"So instead of honoring her memory, you threw me away," I said softly, with heartbreak in my voice, not anger.

I'd moved past the anger. I just needed to finally understand why he'd done what he'd done.

"I squandered my chance at happiness. At family."

His blunt admission stopped me cold.

My father's handsome features crumbled. "She was gone."

"But I was here. I've been here all my life. Waiting for you to come home."

There it was, an admission of my own. All the years of sadness and confusion grew inside me, mixing with the questions and uncertainties the past few months had brought to the surface.

I'd waited twenty years for him to come home, and I'd spent the past three months waiting to see if he'd stay.

I pointed to the ceiling and Ella's bedroom, where I was confident the frightened child sat huddled inside her reading nook.

"What about Ella?" I dropped my voice to a whisper. "What if she reminds you too much of Sydney?"

I kept my voice soft, hoping she wouldn't hear. I wasn't looking for an argument. I was looking for the truth.

But instead of stepping away, my dad stepped closer. "I made you a promise, Destiny. I'm not going anywhere."

He took the photograph from my fingers and stared down into our past. He lifted his focus to me, his gaze intense, all sign of fatigue gone. "You've grown into an amazing young woman."

And then, instead of pushing him away, I pulled him close. I pushed away the past and chose the present. I wrapped my arms around his neck and held on tight, doing the best I could to believe him, to believe in myself. To hope that this time, we'd survive our loss together.

CHAPTER
THIRTY-FOUR

That night I used my mother's recipe cards to bake macaroni and cheese.

Dad had gone upstairs to check on Sydney, and my mind measured time as I cooked.

The time he and I had spent apart. The time we spent together now.

I pushed past the sadness of the missing pieces and focused on the progress we'd made, hoping for our future.

I wished Sydney would be a part of that future, but I knew that wish was one I'd never see come true.

My earlier conversation with Jessica echoed through my thoughts.

Maybe Sydney shouldn't be tucked into a hospital bed upstairs, but this was where she'd settled; this was where she could be loved.

Had she failed more quickly during her time at the hospital, we might not have moved her home. But now that she was here, and her pain was under control, I believed we'd made the best decision we could for our family, Ella included.

I stared into Scarlet's tank as the macaroni and cheese cooked, amazed at the difference in the fish. Where before she'd floated, she now swam. She interacted with anyone who stopped to talk to her, and she happily flitted about her space, fins relaxed, color brilliant.

Who knew Jackson Harding would prove to be a fish whisperer?

We hadn't seen him since the night he'd helped install and fill Ella's nook. I wondered how he was, wondered if he'd stop by again, wondered if a big-city guy like him could ever be interested in a small-town carpenter from Paris, New Jersey.

I tamped down my thoughts.

My life had no room for Jackson.

When the timer sounded, I pulled the casserole dish from the oven and set it on the stove. I wiggled my fingers at Scarlet, who happily watched my every move as if I were about to dish up her very own serving.

At the bottom of the stairs, I peered around the corner of the sitting room.

At some point during my cooking, my father had returned to his favorite chair. He'd propped the snapshot of the two of us against the framed photo of my mother and Sydney, and he'd fallen sound asleep.

"Dad," I called to him softly. "Dinner."

He stirred, and I headed up to Sydney's room. I slowed at the doorway, not wanting to wake her.

"It's OK. I'm up," she said.

I couldn't help but notice that her words slurred slightly, the act of speaking becoming more and more difficult as her disease spread.

I sat lightly on the edge of her bed, adjusting the pillows that supported her shoulders and head. "Good?" I asked.

"Perfect," she answered, giving me a weak smile. "You good?"

"Always," I lied. "I attempted Mom's baked macaroni and cheese recipe. Can I bring you some?"

She closed her eyes and shook her head ever so slightly. "Not hungry. Maybe later?"

I kissed her forehead. "You got it." Then I plucked her water glass from the bedside table and pressed the straw to her lips. "You have to stay hydrated."

"K," she mumbled as she sipped. Then her breathing leveled out, steady and deep, and she slipped that much further away.

I set down her glass and headed for Ella's room, knocking lightly on the doorjamb. When there was no answer, I stepped inside and tapped on the door to her reading nook. Still no answer.

"I attempted mac and cheese," I said. "Grandpa Albert's waiting. Your momma's going to eat later. You ready?"

Silence.

My pulse quickened as I turned the knob, even though I knew my fears were ridiculous. The poor kid had probably fallen asleep.

But when I cracked open the door, darkness greeted me.

I backtracked, checking the hall bathroom, my bedroom, my father's room. But Ella was nowhere to be found.

Ella was gone.

I walked calmly back past Sydney's door, but took the stairs two at a time on the way down. I hurried into the kitchen, where Dad stood fixing plates, waiting for us to join him.

"Did Ella come down while I was in with Sydney?"

He shook his head, concern in his eyes. "Not in her room?"

I shook my head.

"Bathroom?"

"No."

"I'll grab a jacket," he said.

"I'll check Marguerite's."

"What about your sister?"

"Sleeping," I answered. "I think we can leave her for a few minutes. Not a lot longer."

He followed me out the door and around the path to Marguerite's.

"Ella?" I asked when she cracked open her front door.

But Marguerite only shook her head. "I haven't seen her since she walked home from school. Why?"

"Where would she go?" Dad asked.

"Check her room for a note," Marguerite suggested. Then she turned on one heel. "I'll grab my jacket and some flashlights."

I retraced my steps, taking the stairs as quickly as possible, slowing only when I passed Sydney's door, not wanting to wake or frighten her.

Sure enough, I found a short stack of letters sitting on Ella's nightstand. She'd folded notebook paper in quarters, then tied the stack with one of the teal shoelaces she wore in her hair each gym day.

I carefully slid the papers from the stack, reading their hand-printed labels one at a time.

Momma. Grandpa Albert. Marguerite. Scarlet. Auntie D.

I didn't need to unfold the pages to know what they said.

She'd said good-bye.

Had she heard my father and me in the kitchen? Had she heard me asking him if he'd leave if she reminded him too much of Sydney?

Thanks, life, I thought, remembering the pain of being Ella, of knowing my mother was going to die.

Damn it. We'd come so far. Where would she have gone?

Panic tore through me.

I tucked her notes back into the ribbon, and I raced downstairs.

As much as I'd spent my life regretting that everyone in Paris knew my business before I did, I now appreciated the fact that word spread quickly that Ella had gone missing. On every stretch of cobblestone sidewalk, riverbank, and bike trail, friends and neighbors looked high and low for a little girl.

Within fifteen minutes, a text message from Mona Capshaw sounded on my phone.

`Lookout Rock.`

I was six blocks away. I forwarded the message to my dad and took off running, slowing only when I reached the edge of the bike trail, where the asphalt path ended and the dirt path began.

Lookout Rock. How could I not have known?

I kept the beam of my flashlight low, not wanting to trip and roll into the Delaware, but also not wanting to give Ella a chance to run.

Given the gathering of flashlights over at the park, it was likely the kid knew she'd been spotted. And thanks to the town I loved, I knew she wasn't about to get away again.

"Hey," I said softly as I stepped close to the boulder. "I got a little scared when I couldn't find you."

"I'm right here." Frustration and tears mingled in her voice, and my heart hurt.

"Would you mind if I sat with you?"

Ella sniffled. "Probably not."

"Great," I said, hoisting myself up onto the flat surface of the boulder. "Thanks."

"You're welcome."

"Want to tell me what you're doing?" I asked.

Ella shrugged in the darkness.

"That's what I thought," I said. "I figured you needed some alone time, but when you weren't in your nook, I got a little worried. So did they." I pointed to the flashlights.

"They're looking for me?"

"Yeah." I worked to keep my voice calm, when I really wanted to pull her into my arms and tell her never to scare me like this again. "They must like you or something."

"You think?"

I smiled. "I know." Then I asked, "What were you thinking about?"

"I was thinking I should leave now, before Momma dies."

"Why?"

"In case you don't want me here."

My heart broke inside my chest. "Never." I swallowed down the knot of emotion in my throat. "You and I are a team, right?"

"Hope so."

"Know so," I replied.

Ella's voice grew tiny as she spoke her next words, seemingly afraid to share what she was about to say. "I feel like I'm hanging."

"Hanging?" I asked, my mind suddenly filled with horrific, unwanted images.

"Up there in the air." She pointed. "And when Momma dies, I'm going to fall."

I searched for what might possibly be the right thing to say, the comforting thing to say. I was a carpenter with zero people skills and even fewer kid skills. But I'd been in her shoes. I'd sat on the same rock, in this same spot, facing the same fate she faced now.

Most of all, I remembered the fear of being left alone.

Ella twisted up her features and shook her head. "I'm afraid no one will catch me when Momma goes to heaven."

"Oh, baby." I wrapped my arm around her shoulder and pulled her close.

I remembered my heartache, remembered the unknown, and hated that she suffered the same way now.

"Me, Grandpa Albert, Marguerite, Miss Jessica . . . We'll always be there to catch you."

Ella sniffed, and I realized she'd started crying. I wiped her cheek with my sweatshirt sleeve.

"Do you promise to never get sick?" she asked.

The unfairness of life and her question reached into my soul. "I can't make a promise I can't control, but you have my word that I'll be by your side for as long as I am able."

I gave her a squeeze and pressed my lips to her ear. "I love you, Ella. I thank God every day that you and your momma found me, and I am going to do everything in my power to take care of you. I promise. Do you believe me?"

She nodded. "And what about Momma?"

I stared into Ella's dark-brown eyes, seeing so much of the pain I still carried with me all these years after losing my mother. Then I told her what I wish someone had told me. "Just love her. Love her more than you ever thought possible for as long as we've got left."

"It's not fair."

Her words were a knife though my heart.

"It's not."

"I wish I was more like you."

"Like how?"

"Fearless." She sniffled. "Grandpa Albert says you're the most fearless person he knows."

I smiled inside, knowing my dad couldn't be more wrong, but touched beyond words that he'd said as much to Ella.

"You know," I said, "I think you're way more fearless than I am. And don't forget, there's nothing wrong with being afraid."

"But you shouldn't stay afraid, right?"

I made a face. "Sometimes you do. Sometimes you stand up to your fear."

"Like with Momma."

An ache blossomed deep inside me. "Like with Momma." I pulled Ella into the tightest hug I could without smothering the poor kid. "We're going to have to face it, whether we want to or not."

"Grandpa Albert left when your mommy died."

The ache spread and I nodded, wondering again just how much of our discussion she'd heard. "He did, but he's here now, and he's not going anywhere. I'm not going anywhere, either. Running away doesn't change anything," I said, even though some crazy piece inside me wanted to grab my niece and run as far as we could get from Paris. We could change our names, reinvent our lives, and pretend our hearts weren't breaking.

Instead I said, "Ready to go home? Bet your momma would love to see your gorgeous face beside her when she wakes up."

Ella nodded, but there was still fear in her eyes.

"Did I mention there's mac and cheese?" I asked.

She shook her head, then frowned. "Did *you* make it?"

"Hey." I laughed. "I'm doing my best."

"I know, Auntie D." She wrapped her arms around my neck, and I buried my face in her sweet-smelling hair. "Me, too," she whispered.

I kissed the side of her head, holding there a few seconds longer than necessary, searching for the words to communicate what I wanted to say. The truth was, sooner or later life broke everyone. We were all broken pieces. The trick was to gather up our remaining fragments and move forward.

"Life is magical and heartbreaking," I said slowly. "It's wonderful and sad. And even when it doesn't seem fair, our job is to get up every day and be the best Ella and Auntie D we can be." I held out my hand. "Deal?"

Ella shook her head, then held up just her pinkie. "Pinkie promise."

I held up my pinkie and we interlocked our little fingers. "Pinkie promise," I repeated.

Then I pulled her into one more hug and held on tight.

CHAPTER
THIRTY-FIVE

Jackson Harding was working beside my father in the garden the next morning when I stepped outside with two piping-hot cups of coffee.

To say I was startled would be an understatement, considering I'd just thought about him the night before.

For a moment I simply stood on the top step, watching the two men work.

Jackson's standard blazer had been tossed aside, and he'd shoved the sleeves of his pale blue sweater up to his elbows. My father had apparently launched into a detailed explanation of something garden related, and Jackson absorbed his every word, his attention fully focused on Albert, until he spotted me.

"Excuse me," he said to my father and then he stood, never taking his eyes from me.

His expression shifted from surprised to amused, and at the precise moment he smiled, I remembered something.

I was bald.

I instinctively wanted to put a hand to my head and wished I'd grabbed my ball cap that morning. Then I realized I hadn't worn my ball cap since Manny had buzzed my hair.

"Let me help you," Jackson said.

He jogged to the steps and took the coffees from my hands.

"Good morning," he said.

"Good morning." I tipped my chin toward the garden, where my father stood, watching our every move. "Getting an early start on next year's crop?"

"Actually, I missed Scarlet. Figured I was due to check on her." Then he shifted his gaze to my head. "This is a new look for you."

I stiffened. "Surprised?"

He shook his head. "I'm not surprised at all."

I furrowed my brows.

"It's exactly what I'd expect you to do."

An odd sense of humility warmed me deep inside.

"And I think you're even more beautiful than you were the last time I saw you."

His words left me speechless, and he knew it, amusement dancing in his eyes.

The warmth he'd inspired spread, flaring up into my cheeks.

"Here"—he handed back my coffee mug—"this is yours. I'll give your dad his, and then I need to hear all about my fish. How's she doing?"

His fish.

I gestured toward the open door and the hallway. "Why don't you come in and see for yourself? And then you can stay for breakfast."

He hesitated. "I'm not sure I should. I mean, can you cook?"

I laughed then, amazed at how happy seeing him made me. Frightened a little, too. And surprised.

My father, who had walked up behind us, clapped a hand on Jackson's back. "Her pancakes can't hold a candle to mine . . . or her sister's . . . but she can scramble the heck out of a dozen eggs."

As crazy as it sounded, his simple, easy praise touched me as if he'd shouted it to the world.

They climbed the steps together, and Jackson paused beside me just long enough to shoot me a sideways grin. "Let's do it, then."

Jackson visited with Sydney while Dad and I cooked breakfast. We moved together in the kitchen like old pros, passing ingredients back and forth, shifting pans, reaching over one another for utensils.

We were a team, a team I'd once thought lost to me forever.

Ella ran next door to invite Marguerite over to our feast.

From upstairs I could hear Sydney's soft laughter, and I couldn't help but wonder what might have possessed Jackson to pull an early morning pop-in with my father and his family.

As though he'd read my thoughts, Dad spoke, his words casual as he manned the bacon skillet. "You seem pleased to see Jackson."

"I think pleased might be too strong a word. Surprised, actually."

Dad grinned. "I may have called him a time or two. Good man, that one."

I chose not to ask any probing questions about Jackson's intentions, choosing instead to simply enjoy the slow pace of the morning.

After Dad took breakfast up to Sydney, and Marguerite and Ella assumed dish duty, Jackson and I stood in the foyer staring at each other.

"Thanks for being here today," I said. "It's been a nice surprise."

"I can't seem to get your family out of my mind." He hesitated. "And I wanted to see how you were."

The simple kindness of his statement brought me to my emotional knees, but I held it together, keeping the tears that burned the back of my eyes at bay.

"Sydney tells me you like to walk," he said. "I think she's afraid you won't go if you're by yourself."

By myself.

It's just science, Destiny. Her words rang through my brain.

She was going to leave me by myself, Ella by herself, and there was nothing any of us could do to stop it from happening.

Jackson cupped his palm to my elbow. "Walk with me?"

We headed for the river. I pointed out the opera house on the way, detailing the progress I'd made on the restoration with the help of my family and my subcontractors.

He didn't say much, simply walked beside me, listening, letting me ramble. Oddly enough, I felt comfortable, uncharacteristically able to talk about anything.

When we reached the pathway that wound along the banks of the Delaware, he came to a sudden stop.

"What's this?" he said, squatting down to scoop up a painted rock from a crook among the roots of an old maple tree.

Ella.

I smiled as he studied the oval stone in his palm, every inch of surface covered in hearts and rainbows. One of the early designs.

"It's a smile," I said.

Jackson tipped his handsome face toward me, the morning sun lighting the brown of his irises, making them appear to glow. "A smile?"

"Weeks ago, Ella had this idea that if she painted rocks and left them where people might find them, she could make them smile— when they least expected it."

"Huh," Jackson said, as he carefully replaced the stone where he'd found it. "Pretty selfless."

I nodded. Selfless. He had no idea how right he was.

"That's Ella," I said. "All Ella."

"Special kid."

"One in a million," I said a bit too loudly, as though I needed to prove my point. But when it came to Ella, there was nothing to prove. There was only the truth.

"What's going to happen?" he asked.

"There's no family back in Ohio," I said matter-of-factly. "Sydney and I have decided she's better off here, with me."

I realized I hadn't uttered the statement to anyone outside our immediate family before that moment, and although the words still made me nervous, they felt right.

Jackson nodded. "Lucky girl."

I shook my head. "Lucky me."

I dropped my focus to the ground, but Jackson wasn't about to let me avoid his gaze. He brushed two fingers lightly beneath my chin, turning my face toward him.

His touch ignited a longing deep inside me, a desire to know this man well beyond his role as manager to my father, or frequent visitor to my family.

"All my life I wished for a family," I said, forcing my words through the tangle of emotion in my throat. "I had my grandmother, sure. And I had Marguerite and all of Paris, but I saw my dad at Christmas. I'd pretty much forgotten my mom—her voice, her laugh—and then Sydney showed up with Ella.

"They rocked my world," I continued, drawing in a deep breath, fighting to maintain my composure. "I promised myself I'd never let anyone in and—"

Words failed me, and I squeezed my eyes shut, refusing to cry.

Jackson took my hand between his and held on tight. "And life threw you a curveball."

I nodded.

"And now you're facing the same heartbreak you promised you'd never face again."

I nodded again.

"But this time"—he shook my hand, willing me to look up—"this time you get to be the family for Ella that you never really had."

"What if I'm horrible at it?"

He shrugged. "What if you're not?" He grinned. "What if you're the best aunt any artistic little kid who paints rocks for strangers ever had?"

"Thanks."

Suddenly I felt self-conscious, afraid I'd shared too much, exposed too much of my heart.

I blew out a breath, wiped my face, and stood, pulling my fingers free from his.

"I should probably be getting back to the house," I said.

"OK. And I need to get back to the city," he said. "But I'll try to drive over again soon."

And although I knew a man like Jackson Harding probably said things he might not always mean, I trusted him.

CHAPTER
THIRTY-SIX

Although her time in Paris had been short, Sydney had spent four long years battling her ovarian cancer. Four years.

When her turn for the worse came, it seemed sudden to those of us who loved her, yet I'd come to know Sydney well enough to appreciate she'd understood this day was coming from the moment she'd received her diagnosis.

She was a survivor . . . and a realist. She'd gotten more time than many expected she would, and yet the cancer had been relentless, recurring each time she'd beaten it back down.

This time was too much, even for Sydney.

She was the mother of a young girl who needed family, and she'd tracked us down, packed up her life, and road-tripped partway across the country to find us.

I sat beside her on another blustery afternoon. This time the trees outside her bedroom window had been stripped bare, and Sydney slept more than she was awake.

Albert and Jackson had taken Ella into the city to catch a matinee of *Aladdin*, after I'd promised my niece I'd stay by her mother's side every moment she was away.

Marguerite had been summoned by the Clipper Club to teach the art of relaxation through adult coloring books. If Sydney had been awake, we would have laughed about how ridiculous that request was, like grown women needed someone to tell them how to pick up a crayon and color?

"Let yourself be happy," Sydney said, her voice barely discernible.

She grimaced, and I reached for her hand, startled by her sudden statement. "Are you in pain?"

"A little." She worked to force a smile.

"Want me to hit your pump?"

She frowned. "Want you to live the life you want to live."

"Don't you find these wisdoms ironic, considering you showed up in town with your kid in tow and turned the life I wanted to live upside down?"

The beauty of Sydney was that she understood what I meant, what I was doing, and she smiled. Then she struggled to form her next words. "Tough shit."

Her pump hummed, and I knew she'd be lost to sleep within seconds. I pressed my forehead to hers and swallowed against the sob in my throat.

Not now, I thought. *Not yet. Please.*

"I love you," I said.

Then she smiled sweetly and gave one gentle nod of her head as the meds pulled her under.

By the time Ella, Jackson, and Albert returned from New York, Sydney had been asleep for hours. Marguerite had stopped by to sit beside me. We said little to each other, our faces drawn, fatigue and grief weighing us down. Sydney's breathing had gone deeper, slower, and I couldn't wait until the nurse's visit the next morning to pepper her with questions.

The front door burst open with a blast of excited chatter and laughter.

Life.

Ella burst into the room before Marguerite and I could push to our feet.

"Momma, Momma," she called out. "It was amazing, and Grandpa Albert says he once acted on the very same stage."

I raised my finger to my lips to shush Ella, but Sydney stirred, struggling to force her eyes open and lift her head. "Pillow," she said, and Marguerite and I scrambled into motion, simultaneously lifting her and tucking two pillows behind her back. "Thanks." She smiled. Then she looked directly at Ella, her eye contact solid as the excited little girl hopped onto the side of the bed. "Tell me."

And Ella did.

She rambled on about the music and costumes and lights and scenery as Sydney worked to keep her eyes open and focused. The more animated Ella became, the harder Sydney fought to stay in the moment, and I realized this was all she'd fought for—all she still fought for—to be present for her daughter.

Jackson and Albert stood in the doorway, listening to Ella's retelling of their day. Marguerite pushed past them, her pat to Albert's shoulder not going unnoticed by me. "I'll start some dinner," she said. Sydney winced, and I reached for Ella's hand. "Why don't we let your momma rest?"

"Thanks for telling me," Sydney said softly.

Ella pressed a kiss to her forehead and bounded to my side, taking my hand. "Want to watch *Aladdin* with me?"

"Didn't you just watch *Aladdin*?"

"The movie, silly."

I scrunched up my face. "I don't have it."

Jackson held up a DVD case and shook it. "Made a stop on the way back."

I hesitated, reaching one hand for Sydney's, part of me not wanting to leave her, part of me wanting to run and hide. "I might be too old for fairy tales."

"Never," my father said, his voice booming inside Sydney's bedroom. Then he met my gaze, his eyes urging me to go, to escape for a little while.

Sydney wrapped her delicate fingers around my wrist. "Never," she repeated, her voice no more than a raspy whisper.

Ella's features fell, and her brown eyes went huge. I was sure the time would come in which I'd have to say no to the kid on a regular basis, but this was not that time. Plus, I found myself so desperate for a happy ending I began to nod. "Where shall we watch it?"

"In the nook." Ella clapped her hands. "Jackson bought a tiny DVD player for my nook."

"For your *reading* nook?" I shot him a glare and he shrugged.

A few moments later, I waited in the hall as Jackson and Ella readied the nook, and I thought about Sydney, her words bouncing through my mind.

Live the life you want to live.

Ella and Jackson appeared in the doorway, gesturing for me to come inside, and I realized that while I'd imagined many lives, I'd never imagined this one.

I studied Ella's sweet profile, and Jackson's five o'clock shadow and the creases that framed his dark eyes. I thought of my father, who had run in fear during my mother's dying days but now sat beside Sydney, reading aloud to her from *The Velveteen Rabbit*.

Down in the kitchen, pots and pans rattled about, and I knew Marguerite was creating one of her culinary concoctions. Heaven help us.

Even though I had thought I'd been living the life I wanted to live, this life—a life I'd never imagined—was perfect beyond understanding. Perfect in all its imperfections, and challenges, and heartbreaks.

So I settled inside Ella's nook, Ella nestled between me and Jackson, and let myself be present in the moment.

I'd never been one for fairy tales, but for the first time in my life I understood their allure. They offered the hope that just beyond the next bend in the road, beyond the next mountain, there hid a discovery so magical it might change a person's life.

For the first time, I thought about my father's career on stage, the roles he'd played, and the worlds he'd helped create as more than just his escape. He'd helped others feel exactly what I was feeling now. He'd provided a respite for the weary, hope for the hopeless, laughter for the brokenhearted.

I closed my eyes and listened to Ella and Jackson's laughter, my father's soft voice down the hall, and Marguerite's distant conversation with Scarlet. Then I realized something far beyond a new understanding of my father and his love of performing.

I realized how lucky I'd become.

After all, a person didn't always discover her magical life.

Sometimes a magical life discovered her.

CHAPTER
THIRTY-SEVEN

For the next several days I worked odd hours at the opera house, installing the façade that framed the stage.

While Albert covered early mornings with Sydney, I worked. My subcontractors and I transported the finished paneling pieces to the opera house and completed the installation section by section.

Jessica visited most afternoons between school dismissal and dinner time at the café. As Max and Belle played with Ella, she sat with Sydney, holding her hand as she slept. They'd grown close during the time they'd spent together after Halloween, documenting Sydney's messages for Ella. Thoughts, dreams, lessons, hopes, love.

I went home each evening to eat dinner with Sydney, Ella, and Dad, and each night after Ella was tucked in bed, my father and I slept beside Sydney, curled into chairs, wanting only to be close by in case she needed us.

Marguerite, true to form, became an invaluable member of our family, helping Ella each night with schoolwork, packing lunches, running laundry, and maintaining as much normalcy as was possible under the circumstances.

It was Marguerite who sat with Sydney on the day the Paris Opera House Board of Trustees viewed the newly renovated stage frames for the first time.

Albert, Ella, and I headed downtown a little before ten a.m.

The doors hadn't yet been unlocked when we arrived, so Ella knocked, pressing her face to the glass impatiently. Jack Maxwell appeared immediately, ushering us inside and glancing about, acting as though we were about to be made privy to some sort of national treasure.

The nerves that had tormented me back on the morning of my first proposal to the selection committee reappeared now, sending waves of butterflies soaring through my belly.

Ella bounced up and down on the toes of her best sneakers. Up. Down. Up. Down.

"For the love of Pete"—my father pressed a hand to her shoulder, doing his best to press her feet flat to the floor—"this waiting is nerve-racking enough."

So this was what it felt like to be part of a family who stood by your side in times of sorrow and in times of great expectations. My nerves were their nerves. My success would be their success.

Then he turned to me. "Breathe," he said. "In and out. Slow and steady."

My butterflies settled, soothed by the man and the little girl by my side.

"We're ready now," Jack said, gesturing for us to head to the main auditorium. "Byron's got the board assembled by the lower doors," he explained. "We'll enter down there."

So we followed him down the ornately carpeted hall that ran along the curve of the auditorium, paralleling the aisles inside, on a crash course with the back wall of the building and the side entrance to the stage.

Byron smiled as we neared. "Here she is now," he proclaimed. "The woman of the hour and her family."

Her family.

Ella slipped her hand inside mine and squeezed. Albert smiled and nodded, and although his countenance said cool, the twinkle of anticipation in his eyes said anything but.

"Could this blowhard move any slower?" he whispered in my ear.

Ella giggled, and I said, "Dad, knock it off."

And then it was time.

Byron Kennedy and Jack Maxwell pulled open the heavy theater doors, and the fourteen members of the board filed inside, turning to take in the majestic panels, their faux finish, and their intricate woodwork with oohs and aahs that enveloped me like a warm, congratulatory embrace.

"The full paneling along the base of the stage will be next," Byron announced, "followed by the box seats themselves."

But even before those gathered responded, my father, the award-winning actor, leaned close and murmured, "My girl, I think it's time you took a bow."

Erma Leroy began to clap, followed by Polly Klein, Jack Maxwell, and Byron Kennedy himself. And then, as the applause spread and the volume rose to a crescendo, I climbed the steps up to the stage, keeping a firm grip on Ella's hand, and we took a bow together before the appreciative board. The majestic panels hung from floor to ceiling, framing the opera house stage in all its original beauty once more.

And for just a few fleeting moments, my inner ten-year-old pushed aside the thirty-year-old and soaked it all in, wondering if this was how my father had felt at the end of every show.

CHAPTER
THIRTY-EIGHT

Sydney left us in the quiet hours of the morning.

Her breathing had become labored not long after the three of us had returned from the opera house.

Dad had fallen asleep with his hand on hers. Ella had drifted to sleep curled by her side, her slight arm wrapped around Sydney's waist.

Marguerite had fallen asleep in the chair we'd dragged in from my father's room, and I sat waiting. Waiting to say good-bye to the sister I'd just come to know.

When Sydney's labored breathing fell quiet, Ella said, "Momma" softly in her sleep, smiling.

Sydney gasped, her soul leaving midbreath. Her pale lips curved softly, and peace washed across her beautiful face, as if she'd traveled to Ella's dream and danced beside her daughter.

While I'd told myself I was ready, how could I ever be ready to say good-bye to someone like Sydney?

I loved her as much as I'd always imagined I might love a sister.

No.

I loved her more.

Far, far more.

I scrambled to my feet, laying my palm flat to her frail cheek, pressing my lips to her cool forehead. "I love you."

And then I sank to my knees and cried softly, reaching gently to wake my father, while Sydney danced free in her daughter's dreams.

CHAPTER
THIRTY-NINE

The morning after Sydney's funeral, I walked toward Jessica's café. Ella had cried late into the night, finally falling asleep sometime after midnight. My father had fallen asleep in his chair, clutching Sydney's baby photo to his chest. I'd tucked one of her favorite quilts around him before I sneaked out the door, hoping the familiar fabric would bring him comfort when he finally awoke.

The sun had barely peeked over the horizon, and daybreak painted the sky with streaks of coral and violet. Yet, as brilliant as the day promised to be, every step I took felt as though I were slogging through muck or mud. Or life.

I thought of what I'd said to Sydney when she'd first convinced me to try yoga.

I'm going to hurt in places I never knew I had.

That's how you know you're alive, she'd said.

The front door to the café remained locked, even though lights glowed from deep inside the restaurant. Jessica no doubt busied herself for the day, hustling around behind the counter, stocking glasses, nap-kins, and silverware, filling glass-topped pastry dishes with doughnuts and coffee cakes and muffins.

I lifted my hand to knock, but instead let it fall back to my side.

I leaned my forehead against the door and shut my eyes. Every inch of me ached in a way it had never ached before.

I wanted Sydney.

I wanted all the years we hadn't had.

I wanted to ask her why the space between her third and fourth toes was bigger than the space between the rest of her toes. Had she fallen, tripped, stubbed her foot on a piece of furniture? Had she fallen off a bike?

If we'd grown up together, I would have known most everything about her. After all, wasn't that what sisters did?

But I did know her.

Sydney and I had crammed a lifetime of sisterhood into three months. A lifetime of finding our way around each other. A lifetime of laughter, sorrow, hope, and good-bye. And as much as this moment hurt, I wouldn't trade anything that had led to it. I wouldn't trade the betrayal I'd felt when I'd learned she existed, and I wouldn't trade the love I'd discovered as I'd let her into my heart.

The only thing I'd trade would be this thing. Grief. The seemingly unbearable weight of defeat and sorrow and aimlessness that blanketed me now.

A soft click sounded, and the door vibrated beneath me. I straight-ened, opening my eyes to meet Jessica's. Tears ran down her cheeks, two stoic lines of moisture.

She pushed open the door and pulled me inside, wrapping me in her arms. She squeezed, holding on so tightly I remembered all the times we'd knocked each other to the floor as kids with hugs and vows to never let go.

"I'm sorry," she said softly. "So sorry."

My tears came then, hot and fast, pouring down my face. My shoulders heaved and my knees buckled, but Jessica held tight, not letting go, sinking to the floor beside me.

"You'll be all right," she said. "I promise."

"For the love of God, do not tell me she's in a better place," I said, my tone sharp as I pushed away from her. "I heard that so many times yesterday, I thought I'd scream."

Jessica's features softened, and she reached to brush my hair from my face. "Never." She shook her head. "Just a different place." She touched her fingertips to my heart. "And this place."

Jessica pushed to her feet and held out a hand. "I was just about to pour your coffee, and I baked chocolate-chip muffins just for Ella. I set one aside for you."

Small towns. How did people who lived anywhere else survive without them?

I'd just settled at the counter when the bells above the door sounded. Ella raced across the space between us, winding her way between the tables before she climbed into my lap and wrapped her arms around my neck.

Marguerite appeared a few seconds behind her, slightly out of breath, cheeks flushed.

"Did you run all the way here?" I asked Ella. She nodded, the tangle of her hair covering my face.

I tucked her against me and squinted at Marguerite. "Where's my dad? Does he know Ella ran out?"

I spotted the answer in Marguerite's face before she spoke, in the moment in which she adjusted her features, searched for her words.

"He's gone." The heartbreak in her eyes belied the steady cadence of her voice.

I grabbed the counter to maintain my balance, the world suddenly unstable beneath me. "Gone?"

"Nothing in his chair but Momma's quilt and the picture," Ella said, the pain in her voice palpable.

"Luggage?" I asked, unable to believe he'd leave. Not this time.

Marguerite shook her head. "Gone."

"Car?"

"Still in the driveway."

I sat and thought about where Albert might run off to if he hadn't taken my car. There was a bus stop at the far end of town, but to get there he'd have to walk past the one place where I imagined he might stop to think, if only for a moment.

"Come on," I said, setting Ella on her feet and rushing toward the door. "I have an idea. Maybe we can catch him before he gets too far."

We found him less than two blocks away.

"There he is," Ella proclaimed several moments later as we neared Lookout Rock.

My pulse quickened at the sight of my father's figure perched atop the boulder. His luggage sat on the ground, discarded several yards off the edge of the paved path, still a few feet from the massive stone.

I squeezed Ella's shoulder and shot Marguerite a quick look. "Why don't you wait here for a second? Let me talk to Grandpa Albert."

Ella nodded, and I steeled myself as I headed off the path, willing my brain to find the right words, to ask the right questions.

Yet when he turned to face me, his eyes rimmed with tears, I realized the only words I needed were the truth.

"You promised me," I said, as I scrambled up onto the giant rock to sit beside him.

He shook his head, the move sad, beaten. "I did."

"And now?" My heart beat so forcefully against my breastbone, I felt sure he must hear it.

Another shake of his head, this one wordless.

I took his hand in mine, intertwining his slender fingers with my own, callused from work and life.

"You know all those times I told you to leave? It was because I was afraid you actually would." I chuckled. "Actually, I was terrified."

His brows drew together, a question in his eyes.

"I was afraid that if I let you into my life, you'd break my heart again," I said. "It was safer to keep you out."

My father's features crumpled. "And now?"

I inhaled slowly, my breath catching. "Now I'm asking you to stay."

I realized something amazing in that moment. I wasn't scared anymore. If my father left now, I'd survive. Ella would survive.

But I wanted him to stay.

I was willing to run the risk that even if he stayed today, he might leave tomorrow.

"Please stay," I said, forcing the words past the tangle of emotion in my throat. "I love you, Dad."

A sob slipped between his lips then. Just one. Then he gathered himself and dragged his sleeve across his face. He squeezed my hand.

"All my life, other people's emotions have been easier," he said. "But I'm trying."

"I know."

"I love you, Destiny."

His words ignited a warmth deep inside me that helped ease the anguish of losing Sydney.

We sat motionless for several seconds before Ella's voice broke the silence. "Now can I come over there?" she yelled.

I sniffed, unwinding my fingers from my father's. "Someone's waiting for you. I'll grab your bags."

Ella met him halfway between the rock and the path. Dad dropped to one knee, and Ella wrapped her arms around his neck and pulled him into the sort of hug only a nine-year-old can give.

"The man was a genius onstage," Marguerite said a moment later, when I had dragged the luggage to where she stood waiting. "But he couldn't keep your mother alive, and he failed miserably at raising you. I suppose it was easier to stay in New York than it was to face his shortcomings."

"I get that," I said, nodding. "I finally get that."

Marguerite looped her arm through mine. "Watching him with you and Sydney made me realize I'd spent years hating the man because I thought he was a selfish asshole. I never stopped to think he might simply be scared."

She was right.

My father kissed Ella's cheek, then lifted his gaze to meet mine. In his eyes, I spotted raw fear mixed with heartbreak. Yet there he knelt. Still here.

CHAPTER FORTY

My birthday arrived a month later, but I couldn't bring myself to celebrate. Instead, Ella and I walked along the river, continuing the tradition her mother and I had started.

My work continued on the opera house renovation. After the paneling reveal and Sydney's death, the work had become therapeutic for me.

Ella worked most afternoons with me in the shop, and Albert had become a pro at sanding and applying stain.

Sydney would be proud.

My main priority, however, had shifted to school forms, lunches, homework, and braiding hair.

When he wasn't with me in the shop, or working on our garden, Albert gave acting workshops down at the opera house. Nan Michaels had convinced him to join the garden club, and he sat for the occasional painting in Marguerite's backyard.

While Marguerite claimed she was working on her portrait skills, the laughter I heard made me suspect their sessions were more about reminiscing than they were about actual painting. Their truce had finally allowed them to leave the shadows of the past behind.

Jackson Harding had taken to visiting Paris every weekend. He'd stay at the inn and take Ella to brunch at the Paris River Café on Sunday mornings. He'd sit in on Albert's acting classes, and he'd watch me work.

I'd grown to enjoy his visits and his company, and although I'd had little dating experience, I was smart enough to know the man had ulterior motives. Thank goodness.

We'd marked Sydney's grave with a custom-ordered stone. Not gray. Pale pearl, engraved with the image of a mother and daughter, hands joined, spinning.

"I keep forgetting she's gone," Ella said to me now, her hand tucked into mine as we walked. "I wake up and I forget. Then I remember."

And while I wished I had words of wisdom or comfort or something to make sense of the senseless, I could only sigh and offer my love. I wrapped my arm around her shoulders and pulled her close. "Me, too, sweet pea. Me, too."

A broken rock caught my eye. Slate gray. Someone had drawn on it in black pen, the mark looking like a teardrop or a semicircle, then positioned it beneath one of the many giant oaks that lined the bike path.

I pointed. "Is that one of yours?"

Ella scurried to pick it up, her sad pigtails flying in the early December chill. My hair skills needed work. Lots and lots of work.

She plucked the stone from where it had sat, turning it slowly in her hands, studying its every crack and crevice.

"When did you leave that one?" I asked.

"I didn't."

"Maybe your idea's catching on."

She gave a quick lift and drop of her shoulders and smiled, her moment of happiness so genuine it stole my breath. Love welled inside me, an ache deeper than I'd ever imagined possible.

The farther we moved away from Sydney's death, the more Ella let herself smile.

I knew how she felt. I remembered how the ache of losing my mother had never gone away, and I knew the ache of losing Sydney would never completely disappear. But in time it would fade, and Ella would learn to live with the shadows she carried.

Ella pointed to the next giant tree. "Another one!"

She took off running and grabbed the second stone.

I closed the gap between us, and Ella worked to make the two stones fit together. While each had been broken at some point, they were not a match, likely coming from two separate larger stones. Yet, when Ella held them just right, the marks on each aligned to form a familiar shape.

My heart caught inexplicably, and I wondered when I'd morphed from tough guy to sentimentalist.

"A heart," Ella breathed on a whisper.

"A heart," I repeated.

"Wonder who left it?" Her dark gaze shimmered with life and excitement.

A wave of suspicion creeped through me. "Are you sure you didn't leave these?"

"No, silly." Ella bent at the waist and laughed as though I'd said the funniest thing ever. Then she straightened, handed me the stones, and pointed over my shoulder. "He did."

For a split second, I wondered who she meant.

But then he spoke. "I had a little help." The deep timbre of my father's voice rumbled at the exact moment he squeezed my shoulder. "Happy birthday."

He'd remembered.

The grin on my niece's face appeared blurry beyond the sudden surge of moisture in my eyes.

"I'm going to go talk to the ducks," she said. "Then Grandpa Albert says we're going out for cake."

"Don't go too close to the edge," I called out as she raced away. Then I looked down at the small stones. "These are from you?"

Dad nodded, then he shrugged. Both moves sincere, without a trace of melodrama.

My heart sang.

"The rocks reminded me of us"—he pointed back and forth between us—"broken together."

I furrowed my brows, confused.

But my father simply smiled—a lovely, in-the-moment smile. "We're broken. But we're together." He blushed, noticeably embarrassed at his own display of emotion. "You. Me. Ella. Our family."

I held up my hands, cradling the two stones and the awkward heart they formed. "Broken together."

My eyes filled with tears again, and I flashed back on my life before Albert, and Ella, and Sydney. The life in which I'd shut down my dreams of family, shut down my memories of how joyful life could be.

Then I gave silent thanks for my new life . . . and this moment.

Marguerite's words from my childhood bounced through my brain. *You are enough.*

And while that was still true, maybe this was better.

We were enough.

EPILOGUE

My father's garden exploded in color the following spring. Tulips. Daffodils. Hyacinths.

Even the daisies he'd planted grew tall and lush, promising blossoms as soon as the weather warmed enough to coax them forth.

I found one of Ella's superhero stones early one morning as it pushed up through the dirt next to a freshly sprouted tulip.

The teal on the simple stick figure's mask had faded, but her teal ballet slippers remained bright. She stood on her toes, arms over her head. If I had ever taken ballet, or if I had ever paid attention to dance terms, I might have known what the name of this particular superhero's position was. But I hadn't. And I didn't. So I gave it the first name that popped into my head.

Joy.

That was what Sydney had felt when she'd danced with Ella. And that was what Ella had felt when she'd decorated the stone.

Joy.

Ella had forever captured the emotion in a stick figure painted on a stone. And there she stood—triumphant. Emerging from the soil beside all the new life Dad had planted.

Hope welled up inside me, pushing away a measure of my lingering grief.

Perhaps life was like a garden. Even though my mother's flowers had been long dead and the soil had appeared barren, love and time had brought the space back to life.

My mother's azalea, the shrub that hadn't bloomed in twenty years, burst forth in vivid fuchsia flowers.

My father had been right. Some plants did sit dormant for years before they bloomed brighter than ever before.

And Ella's stone sat in the middle of it all.

Joy.

Where my life—and house—had once been empty, it now sat filled to overflowing, and I suspected that was Sydney's greatest gift of all.

Through her dying, she'd taught me how to live.

Where my life had once been nothing but pieces—Dad, Sydney, Ella, Marguerite, Jackson—it was now whole.

There were days in which I caught myself thinking Sydney had been lost, but the truth was, she'd been found.

Her love had united our crazy, fractured family.

Our broken pieces fit.

We weren't perfect. We weren't smooth. But we belonged.

In the end, wasn't that all that mattered?

We're all just walking each other home.

—Ram Dass

RESOURCES

SYMPTOMS OF OVARIAN CANCER

Ovarian cancer is difficult to detect, especially in the early stages. This is partly due to the fact that these two small, almond-shaped organs are deep within the abdominal cavity, one on each side of the uterus. These are some of the potential signs and symptoms of ovarian cancer:

- Bloating
- Pelvic or abdominal pain
- Trouble eating or feeling full quickly
- Feeling the need to urinate urgently or often

Other symptoms of ovarian cancer can include:

- Fatigue
- Upset stomach or heartburn
- Back pain
- Pain during sex
- Constipation or menstrual changes

If symptoms persist for more than two weeks, see your physician.

Source: National Ovarian Cancer Coalition, www.ovarian.org

> *As I look out in the future, I dream of a time when women of all ages will have a reliable early-detection test for ovarian cancer and more humane treatment for those women with late-stage ovarian cancer.*

> —Colleen Drury

Source: Colleen's Dream, www.colleensdream.org

ACKNOWLEDGMENTS

For Ingrid Tornari. With any luck at all, this book will release on your birthday. I only wish you were here to see it. Thank you seems so inadequate for the love and friendship you brought to my life. I miss the sound of your laughter more than you will ever know. I miss your faith. I miss your gorgeous smile. Thank you for showing me how to live.

For Desiree Hernandez, thank you for holding my hand on some of the saddest days of my life. Thank you also for encouraging me as I struggled to put this book into words.

For Danielle Marshall, thank you for giving me a chance to tell this story the way I wanted to tell it. The end result would not have been possible without your patience and your belief.

For Tiffany Yates Martin, thank you for your wise guidance and thoughtful contributions. Never have the words "I couldn't have done this without you" been more true. You rock.

For Dan, thank you once again for supporting your crazy writer wife as she hid away in the office banging on the keyboard. You officially win the award for the husband most willing to order takeout . . . again. I love you.

For Annie, thank you for all the quiet moments you sat beside me in the office, keeping me company. Thank you also for the movie breaks, the dance parties, and the expertly prepared snacks. You, kid, are one in a million. I am the luckiest mom in the world. I love you.

For Mom, thank you for your unfailing support and your continued belief in my dream. Thank you for teaching me to never quit. Your voice in my head got me through this one. How lucky am I to call you Mom? I love you.

Finally, for my readers, thank you for your ongoing support and encouragement. Your notes, emails, and friendships fill me with gratitude. While Destiny's journey may be darker than my previous stories, I hope her love, as well as her hope, will stay with you long after you turn the last page.

ABOUT THE AUTHOR

 Kathleen Long is the author of sixteen novels in the genres of women's fiction, contemporary romance, and romantic suspense. Kathleen has won a RIO Award and is a two-time winner of the Gayle Wilson Award of Excellence. She has also been nominated for a RITA® Award. Her additional honors include award nominations for National Readers' Choice, HOLT Medallion, Booksellers' Best, and Book Buyers Best, as well as appearances on the *USA Today* and *Wall Street Journal* bestseller lists. A native of Wilmington, Delaware, she now divides her time between suburban Philadelphia and the Jersey Shore. When Kathleen is not plotting her next book or teaching creative writing, she spends her time bribing her tween to pick up her clothes and begging the dog to heel. Connect with Kathleen at www.kathleenlong.com.